Through a Glass, Darkly

Also by Donna Leon

Death at La Fenice
Death in a Strange Country
The Anonymous Venetian
A Venetian Reckoning
Acqua Alta
The Death of Faith
A Noble Radiance
Fatal Remedies
Friends in High Places
A Sea of Troubles
Wilful Behaviour
Uniform Justice
Doctored Evidence
Blood from a Stone

Donna Leon

Through a Glass, Darkly

Atlantic Monthly Press
New York

First published in 2006 in the United Kingdom by William Heinemann,
The Random House Group Limited, London

Published simultaneously in Canada
Printed in the United States of America

FIRST AMERICAN EDITION

Library of Congress Cataloging-in-Publication Data
Leon, Donna.
    Through a glass, darkly / Donna Leon.
      p. cm.
    ISBN-10: 0-87113-937-5
    ISBN-13: 978-0-87113-937-5
    1. Brunetti, Guido (Fictitious character)—Fiction. 2. Police—Italy—Venice—
Fiction. 3. Murano (Italy)—Fiction. 4. Watchmen—Crimes against—Fiction.
5. Businessmen—Fiction. 6. Environmentalists—Fiction. 7. Water—Pollution—
Italy—Venice, Lagoon of—Fiction. I. Title.
PS3562.E534T49 2006
813'.54—dc22   2005058859

Atlantic Monthly Press
an imprint of Grove/Atlantic, Inc.
841 Broadway
New York, NY 10003

Distributed by Publishers Group West
www.groveatlantic.com

06 07 08 09 10   10 9 8 7 6 5 4 3 2 1

for Cecilia Bartoli

Da qual tremore insolito
Sento assalir gli spiriti!
Dond'escono quei vortici
Di foco pien d'orror?

What strange fear
Assails my spirits!
Where do they come from,
Those horrible whirlwinds of flame?

Don Giovanni
Mozart

1

Brunetti stood at his window and flirted with springtime. It was there, just on the other side of the canal, evident in the shoots he saw popping up from the earth. Over the last few days, someone – in all these years, he had never seen a person working in the garden – had raked the earth, though he noticed it only now. Tiny white flowers were visible amidst the grass, and those fearless little ones that hugged themselves close to the ground, the names of which he could never remember – the little yellow and pink ones – sprouted from the freshly turned earth.

He opened the windows and felt fresh air flood into his overheated room. It brought with it the scent of new growth or rising sap or whatever it was that led to spring fever and an atavistic urge towards happiness. Birds, he noticed, were busy on the ground, no doubt pleased to discover that the worms had somehow been lured to the surface. Two of them squabbled over something, then one flew away, and Brunetti watched it disappear to the left of the church.

'Excuse me,' he heard someone say behind him. He wiped

away his smile before he turned. It was Vianello, wearing his uniform and looking far more serious than he should on such a lovely day. From the expression on the Inspector's face and the stiffness of his body, Brunetti wondered if he should address him with the formal *Lei*, a grammatical formality they had abandoned on Vianello's promotion to inspector. 'Yes, what is it?' Brunetti asked in a friendly tone while evading the grammatical issue.

'I wondered if you had a moment,' Vianello said, using the familiar *tu* and not referring to Brunetti as 'sir', thus increasing the likelihood that this would be an informal conversation.

Further to relax the atmosphere, Brunetti said, 'I was just looking at those flowers across the way –' gesturing with his head towards the garden – 'and wondering what we were doing inside on a day like this.'

'First day you begin to feel it's spring,' Vianello agreed, smiling at last. 'I always used to play hooky.'

'Me, too,' said Brunetti, who had not. 'What did you do?'

Vianello sat in the chair on the right, his usual chair, and said, 'My older brother delivered fruit to Rialto, so that's where I'd go. Instead of going to school, that is. I'd go over to the market and meet him and help him carry crates of fruit and vegetables all morning, and then go home for lunch at the same time I usually got home from school.' He smiled again and then he laughed. 'My mother always knew. I don't know how she did, but she always asked me how things were at Rialto and why I hadn't brought her any artichokes.' Vianello shook his head at the memory. 'And now Nadia is the same with the kids: it's like she can read their minds and always knows when they haven't gone to school or have done something they shouldn't.' He looked at Brunetti. 'You have any idea how they do it?'

'Who? Mothers?'

'Yes.'

2

'You said, it, Lorenzo. They read minds.' Brunetti judged that the atmosphere was sufficiently relaxed and so asked, 'What was it you wanted?'

His question restored all of Vianello's nervousness. He uncrossed his legs and brought his feet together, sitting up straighter. 'It's about a friend of mine,' he said. 'He's in trouble.'

'What kind of trouble?'

'With us.'

'The police?'

Vianello nodded.

'Here? In Venice?'

Vianello shook his head and said, 'No. In Mestre. That is, in Mogliano, but they were taken to Mestre.'

'Who?'

'The people who were arrested.'

'Which people?'

'The ones outside the factory.'

'The paint factory?' Brunetti asked, recalling an article he had seen in that morning's paper.

'Yes.'

The *Gazzettino* had devoted the front page of its second section to a report of the arrest of six people during a 'No Global' protest in front of a paint factory in Mogliano Veneto the previous day. The factory had been repeatedly fined for its failure to observe regulations on the disposal of toxic waste but had continued to operate regardless, choosing to pay the derisory fines rather than invest in changes to its production methods. The protesters were demanding that the factory be closed and had tried to prevent the workers from entering. This had led to a confrontation between the protesters and the workers, during which the police had intervened and arrested seven people.

'Is he a worker or a "No Global"?' Brunetti asked.

'Neither,' Vianello answered, then qualified his response

3

by adding, 'Well, not a real "No Global," that is. Any more than I am.' This sounded, apparently even to Vianello himself, like a dead end as an explanation, so he took a breath and began again. 'Marco and I were at school together, but then he went to university and became an engineer. He's always been interested in ecology: that's how we know one another, from meetings and things. Once in a while we have a drink together, after a meeting.'

Brunetti chose not to inquire about these meetings. The Inspector continued. 'He's very concerned about what's going on at that factory. And in Marghera. I know he's been at the protests there, too, but he's never been involved in anything like this.'

'Like what?'

'When things get violent.'

'I didn't know that was the case,' Brunetti said. The paper had reported only that people had been arrested; there had been no mention of violence. 'What happened?' he asked. 'Who started it?' He knew how people always answered this question, whether for themselves or for their friends: it was always the other guy.

Vianello sat back in his chair and crossed his legs again. 'I don't know. I only spoke to his wife. That is, she called me this morning and asked me if I could think of some way to help him.'

'Only this morning?' Brunetti asked.

Vianello nodded. 'She said he called her last night, from the jail in Mestre, and he asked her to call me, but not until the morning. She got hold of me just as I was leaving for work.' Vianello returned to Brunetti's question. 'So I don't know who started it. It could have been the workers, or it could have been some of the "No Globals".'

Brunetti was surprised to hear Vianello admit this as a possibility. The Inspector went on, 'Marco's a peaceful guy: he wouldn't start anything. I know that, but some of the

4

people who go to these things, well, I think they use it as a way to have some fun.'

'That's a strange choice of word: "fun".'

Vianello raised a hand and let it fall to his lap. 'I know it is, but that's the way some of these people look at it. Marco's talked about them, says he doesn't like them and doesn't like it when they join a protest, because it increases the risk of trouble.'

'Does he know who the violent ones are?' Brunetti asked.

'He's never said, only that they make him nervous.'

Brunetti decided to bring the conversation back to its original purpose. 'But what did you want to ask me?'

'You know the people in Mestre. Better than I do. And the magistrates, though I don't know who this has been given to. So I wondered if you could call and see what you could find out.'

'I still don't understand why you don't do it,' Brunetti said, making this sound like what it was – a request for information – and not what it was not, a suggestion that Vianello take care of it himself.

'I think it would be better if the inquiry came from a commissario.'

Brunetti considered this for a moment and then said, 'Yes; maybe. Do you know what the charge is?' he asked.

'No. Probably causing a disturbance or resisting a public official in pursuit of his duties. Marco's wife didn't say. I told her not to do anything until I had time to talk to you. I figured you, or we, might be able to do something . . . well, informally. It would save him a lot of trouble.'

'Did she tell you anything at all about what happened?'

'Just what Marco told her: that he was standing there with a placard, along with the other people from his group: about a dozen of them. Suddenly there were three or four men they didn't know, shouting at the workers and spitting at them, and then someone threw a rock.' Before Brunetti could ask,

5

Vianello said, 'No, he didn't know who did it; he said he didn't see anything. Someone else told him about the rock. And then the police were there, and he got thrown to the ground and then they put him in a truck and took him to Mestre.'

None of this surprised Brunetti in any way. Unless someone had been there with a video camera, they would never know who had thrown the first punch, or rock, so it really was anyone's guess what the charges would be and whom they would be brought against.

After a brief pause, Brunetti said, 'You're right, but we better do this in person.' If nothing else, Brunetti caught himself thinking, it would be an excuse to get out of his office. 'You ready to go?'

'Yes,' said Vianello, getting to his feet.

2

As they left the Questura, Brunetti saw one of the launches approaching. The new pilot, Foa, stood at the wheel and he gave Brunetti a smile and Vianello a wave as he pulled up to the dock. 'Where are you going?' Foa asked, and then added, 'sir', to make it clear whom he was addressing.

'Piazzale Roma,' Brunetti said. He had called the sub-station there and asked that a car be ready for them. Because there had been no launch visible from his window, he had assumed that he and Vianello would have to take the vaporetto.

Foa looked at his watch. 'I don't have to be anywhere until eleven, sir, so I could easily take you there and get back.' Then to Vianello, 'Come on, Lorenzo: the weather's perfect today.'

They needed no more to lure them on to the deck, where they remained while Foa took them up the Grand Canal. At Rialto, Brunetti turned to Vianello and observed, 'First day of spring, and we're both playing hooky again.'

Vianello laughed, not so much at what Brunetti had said

but at the perfect day, the certain slant of light on the water in front of them, and at the joy of playing hooky on the first day of spring.

As the boat slipped into one of the taxi ranks at Piazzale Roma, both men thanked the pilot and stepped up on to the dock. Beyond the ACTV building, a police car waited, engine running, and as soon as they got in, it pulled out into the traffic leading across the causeway to the mainland.

At the Mestre headquarters, Brunetti quickly learned that the case of the detained protesters had been assigned to Giuseppe Zedda, a commissario he had worked with some years before. A Sicilian and almost a head shorter than Brunetti, Zedda had impressed him then with his rigorous honesty. They had not become friends, but as colleagues they had shared a mutual respect. Brunetti trusted Zedda to see that things were done fairly and well and that none of the people arrested would be prevailed upon to give statements they might later retract.

'Could we speak to one of them?' Brunetti asked, after he and Vianello had turned down Zedda's offer to have a coffee in his office.

'Which one?' Zedda asked, and Brunetti realized he knew nothing more about the man under arrest than that his name was Marco and he was a friend of Vianello's.

'Ribetti,' Vianello supplied.

'Come with me,' Zedda said. 'I'll put you in one of the interrogation rooms and get him for you.'

The room was like every interrogation room Brunetti had ever known: the floor might have been washed that morning – it might have been washed ten minutes ago – but grit crunched underfoot, and two plastic coffee cups lay on the floor beside the wastepaper basket. It smelled of smoke and unwashed clothing and defeat. Entering it, Brunetti wanted to confess to something, anything, if only it would get him out of there quickly.

After about ten minutes Zedda came back, leading a man taller than himself yet at least ten pounds lighter. Brunetti often noticed that people who were arrested or held overnight in police custody quickly came to shrink inside their clothing: such was the case here. The bottoms of the man's trousers touched the ground, and his shirt bunched up and overflowed his buttoned jacket. He had apparently not been able to shave that morning, and his hair, thick and dark, stuck up on one side. His ears jutted out and gave him an ungainly look that went with the outsize clothing. He looked at Brunetti without expression, but on seeing Vianello he smiled with relief and pleasure, and when his face softened Brunetti saw that he was younger than he had first seemed, perhaps in his midthirties.

'Assunta found you?' the man asked, embracing Vianello and clapping him on the back.

The Inspector seemed surprised at the warmth of the greeting but returned Ribetti's embrace and said, 'Yes, she called me before I left for work and asked if there was anything I could do.' He took a step back and turned to Brunetti. 'This is my commander, Commissario Brunetti. He offered to come with me.'

Ribetti put out his hand and shook Brunetti's. 'Thank you for coming, Commissario.' He looked at Vianello, at Brunetti, then back to Vianello. 'I didn't want to . . .' he left the sentence unfinished. 'That is, I didn't want to cause you so much trouble, Lorenzo.' And to Brunetti, 'Or you, Commissario.'

Vianello walked over to the table, saying, 'It's no trouble, Marco. It's what we do all the time, anyway: talk to people.' He pulled out two of the chairs on one side of the table and then the one at the head, which he held for Ribetti.

When they were all seated, Vianello turned to Brunetti, as if handing over to him. 'Tell us what happened,' Brunetti said.

'Everything?' Ribetti asked.

9

'Everything,' Brunetti answered.

'We've been out there for three days,' Ribetti began, looking at the two men to see if they knew about the protest. When both nodded in acknowledgement, he said, 'Yesterday there were about ten of us. With placards. We've been trying to convince the workers that what they're doing is bad for all of us.'

Brunetti had few illusions as to how willing workers would be to give up their jobs when told that what they were doing was bad for countless people they didn't know, but he nodded again.

Ribetti folded his hands on the table and looked at his fingers.

'What time did you get there?' Brunetti asked.

'It was in the afternoon, about three-thirty,' he answered, looking at Brunetti. 'Most of us on the committee have jobs, so we can go out only after lunch. The workers come back at four, and we like them to see us, maybe even listen to us or talk to us, when they go in.' A look of great perplexity came over his face, reminding Brunetti of his son, as Ribetti said, 'If we can make them understand what the factory is doing, not only to them, but to everyone, then maybe . . .'

Again, Brunetti kept his thoughts to himself. It was Vianello who broke the silence by asking, 'Does it do any good, talking to them?'

Ribetti answered this with a smile. 'Who knows? If they're alone, sometimes they listen. If there's more than one of them, though, they just walk past us, or sometimes they say things.'

'What sort of things?'

He looked at the two policemen, then at his hands. 'Oh, they tell us they aren't interested, they have to work, they have families,' Ribetti answered, then added, 'or they get abusive.'

'But no violence?' Vianello asked.

Ribetti looked at him and shook his head. 'No, nothing.

We've all been trained not to react, not to argue with them, never to do anything that could provoke them.' He continued to look at Vianello, as if to convince him of the truth of this by the sincerity of his expression. 'We're there to help them,' he said, and Brunetti believed he meant it.

'But this time?' Brunetti asked.

Ribetti shook his head a few times. 'I have no idea what happened. Some people came up to us – I don't know where they came from or whether they were with us or were workers – they started to shout, and then the workers did, too. Then someone pushed me and I dropped the placard I was carrying, and after I picked it up, it looked like everyone had suddenly gone crazy. People were shoving and pushing one another, then I heard the police sirens, and then I was on the ground again. Two men pulled me up and put me in the back of a van, and they brought us here. It wasn't until almost midnight that a woman in uniform came into the cell and said I could call someone.' He hurried through this summary, his voice sounding as confused as the events he described.

He turned back and forth between Brunetti and Vianello, then said to the latter, 'I called Assunta and told her where I was, what had happened, and then I thought of you. And I asked her to see if she could find you and tell you what had happened.' His voice changed as he asked, 'She didn't call you then, did she?' he asked, forgetting that Vianello had already told him.

Vianello smiled. 'No, not until this morning.' Brunetti noticed that Ribetti seemed relieved to hear this.

'But you didn't have to come all the way out here for me,' Ribetti said, using the plural. 'Really, Lorenzo: I don't know what I was thinking of when I asked her to call you. I guess I panicked. I thought you could make a phone call to someone here or something, and everything would be all right.' He raised a hand in Vianello's direction and said, 'Really, it never occurred to me that you'd have to come out here.' Then, to

11

Brunetti, 'Or that you'd have to come, Commissario.' He looked at his hands again. 'I didn't know what to do.'

'Have you ever been arrested before, Signor Ribetti?' Brunetti asked.

Ribetti looked at him with an astonishment he could not disguise: Brunetti might as well have slapped him. 'Of course not,' he said.

Vianello interrupted to ask, 'Do you know if any of the others have ever been arrested?'

'No, never,' Ribetti said, voice rising with the force of his insistence. 'I told you: we're trained not to cause trouble.'

'Isn't a protest like yours a form of trouble?' Brunetti asked.

Ribetti paused, as if he were playing the question back in his mind to check for sarcasm. Apparently finding none, he said, 'Of course it is. But it's non-violent, and all we're trying to do is make the workers understand how dangerous what they do is. Not only for us, but for themselves even more.'

Brunetti noticed that Vianello accepted this, so he asked, 'What dangers, Signor Ribetti?'

Ribetti looked at Brunetti as though he had just asked the sum of two plus two, but he wiped the expression away and said, 'The solvents and chemicals they work with, more than anything else. At least at the paint factory. They spill them and splash them on themselves and breathe them in all day. And that's not even to mention all the waste they have to get rid of. Somewhere.'

Brunetti, who had been hearing this kind of thing from Vianello for some time, avoided the Inspector's glance. He asked, 'And do you think your protests will change things, Signor Ribetti?'

Ribetti threw his open hands in the air. 'God knows. But at least it's something, some little protest. And maybe other people will see that it's possible to protest. If we don't,' he said, his voice mournful and filled with conviction, 'they'll kill us all.'

Precisely because he had had this kind of conversation with Vianello many times, Brunetti did not have to ask Ribetti who 'they' were. Brunetti realized how much he too had come to believe, how much he had been converted, in recent years, and not only because of Vianello's ecological conscience. He increasingly noticed articles about global warming, about the ecomafia and their unbridled dumping of toxic waste all over the South; he had even come to believe that there was a connection between the murder of a RAI television journalist in Somalia some years before and the dumping of toxic waste in that poor afflicted country. What surprised him was that there were people who could still believe that protesting against such things, in their small way, would make some difference. And, he confessed to himself, he did not like to admit that it surprised him.

'But to more practical matters,' Brunetti said abruptly. 'If you've never had any trouble with the police before, then it might be possible for us to do something.' He looked at Vianello. 'If you stay here, I'll go and talk to Zedda and have a look at the report. If no one's been hurt and if no charges have been brought, then I see no reason why Signor Ribetti has to remain in custody.'

Ribetti cast him a glance of mingled fear and relief. 'Thank you, Commissario,' he said, and then quickly added, 'Even if you can't do anything or if nothing happens, still, thank you.'

Brunetti stood up. He went to the door and was glad to find it unlocked. Out in the corridor, he asked for Zedda, whom he found in his office, an office only a quarter the size of his own, with one window that looked out over a parking lot.

Even before Brunetti could ask, Zedda said, 'Take him home, Brunetti. Nothing's going to come of this. No one got hurt, no one has made a *denuncia*, and we certainly don't want any trouble with them. They're a pain in the ass, but

13

they're harmless. So just pack up your friend and take him home.'

A younger Brunetti might have thought it necessary to make clear that Ribetti was Vianello's friend and not his, but after so many years working with the Inspector, Brunetti could no longer make this distinction, so he thanked Zedda and asked if there were any forms to be signed. Zedda waved him away, saying that it had been good to see Brunetti again, and came around his desk to shake hands.

Brunetti returned to the interrogation room, told Ribetti that he was free to go and could come with them if he chose, then led the others out to the waiting police car.

3

The three of them emerged from the main entrance of the Mestre Questura and started down the steps. Vianello put an arm around Ribetti's shoulder and said, 'Come on, Marco, the least we can do is give you a ride back to Piazzale Roma.' Ribetti smiled and thanked him. He wiped a hand over his eyes and drew it down one side of his face, and Brunetti could almost feel it graze across his unshaven cheek. As they continued down the steps towards the waiting car, a taxi pulled up and a short, squat man with white hair got out. He leaned in to hand money to the driver and turned to look up at the building. And saw them.

He gave a savage shove to the door of the taxi, slamming it shut behind him. 'You stupid bastard!' he shouted, starting across the pavement. The taxi drove off. The old man stopped, one hand raised, waving it at them. 'You stupid bastard,' he shouted again and started up the steps towards them. Brunetti and the others stopped halfway down, frozen with astonishment.

The man's face was distorted with anger and livid with

years of drink. So short he would not reach Brunetti's shoulder, he was almost twice as broad, with a thick torso that was moving downward as muscle turned to paunch. 'You and your animals and your trees and your nature, nature, nature. Go out there and cause trouble and get arrested and get your name in the paper. Stupid bastard. You never had any sense. Now those bastards at the *Gazzettino* are calling *me*.'

Brunetti placed himself between the old man and Ribetti. 'I'm afraid there's been some misunderstanding, Signore. Signor Ribetti has not been arrested. Quite the contrary: he's here to help the police with their inquiries.' Brunetti had no idea why he lied. There would be no investigation, so there was no way Ribetti could help with it, but the old man needed to be stopped, and usually people of his age were most easily stopped by mention of the forces of order.

'And who the hell do you think you are?' the old man demanded, tilting his head back to stare up at Brunetti. Without waiting for an answer, he tried to step around Brunetti, who moved to the left and then to the right to stand in his way.

The old man stood still and raised a finger to the height of his own shoulder and poked Brunetti in the chest, saying, 'Look, you bastard, get out of my way. I don't want any inter- ference from strangers.' He took a half-step to the left, but Brunetti blocked him again. 'I said get out of my way!' the old man shouted, this time putting his hand on Brunetti's arm. It could not be said that the old man grabbed Brunetti's arm, nor that he pulled at it, but it was certainly not the casual contact of a man trying to get his friend's attention to make a point.

Vianello came down two steps and stood to the old man's left. 'I think you'd better take your hand off the Commissario, Signore.'

The old man, however, had been carried beyond hearing by his fury. He tore his hand from Brunetti's arm and pointed at Vianello. 'And don't you think you can get in my way, either, you bastard.' His face had grown puce, and Brunetti wondered if he would have some sort of seizure: he had seldom seen a man so easily catapult himself into rage. Sweat stood on the old man's forehead, and Brunetti saw his hands tremble. Spittle had collected at the corners of his mouth, and his eyes, small and dark, appeared to have grown even smaller.

From behind him, Brunetti heard Ribetti say, 'Please, Commissario; he won't cause any trouble.'

Vianello could not hide his surprise, and Brunetti's was apparent to the old man. 'That's right, Signor Commissario whoever you are: I won't cause any trouble. He's the one who causes trouble. Stupid bastard.' He turned his glance from Brunetti to Ribetti, who now stood to Brunetti's left. 'He knows me because he married that fool, my daughter. Went right where he knew the money was and married her. And then filled her with his shitty ideas.' The old man made as if to spit at Ribetti but changed his mind. 'And gets himself arrested,' he added, looking at Brunetti to make it clear that he did not believe what he had been told.

Ribetti caught Brunetti's attention by placing his hand on his arm. 'Thank you, Commissario,' he said, and then to Vianello, 'And you, too, Lorenzo.' Ignoring the old man completely, he moved off to the left and started down the steps. When he reached the sidewalk, Brunetti saw him look at the parked police car, but he continued past it, walked to the next corner, and disappeared around it.

'Coward,' the old man shouted after him. 'You're brave enough when you try to save your goddamn animals or your goddamn trees. But when you have to face a real man . . .' Suddenly the old man ran out of abuse. He looked at Vianello and Brunetti as if he wanted to commit their faces to memory, then pushed past them and went up the steps and into the Questura.

17

'Well?' Brunetti asked.

'I'll tell you about it on the way back,' Vianello said.

The story that Vianello told Brunetti on the way back to Venice was one he had followed during the six months that a former classmate of his had worked as a *maestro* in the glass factory of Giovanni De Cal, the old man on the steps, before quitting and moving to a different *fornace*. It began as a typical story of romance and marriage. She dropped a bag full of oranges at Rialto, and a stranger turned around from buying shrimp to chase the oranges and try to collect them for her. She laughed and thanked him, offered him a coffee for his help, and they talked for an hour over the coffee. He walked her to her boat, took her *telefonino* number, subsequently called and asked her if she wanted to see a film, and four months later they were living together. Her father, Giovanni De Cal, objected, insisted the young man was a fortune hunter. No longer young, never very pretty, the only job Assunta had ever had was in her father's factory . . . who'd want a woman like that if not for her money? Behind this was the less publicly expressed question of who would look after him if she married and left him, a widower, alone in a ten-room house, too busy running his business to be able to take care of it himself.

Reader, she married him. Worse was in store when the young man's principles and politics, his concern for the environment and suspicion of the current government, came into conflict with his father-in-law's philosophy: it's a dog-eat-dog world, and workers are meant to work, not to lie around collecting money from their employers for doing nothing; growth and progress are always good, and more is better.

Even worse, from the old man's point of view, were the young man's education and profession. Not only was he a university graduate and thus one of those useless '*dottori*' who had studied everything and yet knew nothing; he compounded the fault by working as an engineer for the French company that had won the contract to build garbage dumps in the Veneto, for which he conducted site analyses of location, proximity to rivers and ground water, and soil composition. He wrote reports that obstructed the building of garbage dumps, wrote further reports that made their construction more expensive, and all paid for by money taken from the pockets of people like factory owners, who paid taxes so that the lazy and weak could suck off the public tit and engineers could force cities to spend money just so that some fish and animals wouldn't get dirty or sick.

Ribetti and his wife, Assunta De Cal, lived in a house on Murano that had been left to her by her mother. Caught between father and husband, she tried to keep both peace and house: because she worked in her father's factory all day, neither task was easy. De Cal, as Brunetti and Vianello had observed, was a choleric man, the owner of a glass factory on Murano that had been in his family for six generations.

Vianello paused at this point in the story and said, 'You know, hearing myself tell you all this, I'm not sure why I know this much about them. It's not as if Pietro told me all this while he was working there. I mean, even though Marco and I went to school together, we lost touch until about three years ago, so it doesn't make any sense that I know all this. It's not like we're close friends or anything, and he's never talked about the old man.' Vianello was sitting in the back seat of the car taking them across the Ponte della Libertà, so as he spoke, he saw Brunetti's head framed by the smokestacks of Marghera.

It occurred to Brunetti that Vianello might still, after all this time, not realize the full extent of his ability to draw people into conversation and then into confidence with him. Perhaps it was a natural gift, like perfect pitch or the ability

19

to dance, and those who had it were incapable of seeing it as in any way unusual.

Vianello recaptured Brunetti's attention by waving at the Marghera factories and saying, 'You know I agree with him, don't you?'

'About the protests?'

'Yes,' Vianello answered. 'I can't join them, not with this job, but that doesn't stop me from thinking they should protest and hoping that they continue to do it.'

'What about De Cal?' Brunetti asked, realizing that they would reach Piazzale Roma in a few minutes and eager to prevent Vianello from launching into another discussion about the fate of the planet.

'Oh, he's a bastard,' Vianello said, 'as you saw. He's fought with everyone on Murano: over houses, over salaries, over . . . well, over anything people *can* fight about.'

'How does he manage to keep his workmen?' Brunetti asked.

'Well, he does and he doesn't,' Vianello said. 'At least that's what I've heard.'

'From Ribetti?'

'No, not from him,' Vianello answered. 'I told you he doesn't talk about the old man, and he doesn't have anything to do with the *fornace*. But I've got relatives on Murano, and a couple of them work in the *fornaci*. And everyone knows everybody's business.'

'What do they say?'

'He's kept the same two *maestri* for the last couple of years,' Vianello said, then added, 'That's something of a record for him, even if they're not very good. Not that it matters so much, I suppose.'

'Why not?' Behind Vianello's head Brunetti saw the side of the Panorama bus: they would soon be there.

'All they make is that tourist crap. You know, the porpoises leaping up out of the waves. And toreadors.'

20

'With the capes and the black pants?' Brunetti asked.

'Yes, can you believe it, like we had toreadors here. Or porpoises, for that matter.'

'I thought they were all made in China or Bohemia by now,' Brunetti said, repeating something he had heard frequently, and from people who should know.

'Lots of it is,' Vianello said, 'but they still can't do the big pieces, at least not yet. Wait five years and it'll all be coming from China.'

'And your relatives?'

Vianello turned his palms up in a gesture of hopelessness. 'Either they'll learn how to do something else, or everyone will end up like your wife says we will: dressing in seventeenth-century costumes and walking around, speaking Veneziano, to amuse the tourists.'

'Even us?' Brunetti asked. 'The police?'

'Yes,' Vianello answered. 'Can you imagine Alvise with a crossbow?'

Laughter put an end to their conversation, and the matter lapsed, merging into the stream of gossip that flowed through Venice, much of it no cleaner than the water that flowed in the canals.

When they were back at the Questura, Brunetti went to Signorina Elettra's office to see if the staffing list had been prepared for the Easter holiday. 'Ah, Commissario,' she said as he entered the office, 'I've been looking for you.'

'Yes?' he asked.

'It's the lottery, you see,' she said easily, as if he should know what she was talking about. 'I wondered if you'd like to buy a ticket.'

Even before he considered what sort of a lottery she was referring to, whether related to Easter or to one of Vianello's green projects, he answered, 'Of course', reached into his back pocket and took out his wallet. 'How much?'

21

'Only five Euros, sir,' she said. 'We figured we'd sell so many tickets that we could keep the price down.'

'Fine, then,' he said, taking out a note, only half listening.

She thanked him and drew a block of notepaper towards her. 'What date would you like, sir?' She looked around her desk, hunting for a pen, then looked up at him again. 'Any time after the first of May, sir.'

For a moment, Brunetti toyed with the idea of choosing the tenth of May, Paola's birthday, and not inquiring further, but curiosity overcame him and he said, 'I don't think I understand, Signorina.'

'You have to choose a date, sir. The person who gets the right date wins everything that's been bet.' She smiled, adding, 'And yes, you can choose more than one date, so long as you pay five Euros for each one.'

'All right,' Brunetti said. 'I confess. I don't know what you're talking about.'

Signorina Elettra put her hand to her mouth, and he thought he saw a faint blush cross her cheeks. 'Ah . . .' she let escape a long sigh, as though she were a soccer ball and someone had let the air out of her. He watched the play of expressions on her face, saw her toy with the idea of lying, then opt for the truth. Brunetti knew all of this, but didn't know why or how he knew it.

'It's about the Vice-Questore, sir,' she said.

'What about him?' Brunetti asked without impatience.

'About the Interpol job.'

'You mean he applied?' Brunetti asked, unable to contain his surprise that Patta had actually done it. It is perhaps more accurate to say that he was surprised that he had not been told that Patta had applied for the position – at Patta's level, jobs were called positions.

'Yes, sir. Four months ago.'

Brunetti could no longer remember the precise nature of the position his superior had been interested in. He had a vague memory that it involved working with – or, as people with positions said, 'liaising' with – the police of some other nation the language of which Patta did not speak, but he could no longer recall which one.

Into his silence, she supplied the answer. 'In London, sir. With Scotland Yard, as their expert on the Mafia.'

As so often happened when he learned of developments in Patta's professional life, Brunetti found himself without suitable words. 'And the lottery?' he finally asked.

'The date he gets the rejection letter,' she said, voice implacable.

He cared nothing for the details, but he wanted to know. But how to put it? 'You seem rather certain of that outcome, Signorina.' Yes, that was how to put it.

'I am,' she said but offered no explanation. Smiling, she waved the pen over the block of paper. 'And the date, sir?'

'May the tenth, please.'

She wrote the date on the top of a small sheet of paper, tore it off, and handed it to him. 'Don't lose it, sir.'

'In the case of a tie?' he asked as he slipped the paper into his wallet.

'Oh, that's already decided, sir. There are a few dates a number of people want, but it's been suggested that, in the case of a tie, we give all the money to Greenpeace.'

'He would, wouldn't he?' Brunetti asked.

'Who would what, sir?' she asked with every appearance of confusion.

He let out a little puff of air, as if to suggest that even the blind could see the mind at work behind that suggestion. 'Vianello.'

'As a matter of fact, sir,' she said, no change in the sweetness of her smile, 'the idea was mine.'

'In that case,' he picked up seamlessly, 'I'll live in the single hope that I win in a tie so that I can be a part of the money's going to such a noble cause.'

She looked at him, her expression neutral, but then the smile returned and she said, 'Ah, just listen to the falseness of the man.'

Brunetti was surprised by how flattered he felt and went back to his office, all thought of holiday staffing forgotten.

4

Spring advanced, and Brunetti continued to measure it florally. The first lilacs appeared in the flower shops, and he took an enormous bouquet home to Paola; the little pink and yellow flowers made their full appearance in the garden across the canal, were succeeded by random daffodils, and then by ordered rows of tulips at the side of the path bordering the garden. And then one Saturday Paola commandeered him into moving the large terracotta vases from the cool, dark *sottotetto* where they spent the winter back on to the terrace, where they would remain until November. From the terrace, he noticed that the flower boxes on the balcony on the other side of the *calle* and one floor below had been planted with the red geraniums Brunetti so much disliked.

Then there was Palm Sunday, which he was aware of only when he saw people walking around with olive branches in their hands. And then Easter and explosions of flowers in the windows of Biancat, displays so excessive that Brunetti was forced to stop every evening on the way home from work to consider them.

On Easter Sunday, they had lunch with Paola's parents; this year her aunt Ugolina was also in attendance, wearing a straw hat covered with tiny paper roses that saw the light of day, perhaps, once a year. They took with them – because there was nothing to take to the Faliers that they did not already have and did not already have in a superior form – flowers. The *palazzo* was already filled with them, but this did not prevent the Countess from gushing over the roses as though they heralded a new species. The excess of flowers also set Chiara off into an impromptu lecture on the ecological wastefulness of hothouse flowers, a discourse she found no one willing to listen to.

The floral note was continued on an invitation Paola received to a gallery opening that was to present the work of three young artists working in glass. From what Brunetti saw from the photos in the invitation, one produced flat panels using gold leaf and coloured glass; the second made vases with lips that resembled the petals of the flowers that would be put inside; and the third used a more traditional style to create cylindrical vases with smooth lips.

The gallery was new, run by the friend of a colleague of Paola's at the university who suggested that they attend. The level of crime in Venice was as low as the waters of that year's spring tides, and so Brunetti was happy to accept; because the gallery was on Murano, he wondered if he would get to meet Ribetti and his wife: he hardly thought a gallery opening was the sort of place where he would re-encounter De Cal.

The opening was scheduled to begin at six on a Friday evening, which would allow people time to see the artists' work, have a glass of prosecco, nibble on something, and then go out to dinner or go home on time to eat. As they boarded the 41 at Fondamenta Nuove, Brunetti realized that years had passed since he had been out to Murano. He had gone there as a boy, when his father had worked in one of the factories for a time, but since then he had been there infrequently, since none of their friends lived on Murano, and he had never had reason to go there professionally.

Three or four other couples left the boat at Faro and also started down Viale Garibaldi. 'The one in red,' Paola said, moving closer to Brunetti and taking his arm in hers, 'is Professoressa Amadori.'

'And is that the Professor?' Brunetti asked, pointing with his other hand at a tall man with silver hair who walked at the side of the elderly woman in the red coat.

Paola nodded. 'Behave yourself, look attentive and inferior, and perhaps I'll introduce you to her,' she promised.

'Is she that bad?' Brunetti asked, glancing again at what appeared to be a completely ordinary woman, the sort one would see at Rialto, haggling over the price of mullet. From behind, her legs were slightly bowed, her feet stuffed into what looked like very uncomfortable shoes, or perhaps that impression resulted from her walk – tiny steps with inturned toes.

'She's worse,' Paola said. 'I've seen male students come out of their oral exams with her in tears: it's almost a point of pride with her never to be satisfied with their performance.' She paused for a moment, her attention drawn by something in a window, then turned away and continued walking. 'I've known other students who have cancelled exams, even produced doctor's certificates, once they learned that she would be on the examining committee.'

'Could it be that she's only very demanding of them?' he asked.

That stopped her in her tracks. She pulled back a step and looked him in the face. 'You have been living with me for the last twenty years, haven't you, Signore?' she asked. 'And you have heard me mention her a few times?'

'Six hundred and twenty-seven,' Brunetti said. 'If that's a few.'

'Good,' she said, taking his arm and starting to walk again.

'Then you know that it has nothing to do with being demanding, only with being a jealous bitch who doesn't want anyone, ever, to have a chance at getting anything she's got.'

'By failing students in their exams?' Brunetti asked.

'Then they can't get their degrees, which means there's no chance they can join the faculty, and because there's no chance they'll become colleagues, there's no chance they'll ever get an appointment or a promotion or a grant that she might want.'

'That's crazy,' Brunetti said.

She stopped again. 'Is this the same man who works for Vice-Questore Giuseppe Patta?' she demanded.

'That's different,' Brunetti was quick to protest.

'How?' she demanded, stopping again and no doubt unwilling to move until he answered.

'He doesn't have any power over what I do. He can't fail me in an exam.'

She looked at him as though he had started to foam at the mouth and howl. 'No power over what you do?' she asked.

Brunetti smiled and shrugged. 'All right, but he can't fail me in an exam.'

She smiled back at him and took his arm. 'Believe me about this, Guido. She's a bitch.'

'I stand warned,' he said affably. 'The Professor?'

'A marriage made in heaven,' was all she was willing to volunteer by way of information on that subject.

When they reached the canal, they turned left and then crossed Ponte Ballarin, turning right at the bottom. 'It's got to be along here somewhere,' Paola said, slowing her steps and looking into the windows of the shops and galleries they passed.

'It should be on the invitation,' Brunetti said.

'I know,' she said. 'But I forgot to bring it.'

They continued walking down the *riva*, attentive to the windows on their left. Past the *pescheria* they went, past a few more shops, some still open, some already closed. Three people emerged from a doorway in front of them and paused to light cigarettes, holding each other's drinks while they did so.

'That's got to be it,' Paola said. A man and a woman walked out, without drinks, and went off hand in hand in the opposite direction.

When they reached the doorway, two more people emerged, cigarettes already lit, and went to stand with the three other smokers, all leaning against the wall of the embankment and using it as a table for their glasses.

The door was open. Paola went in, paused just inside the threshold and looked around for someone she knew. Brunetti did the same, though with less hope of success. He saw some people he recognized, but it was in a Venetian way that he recognized them, from walking past them on the street over the course of years, perhaps decades, without ever learning who they were or what they did. He could hardly go up to the man who had lost so much of his hair and begin a conversation about that, nor could he ask the woman with the newly blonde hair why she had gained so much weight.

Through a small gap in the wall of people he saw the double row of display cases. He walked towards them, leaving Paola to find someone she knew, or meet someone new, and examined the contents of the first case, which was raised on thin legs to chest height. Upright, gold on one side, cobalt blue on the other, stood a rectangle of worked glass a little bit bigger than a copy of *Espresso*. The surface was textured, but in no regular, orderly way: it looked more as if someone had dragged their fingers in wet clay from bottom to top and then down again, creating shallow runnels where the light glittered and played. The next case contained another panel: though the size was the same, the texture and colours, even the colour of the gold, were entirely different, making it as unlike the first one as it was like it in size. The third

29

case held four thick glass rectangles with alternating stripes of what appeared to be silver and gold. They were as other-worldly as the others, and quite as beautiful.

An empty glass had been left on top of the third case, and Brunetti removed it, annoyed to find it there. The almost sandy dregs of red wine clashed with the supple smoothness of the glass objects.

The next case held three of the flower-like vases on the invitation, all in the faintest of pastels. Brunetti found them far smaller than he had expected. Nor was the work as deli-cate: what might have been flower petals were thicker than the real thing, thicker than what he knew a good *maestro* could create. Another case held three more of them, though these were in stronger, darker colours. The workmanship continued to displease him, and he walked quickly past them to the next case.

These vases were cylindrical, all of them rising up to deli-cate lips, the sort of lips that the others should have had, Brunetti thought. The vases varied in height and in diameter, but each managed to achieve a perfect harmony between the two. The final case held objects of no definite shape: they didn't resemble anything, had no discernible use, seemed to be little more than swerves and swirls of glass, each curve blending into another of a faintly lighter or darker colour.

'Do you like them?' a young woman asked Brunetti.

He looked away from the objects in the last case, smiled, and said, 'Yes, I think I do.' He turned back to the objects and studied them, then moved to the other side of the Plexiglas case to see them from a different perspective. Now they appeared entirely different and he doubted that he would be able to recognize them from this side, though he had just studied them from the other.

When he looked up, the young woman was back, two glasses of prosecco in her hands. She offered him a glass, and he took it with a smile and a nod. Finding himself now with two glasses, he reached down and set the empty one on the floor against the wall. He took a sip of the wine. 'You like it?' she asked, leaving him in some doubt as to whether she intended the prosecco or the art.

'The wine's excellent,' he said, which was true: for this sort of show, it was good. Usually they served the sort of still red that came in large bottles, and instead of the thin glass he had in his hand, the wine was served in plastic cups.

'And those?' she asked.

'I think I think they're beautiful,' he said and took another sip.

'Only *think* you think?'

'Yes,' Brunetti confirmed. 'They're too unlike what I'm used to seeing in glass, so I need to think about them for a while before I decide.'

'You think about the things you see?' the woman asked, sounding not a little surprised at this. She appeared to be in her late twenties, and had a faint Roman accent and a nose that looked as if it had the same origins. Her eyes were dark and bore no trace of makeup, though her mouth had been enlarged by dark red lipstick.

'It's my job,' he said. 'I'm a policeman.' He had no idea what imp of the perverse had made him say that. Perhaps it had been the sight of the people in the room, or the presence of Professoressa Amadori and her husband, the sort of lofty academics he had suffered under for so many years at university.

He took another sip of prosecco and asked, 'What do you do?'

'I teach at the university,' she said.

Paola had never mentioned anyone like this young woman, but that did not necessarily mean anything: Paola, if she discussed her work, usually talked about books rather than about her colleagues. 'Teach what?' Brunetti asked in what he hoped was a friendly manner.

31

'Applied Mathematics,' she said, smiled, and added, 'and you don't have to ask. I find it interesting but few other people do.'

He believed her and felt relieved of the burden of having to feign polite interest. He gestured with his glass toward the objects in the two lines of cases. 'And these? Do you like them?'

'The rectangular ones, yes; and these,' she said, 'especially these last ones. I find them very . . . very peaceful, though I don't know why I say that.'

Brunetti talked with the young woman for a few minutes more, then, finding his glass empty, excused himself and went back to the bar. He searched the room for Paola and saw her on the other side, talking to someone who, had he been able to see him from the back, he might have been able to identify as Professore Amadori. Whether it was he or not, Brunetti could read Paola's expression and made his way across the room to her side.

'Ah,' she said as he came up, 'here's my husband. Guido, this is Professore Amadori, the husband of a colleague of mine.'

The professor nodded to acknowledge Brunetti but did not bother to extend his hand. 'As I was saying, Professoressa,' he went on, 'the chief burden of our society is the influx of people of other cultures. They have no understanding of our traditions, no respect for . . .' Brunetti sipped at his wine, playing over in his memory the smooth surfaces of the first pieces he'd seen, marvelling at how harmonious they were. The professor, when Brunetti tuned back in, had moved on to Christian values, and Brunetti's mind moved on to the second set of vases. There had been no prices, but there was sure to be a price list somewhere, placed in a discreet, dark-covered folder. The professor moved on to the Puritan ethic of work and respect for time, and Brunetti moved on to a consideration of where such a piece could be put in their house and how it could be displayed without their having to get an individual display case for it.

Like a seal coming up to a hole in the ice to take a breath, Brunetti again tuned in to the monologue and heard 'oppression of women', and quickly pulled his head back under the water.

Had the professor been a singer, he might well have performed this entire aria on one breath; certainly it had all been sung on the same note. He wondered if this man or his wife could affect Paola's career in any way, and then it occurred to him that, regardless, they could not affect his own, and so he turned to Paola and said, interrupting the professor, 'I need another drink. Would you like one?'

She smiled at him, smiled at the astonished professor, and said, 'Yes. But let me get them, Guido.' Oh, she was a sly one, his wife: a snake, a viper, a weasel.

'No, let me,' he insisted and then compromised. 'Or come with me and meet this young woman who has just been telling me the most fascinating things about algorithms and theorems.' He smiled and made a small bow to the professor, muttered a word that could have been 'fascinating', or could have been 'hallucinating', said they would just be gone a moment, and fled, pulling his wife to safety by one hand.

She tried to speak but he held up a hand to indicate that it was not necessary: 'I cannot allow the oppression of women,' Brunetti said.

Together, they went and collected fresh glasses of prosecco; he noticed that Paola drank half of hers thirstily.

He asked if she had looked at the works, then went with her as she walked around each of the cases. When she was finished, she said, 'Displaying it would be a problem, though', just as if he had asked her if they should buy one and, if so, which.

Brunetti looked around at the crowd, which had grown

denser. A bearded scarecrow of a man, he saw, had been caught by Professore Amadori, who seemed to have been switched back to PLAY. A tall woman wearing a miniskirt with a fringe of glass baubles dangling from the hem walked past the professor, but his gaze remained on his listener, whose eyes, however, ached after the miniskirt.

A man and woman appeared by the first display case. They wore matching crocheted white skullcaps and ponchos made of rough wool, as though they had passed through Damascus on their way home from Machu Picchu. The man pointed at each piece in turn, and the woman fluttered her hands in praise or condemnation, Brunetti had no idea which.

When he turned back to Paola, she was gone. Instead, standing less than a metre from him and speaking to a woman with short dark hair, he saw Ribetti. He looked better than he had at their first encounter, and happier. He looked better not only because he was wearing a suit and tie and not the trousers and wrinkled jacket he had been wearing when Brunetti saw him the last time, the clothes he had been wearing when he was pushed to the ground and then detained by the police. The suit fitted him, but it seemed that the woman's company fitted him even better.

Brunetti looked down into his glass, not quite sure of the etiquette involved in a social meeting with a person he had saved from arrest. Ribetti, however, made Brunetti's reticence unnecessary for, as soon as he saw the Commissario, he said something to the woman and came across. 'Commissario, how nice to see you,' he said with what appeared to be real pleasure. Then, after a pause, 'I didn't expect to see you here.' Realizing this could be construed as doubt that a policeman could have any interest in art, he added an explanation, 'I mean on Murano, that is. Not here.' He stopped, as if aware that anything else he might say would only dig him in deeper. He glanced back at the woman and said to Brunetti, 'Come and meet my wife.'

Brunetti followed him over to the woman, who smiled at the approach of her husband. She had short hair in which Brunetti noticed quite a bit of grey. On closer inspection, he saw that she was older than her husband, perhaps by as much as ten years. 'This is the man who didn't arrest me, Assunta,' Ribetti said. He stood beside her and wrapped an arm around her shoulder.

She smiled at Brunetti and toasted him with her prosecco. 'I'm not at all sure what the protocol might be here,' she said, echoing Brunetti's concern.

Ribetti raised his glass and said, 'I think the protocol is we raise our glasses and give thanks I'm not in the slammer.' He finished what was left of his prosecco, holding the glass in the air for a moment.

'I'd like to thank you for helping Marco,' his wife said. 'I didn't know what to do, so I called Lorenzo, but I never imagined he'd involve anyone else.' Her glass remained forgotten in her hand as she spoke to Brunetti. 'In fact, I don't know what I thought he'd do. Just that he'd do something.' Her brown eyes were set under unfashionably thick eyebrows, and her nose was broad at the tip and slightly turned up, but softness had found its way into her face with her mouth, which seemed made for smiles.

'I really didn't do anything, Signora; I assure you. By the time we got there, the magistrate had already decided to release everyone. There was no way charges could have been brought against them.'

'Why is that?' she asked. 'I don't see how they could have been taken there if they weren't going to be arrested.'

Brunetti had no desire to explain the vagaries of police procedure, certainly not now, with a glass of prosecco growing warm in his hand and his wife making her way through the crowd towards him, so he said, 'No one ever made it clear what happened, so no charges were brought.' Before either of them could say anything, he sensed Paola's presence at his side and he said, 'This is my wife.' And to Paola, 'Assunta De Cal and Marco Ribetti.'

Paola smiled and said the right things about the pieces on display, then asked how it was they were at the opening. She was delighted to learn that Assunta was the daughter of the owner of the *fornace* where one of the artists' work had been made.

'The flat panels,' Assunta explained. 'He's a young man from here. The nephew of a woman I went to school with, as a matter of fact. That's why he used my father's *fornace*. She called me and asked, and I talked to the *maestro* and then brought Lino to talk to him, and they liked one another's work, so he commissioned the *maestro* to fire the pieces.'

How Venetian a solution, Brunetti thought: someone knew someone who had gone to school with someone, and so the deal was done.

'Couldn't he do the work himself?' Paola asked. When Assunta and Ribetti seemed not to understand, she pointed to the pieces in the display cabinet and said, 'The artist. Couldn't he make them himself?'

Assunta held up a hand as if to ward away evil. 'No, never. It takes years, decades, before you can fire something. You have to know about the composition of the glass, how to prepare the *miscela* to get the colours you want, what sort of furnace you're working with, who your *servente* is, how fast and how reliable he is with the things you have to do for that particular piece.' She stopped as if suddenly exhausted by this long list. 'And that's just the beginning,' she added, and her listeners laughed.

'You sound like you could do it yourself,' Paola said with every sign of respect.

'Oh, no,' Assunta said, 'I'm too small. You really do have to be a man, well, be as strong as a man.' Here she held up her hand, which was little larger than a child's. 'And I'm not that, as you can see.' She let her hand fall to her side. 'But

I've been in and out of the *fornace* since I was a little girl, so I guess I've got glass or sand in my blood.'

'You work for your father?' Paola asked.

The question seemed to puzzle her, as if it had never occurred to her that there might have been anything else she could have done in life. 'Yes. I help him run the *fornace*. I was there even before I was in school.'

'She's the paid slave,' Rubetti said and ruffled her hair.

She bowed her head as if to escape his hand, but it was obvious that she enjoyed both the attention and the contact. 'Oh, stop it, Marco. You know I love it.' She looked at Paola and asked, 'What do you do, Signora?'

'Call me Paola,' she offered, slipping automatically into the familiar *tu*. 'I teach English literature at the university.'

'Do you love it?' Assunta asked with surprising directness. 'Yes.'

'Then you understand,' Assunta said. Brunetti was glad she did not think to ask him the same question, for he had no idea how he would have answered. She put a hand on Paola's arm and continued, 'I love to see the things grow and change and become more beautiful, even love to see them resting there overnight in the *fornace*.' She put her palm flat against the side of the display cabinet. 'And these objects, I love them because they seem to be so alive. Well, at least to me.'

'Then I'd say you have the perfect job,' Brunetti told her.

Assunta smiled and moved, if possible, closer to her husband. Brunetti waited for her to announce that she had also found the perfect man, but instead she said, 'I just hope I can keep it.'

Paola made no attempt to disguise her concern and asked, 'Why? It's not a job you're afraid of losing, is it?'

Paola was looking at Assunta's face, so she missed the glance Ribetti gave her, a slight shake of the head and a momentary narrowing of the eyes. But his wife saw it and immediately said, 'Oh, no, of course not.' Brunetti watched her search for something else to say, other than what she had been about to say. After a long pause, Assunta went on, 'You just want these things to last for ever, I guess.'

'Yes, of course,' Brunetti said, smiling and pretending that he had not observed Ribetti's glance and had not registered the change of atmosphere, the lowering of the human temperature of the conversation. He put his arm around Paola's shoulder and said, 'I'm afraid I've got to drag us away, though.' He looked at his watch. 'We've got to meet people for dinner, and we're already late.'

Paola, no slouch as a liar, looked at her watch and gasped, 'Oh my God, Guido. We *are* late. And we've got to get to Saraceno.' She reached into her bag, searching for something, finally abandoned the search, and asked Brunetti, 'I forgot my *telefonino*. Can you call Silvio and Veronica and tell them we'll be late?'

'Of course,' Brunetti said smoothly, though Paola had never had a *telefonino*, and none of their friends were called Silvio. 'I'll do it from outside. The reception will be better.'

There followed the usual exchange of pleasantries, the two women kissing on the cheek while the two men tried to jockey around the business of choosing between *Lei* and *tu*.

It wasn't until they were outside on the *riva* that he could look Paola in the eye and ask, 'Silvio and Veronica?'

'Every woman must have her dream,' she intoned piously and then turned to begin to walk towards the vaporetto that would take them back to Venice and home.

5

The return of spring also brought the return of tourists to the city, and that brought in its wake the usual mess, just as the migration of wildebeest lures the jackals and hyenas. The Romanians with the die hidden under one of three cups appeared on the tops of bridges, from which their sentries could watch for the arrival of the police. The *vu cumprà* fished into their capacious hold-alls and produced the new models just launched by the designer bag-makers. And both the *Carabinieri* and the *Polizia Municipale* handed endless copies of the proper forms to the people who had had their pockets or purses picked. Springtime in Venice.

Late one afternoon, Brunetti stopped by Signorina Elettra's office, but she was not at her desk. He had hoped to have a word with the Vice-Questore, but when he saw that the door to Patta's office was open, Brunetti came to the conclusion that they had both decided to leave for the day. In Patta's case, this was only to be expected, but Signorina Elettra, since this was the day when she did not arrive until after lunch, usually stayed until at least seven.

He was about to retreat from her room and take the papers he had brought with him back up to his own office, when the impulse to be certain forced him nearer to the door to Patta's office. He was surprised to hear Signorina Elettra speaking English very slowly and enunciating every word as if for the benefit of the hearing impaired, saying, 'May I have some strawberry jam with my scones, please?'

After a longish pause, this was followed by Patta's voice, saying, 'May E ev som strubbry cham per mio sgonzes, pliz?'

'Does this bus go to Hammersmith?'

And on it went, through four phrases of dubious utility until Brunetti heard, once again, the pained request for strawberry jam. Fearing he might be there some time, he went back to the door to her office and knocked loudly, calling out, 'Signorina Elettra, are you there?'

Within seconds she appeared at Patta's doorway, a look of stunned relief illuminating her face, as though Brunetti's voice had just pulled her from quicksand. 'Ah, Commissario,' she said, 'I was just about to call you.' Her voice caressed every syllable of the Italian, as though she were Francesca, the language her Paolo, and this her last chance to speak their love.

'I'd like to have a word with the Vice-Questore, if that's possible,' he said.

'Ah, yes,' she said, stepping clear of Patta's door. 'He's free at the moment.'

Brunetti excused himself and walked past her. Patta sat at his desk, elbows propped on the surface, chin cupped in his palms, as he studied the book in front of him. Brunetti approached and, glancing down, recognized the photo of Tower Bridge on the left-hand page, the black-hatted Beefeater on the right. '*Mi scusi, Dottore,*' he said, careful to speak softly and enunciate clearly.

Patta's eyes drifted towards Brunetti and he said, '*Sì?*'

'I wondered if I might have a word with you, sir?' Brunetti said.

With a slow motion full of resignation, Patta shut the book and moved it to one side. 'Yes? Have a seat, Brunetti. What is it?'

Brunetti did as he was told, careful to keep his eyes away from the book, though it was impossible not to notice the Union Jack waving across the cover. 'It's about the juveniles, sir,' Brunetti said.

It took Patta some time to cross the Channel and return to his desk, but he eventually responded. 'What juveniles?'

'The ones we keep arresting, sir.'

'Ah,' Patta said, 'those juveniles.' Brunetti watched his superior trying to recall the documents or arrest reports that had passed his desk in recent weeks, and saw him fail.

Patta straightened himself in his chair and asked, 'There's a directive from the Ministry, isn't there?'

Brunetti refused the temptation to answer that there was a directive from the Ministry prescribing the number of buttons on the officers' uniform jackets and, instead, said, 'Yes, sir, there is.'

'Then those are the orders we have to follow, Brunetti.' He thought Patta would be content to leave it at that, given that it was so close to the time he usually went home, but something drove Patta to add, 'I think we've had this conversation before. It is your duty to enforce the law, not to question it.'

Nothing in his statement, or in his manner, Brunetti knew, had suggested any questioning or desire to question the law. Yet from force of habit, habit worn deep by years of exposure to his subordinate, Patta had but to hear Brunetti mention a regulation in order to hear some phantom voice rise up in criticism or doubt.

Patta's comment pressed Brunetti into the role of troublemaker. 'Mine is more a procedural question, sir.'

'Yes? What?' Patta asked with some surprise.

'It's about these juveniles, as I said, sir. Each time we arrest them, we take their photos.'

41

'I know that,' interrupted Patta. 'It's part of the orders in the directive.'

'Exactly,' Brunetti said with a smile he realized more clearly resembled that of a shark than that of a dutiful subordinate.

'Then what is it?' Patta said with a glance at his watch he made neither swift nor covert.

'We're in some uncertainty about how to list them, sir.'

'I don't follow you, Brunetti.'

'The directive says we're to catalogue them according to age, sir.'

'I know that,' said Patta, who probably did not.

'But each time they're arrested and photographed, they give us a different name and a different age, and then a different parent comes to collect them and brings a different piece of identification.' Patta started to speak, but Brunetti rolled right over him. 'So what we wondered, sir, was whether we should list them under the age they give, or under the name, or perhaps according to their photo.' He paused, watching Patta's confusion, then said, 'Perhaps we could institute some system of filing them by photo, sir.'

He saw Patta draw himself up, but before the Vice-Questore could answer, Brunetti thought of one case his officers had complained about that morning, and said, 'There's one we've arrested six times in the last ten days, and each time we have the same photo, sir, but we've got . . .' he looked down at the papers he had intended to give Signorina Elettra, which had nothing at all to do with the young man he was talking about, and said, 'six different names and four different ages.' He looked up and gave his most subservient smile. 'So we were hoping you could tell us where to file him.'

If he had expected, or hoped, to goad Patta to anger, Brunetti failed. The closest he got was for the Vice-Questore to drop his chin into one hand, stare at Brunetti for almost a minute, and then say, 'There are times when you try my patience, Commissario.' He got to his feet. 'I've got a meeting now,' he said.

Graceful and sleek as an otter, Patta never failed to impress Brunetti with his appearance of power and competence, and so it was now. He ran a hand through his still-thick silvering hair and went to the *armadio* against the wall, from which he removed a light topcoat. He drew a white silk scarf from one of the sleeves and wrapped it around his neck, then put the coat on. He went to the door of his office and turned back to Brunetti, who still sat in front of his superior's desk. 'As I said, the rules are spelled out in the directive from the Ministry, Commissario.' And he was gone.

Curiosity led Brunetti to lean forward and pick up Patta's book; he flipped through the pages. He saw the usual photos of boy meeting girl, girl meeting boy, then noted how carefully they took turns asking where the other came from and how many people were in their families, before the boy asked the girl if she would like to go and have a cup of tea with him. Brunetti dropped the book back on Patta's desk.

Outside, Signorina Elettra sat at her desk. Sufficient time had passed for her to have returned to some semblance of serenity. 'Does this bus go to Hammersmith?' Brunetti asked in English, straight faced.

Signorina Elettra's expression quit the world of Dante and turned to scripture: her face could have been that of the fleeing Eve on any one of a number of medieval frescos. Ignoring his English, she responded in Veneziano, a language she seldom used with him. 'This bus will take you straight to *remengo* if you're not careful, *Dottore*.'

Where <u>was</u> *remengo*, Brunetti wondered? Like most Venetians, he had been told to go there and had been telling people to go there for decades, yet he had never paused to consider whether it was reachable by foot or boat or, in this case, bus. And was it a place like a city, meant to be written with a capital letter, or a more theoretical location like

43

desperation or the devil and thus reachable only by means of imprecation?

'. . . can't bring myself to be the one to tell him it's hopeless.' Signorina Elettra's words brought him back to the present.

'But you're still giving him English lessons?'

'I used to be able to resist him,' she said. 'But then he became vulnerable when I knew he was going to be rejected and he thought there was still a chance, and now I can't keep myself from trying to help.' She shook her head at the madness of it.

'Even though you know there's no hope he'll get the job?'

She shrugged and repeated, 'Even though I know there's no hope he'll get the job. Everything was fine until I saw his weakness – how much he wants this job – it was enough to make him human. Or very close. I closed my eyes for a minute and he slipped beneath my radar.' She tried to shake the thought away but failed.

Brunetti resisted the temptation to ask her how it was that she was so certain the Vice-Questore had no chance at the job, wished her a good evening and, deciding to walk home, turned left rather than right when he left the Questura. The same magic hand that had been poised over the city for a week remained in place, warding off rain and cold and beckoning forward ever milder temperatures. Urged by some secret motion, plants sprang up everywhere. In passing an iron railing, he noticed vines trailing over the top in an attempt to escape into the *calle* from the garden where they were being kept prisoner. A dog ran past him, followed by another, busy with doggy things. Perched on the wall of an embankment in the increasing chill of the evening were two young men in T-shirts and jeans, a sight which called Brunetti back to his senses, forcing him to button his jacket.

Paola had said something about lamb that morning, and

Brunetti started thinking about the many interesting things that could be done to lamb. With rosemary and black olives or with rosemary and hot chilli peppers. And what was that one that Erizzo liked so much: the stew with balsamico and green beans? Or simply white wine and rosemary – and why was it that lamb cried out for rosemary more than any other herb? Following the trail of lamb, Brunetti found himself on the top of the Rialto, gazing south toward Cà Farsetti and the scaffolding that still covered the façade of the university down at the bend, the buildings softened by the evening light. Look at those *palazzi*, he told some silent audience of non-Venetians. Look at them and tell me who could build them today. Who could come and stack those blocks of marble one on top of the other and have the finished products display such effortless grace?

Look at them, he went on, look at the homes of the Manins, the Bembos, the Dandolos, or look farther down to what the Grimanis and the Contarinis and the Trons built in their names. Look on those things and tell me we did not once know greatness.

A man hurrying across the bridge bumped lightly into Brunetti, excused himself, and ran down the other side. When Brunetti looked back up the canal, the *palazzi* looked much as they always did, massive and grand, but the magic had dimmed, and now they also looked slightly in need of repair. He walked down the stairs on his side of the bridge and cut along the *riva*. He didn't want to have to push his way through whatever crowds still lingered near the market or walk the gauntlet of cheap masks and plastic gondolas.

Lamb it was, lamb with balsamic vinegar and green beans. No antipasto and only a salad to follow. This could mean one of a number of things, and as he ate, Brunetti used his professional skills to seek out the possible cause. Either his wife had been so caught up in the reading of some text – Henry James tended to make her most careless about dinner – or

45

she was in a bad mood, but there was no sign of that. Her suitcase was not standing open on their bed, so he excluded the possibility that she was preparing to run off with the butcher, though the lamb would have been more than suffi-cient inducement for most women. He approached the next course with mounting anticipation and increasing hope: it might involve an explosive dessert, something they had not had for some time.

The detective finished the beans, keeping an eye on the suspects around the table. Whatever it was, the wife and the daughter were in it together. Every so often they exchanged a secret glance, and the girl had trouble disguising her excite-ment. The boy appeared not to be involved in whatever was going on. He polished off the lamb and ate a slice of bread, looked over at the beans and made no attempt to hide his disappointment that his father had beaten him to them. The woman shot a glance at the boy's plate, and did he detect a smile on her face when she saw that it was empty? The detec-tive glanced away so she would not catch him watching them so closely. To lead them astray, he poured himself a half-glass of Tignanello and said 'Wonderful meal', as if that were the end of it.

The girl looked worried, glanced at the woman, who smiled calmly. The girl got to her feet and stacked the plates. She carried them over to the sink and said, her back to the others, 'Anyone interested in dessert?'

A man kept on short rations at his own table – certainly he was interested in dessert. But he left it to the boy to speak, contenting himself with another sip of wine.

The woman got up and went over to the door leading to the back terrace, the one facing north, where she kept things that wouldn't fit in the refrigerator. But when she heard the girl setting the dishes in the sink, she called her over, and they had a whispered conversation. The detective watched the woman go to the cabinet where the dishes were kept and take down shallow bowls. Not fruit salad, for heaven's sake. And not one of those stupid puddings filled with bread.

The detective picked up the bottle and checked to see what was left. Might as well finish it: it was too good to leave uncorked overnight.

The woman came back with four tiny glasses, and things began to look up. What would be served with sweet wine? No sooner had he begun to hope than realism intervened: this might be another attempt to deceive him, and there might be nothing more than almond cookies, but then the girl turned from the door to the terrace and came towards the table with a dark brown oval resting on a plate in front of her. The detective had time to think of Judith, and Salome, when his suspicions were obliterated by three voices calling in unison, 'Chocolate mousse. Chocolate mousse', and he glanced aside just in time to see the woman pull an enormous bowl of whipped cream from the refrigerator.

It wasn't until considerably later that a sated Brunetti and a contented Paola sat together on the sofa, he feeling virtuous at having refused the sweet wine and then the grappa that was offered in its place.

'I had a call from Assunta,' she said, confusing him.

'Assunta who?' he asked, his feet crossed on the low table in front of them.

'Assunta De Cal,' she said.

'Whatever for?' he asked. Then he remembered that it was in her father's *fornace* that the glass panels had been made and wondered if Paola wanted to see more of the artist's work.

'She's worried about her father.'

Brunetti was tempted to inquire what his involvement in that might be but asked only, 'Worried about what?'

'She said he's getting more and more violent towards her husband.'

'Violent violent or talk violent?'

'So far, only talk violent, but she's worried – Guido, I really think she is – that the old man will do something.'

'Marco's at least thirty years younger than De Cal, isn't he?' When she nodded, Brunetti said, 'Then he can defend himself or he can just run away. Walk away, from what I remember of the old man.'

'It's not that,' Paola said.

'Then what is it?' he asked kindly.

'She's afraid that her father will get in trouble by doing something to him. By hitting him or, oh, I don't know. She says she's never seen him so angry, not ever in her life, and she doesn't know why he is.'

'What sort of things does he say?' Brunetti asked, knowing from experience that the violent often announce their intentions, sometimes in the hope that they will be prevented from carrying them out.

'That Ribetti's a troublemaker and that he married her for her money and to get his hands on the *fornace*. But he says that only when he's drunk, Assunta said, about the *fornace*.'

'Who in their right mind would want to take over a *fornace* in Murano these days?' Brunetti asked in an exasperated voice. 'Especially someone who has no experience of glass-making?'

'I don't know.'

'Why did she call you, then?'

'To ask if she could come and talk to you,' Paola said, sounding faintly nervous about passing on the request.

'Of course, she can come,' Brunetti said and patted her thigh.

'You'll be nice to her?' Paola asked.

'Yes, Paola,' he said, leaning over to kiss her on the cheek. 'I'll be nice to her.'

6

Assunta De Cal came to the Questura a little after ten the following morning. An officer called from the entrance to say Brunetti had a visitor, then accompanied her to the Commissario's office. She stopped just inside the door, and Brunetti got to his feet and went over to shake her hand. 'How nice that we see one another again,' he said, using the plural to avoid addressing her either formally or informally. If she had looked older than her husband at the gallery opening, she looked even more so now. Her skin was sallow, and the lines running from her nose down either side of her mouth were more pronounced. Her hair was freshly washed and she wore makeup, but she had not managed to disguise her nervousness or the stress she seemed to be under.

She had apparently decided that he was to share in the same grammatical dispensation as Paola and addressed him as *tu* when she thanked him and said it was kind of him to take time to listen to her.

Brunetti led her to the chairs in front of his desk, held one for her, and took the other as soon as she was seated.

'Paola said you wanted to talk to me about your father,' he began.

She sat upright in the chair, like a schoolchild asked into the office of the *preside* to be reprimanded. She nodded a few times. 'It's terrible,' she finally said.

'Why do you say that, Assunta?'

'I told Paola,' she said, as though she were reluctant or embarrassed and perhaps hoped to learn that Paola had told Brunetti everything.

'I'd like you to tell me about it, as well,' Brunetti encouraged her.

She took a deep breath, brought her lips together, opened her mouth to sigh, and said, 'He says that Marco doesn't love me and that he married me for my money.' She did not look at him as she said this.

Brunetti could understand her embarrassment at repeating her father's remarks about her desirability, but these were not the threats Paola had mentioned. '*Do* you have any money, Signora?'

'That's the crazy thing,' she said, turning to him and stretching out a hand. She drew it back just before it touched his arm, and she said, 'I don't have any. I own the house my mother left me, but Marco owns his mother's house in Venice, which is bigger.'

'Who's in that house?' Brunetti asked.

'We let it,' she said.

'And the money which comes from that? Is it enough to make you rich?'

She laughed at the idea. 'No, he lets it to his cousin and her husband. They're paying four hundred Euros a month. That's not going to make anyone rich,' she said.

'Do you have any savings?' he asked, thinking of the many stories he had heard, over the years, of people who had hoarded away their salaries and become millionaires.

'No, not at all. I used most of my savings when I inherited the house from my mother and had it restored. I thought I could let it and continue to live in my father's house, but then I met Marco and we decided we wanted our own house.'

'Why did you decide to live on Murano instead of here in the city?' From what Vianello had told him of Ribetti's work, the engineer would have to spend a lot of time on the mainland, and that would probably be easier from Venice than from Murano.

'I work in the factory, and sometimes, if there's a problem, I have to go in at night. Marco goes to the terra ferma a few times a week for his work, but he can get to Piazzale Roma easily enough from there, so we decided to stay on Murano. Besides,' she added, 'his cousin has been in the house a long time.'

Brunetti realized that this was a coded way of explaining that the cousin either would not get out of the house without a court order forcing her to do so or that Ribetti was unwilling to ask her to leave. It was not important to Brunetti which of these was true, so he abandoned the subject and asked, searching for the proper way to refer to future inheritance, 'Do you have prospects?'

'You mean the *fornace*? When my father dies?' she asked: so much for Brunetti's attempts at delicacy.

'Yes.'

'I think I'll inherit it. My father has never said anything, and I've never asked. But what else would he do with it?'

'Have you any idea what a *fornace* like your father's would be worth?'

He watched her calculate, and then she said, 'I'd guess somewhere around a million Euros.'

'Are you sure of that sum?' he asked.

'Not exactly, no, but it's a good estimate, I think. You see, I've kept the accounts for years, and I listen to what the other owners say, so I know what the other *fornaci* are worth, or at least what their owners think they're worth.' She looked at

him, then away for an instant and then back, and Brunetti
sensed that he was finally getting close to what she had come
to talk about. 'But that's another thing that bothers me.'

'What?'

'I think my father might be trying to sell it.'

'Why do you say that?'

She looked away for a long time, perhaps formulating an
answer, then back at him before she said, 'It's nothing, really.
Well, nothing I can describe or be sure of. It's the way he acts,
and some of the things he says.'

'What sort of things?'

'Once, I told one of the men to do something, and he – my
father, that is – asked me what it would be like if I couldn't
order men around any more.' She paused to see how Brunetti
reacted to this and then went on. 'And another time, when
we were ordering sand, I told him we should double the
order so we could save on the transport, and he said it would
be best to order enough only for the next six months. But the
way he said it was strange, as if he thought . . . oh, I don't
know, as if we weren't going to be there in six months.
Something like that.'

'How long ago was this?'

'About six weeks, maybe less.'

Brunetti thought about asking her if she would like something to drink, but he knew better than to break the rhythm
into which their conversation had fallen. 'I'd like to go back
to the things your father has said about Marco. Has he ever
talked about wanting to do anything to him?' Obviously, she
must realize that Paola would have repeated to him what she
had said but perhaps it helped her to pretend she had not
revealed family secrets and let him coax the story out of her.

'You mean threaten him?'

'Yes.'

She considered this for some time, perhaps trying to find
a way to continue denying it. Finally she said, 'I've heard

him say what he hopes will happen to him.' It was an evasive answer, Brunetti knew, but at least she had begun to talk.

'But that's not exactly a threat, is it?' Brunetti asked.

'No, not really,' she surprised him by agreeing. 'I know how men talk, especially men who work in the *fornaci*. They're always saying that they'll break someone's head or break his leg. It's just the way they talk.'

'Do you think that's the case with your father?' Brunetti asked.

'I wouldn't be here if I thought that,' she said in a voice that had suddenly grown serious, almost reproving him that he could ask such a thing or treat her visit so lightly.

'Of course,' Brunetti agreed. 'Then has your father made real threats?' When she made no move to answer, he asked, 'Did Marco tell you?' He thought it would be best to speak of Marco familiarly and thus make the atmosphere more friendly again, if only to induce her to speak more openly.

'No, he'd never repeat things like that.'

'Then how did you learn about it?'

'Men at the *fornace*,' she said. 'They heard him – my father – talking.'

'Who?'

'Workers.'

'And they told you?'

'Yes. And another man I know.'

'Would you tell me their names?'

This time she did put a hand on his arm and asked, her concern audible, 'Is this going to get them into trouble?'

'If you tell me their names or if I talk to them?'

'Both.'

'I don't see any way that it could. As you said, men talk like this, and most often it's nothing, just talk. But before I can know if that's all it is, I need to talk to the men who heard your father say these things. That is,' he added, 'if they'll talk to me.'

'I don't know that they will,' she said.

'Neither do I,' Brunetti said with a small, resigned grin. 'Not until I ask them.' He waited for her to volunteer the names; when she didn't, he asked, 'What did they tell you?'

'He told one of them that he'd like to kill Marco,' she said, her voice unsteady.

Brunetti did not waste time trying to explain that a remark like this depended on context and tone for its meaning. He hardly wanted to begin to sound like an apologist for De Cal, but the little he had seen of the man led him to suspect that he would be prone to say such things without any serious intent.

'What else?'

'That he'd see him dead before he'd let him have the *fornace*. The man who told me this said my father was drunk when he said it and was talking about the history of the family and not wanting it to be destroyed by some outsider.' She looked at Brunetti and tried to smile but didn't make a very good job of it. 'Anyone who's not from Murano is an outsider for him.'

Trying to lighten the mood, Brunetti said, 'My father felt that way about anyone who wasn't from Castello.'

She smiled at this but returned immediately to what she had been saying. 'It doesn't make any sense for him to say that, no sense at all. The last thing in the world Marco wants is to have anything to do with the *fornace*. He listens to me when I talk about work, but that's politeness. He has no interest in it.'

'Then why would your father think he did?'

She shook her head. 'I don't know. Believe me, I don't know.'

He waited a while and then said, 'Assunta, I'd like to tell you that people who talk about violence never do it, but that's not true. Usually they don't. But sometimes they do. Often all they want to do is complain and get people to listen to

54

them. But I don't know your father well enough to be able to tell if that's true about him.'

He spoke slowly and without judgement or criticism. 'I'd like very much to speak to these men and get a clearer idea of what he said and how he said it.' She started to ask a question but he went on, 'I'm not asking you as a policeman, because there's no question of a crime here, nothing at all. I'd simply like to go and talk to these people and settle this, if I can.'

'And to my father?' she said fearfully.

'Not unless I think there's reason to do that,' Brunetti answered, which was the truth. He had no desire to speak to De Cal again; further, he did not think her father a man much given to listening to the voice of sweet reason.

'You want me to tell you their names?' she asked, her voice suddenly softer, as if by making it smaller she could more easily hide from the answer.

'Yes.'

She looked at him for a long time. Finally she said, 'Giorgio Tassini, *l'uomo di notte*. For my father and for the *fornace* next door. And Paolo Bovo. He doesn't work for us, but he heard him talking.'

Brunetti asked for their addresses, and she wrote them down on a piece of paper he gave her, asking him if he would try to talk to Tassini away from the *fornace*. Brunetti was happy to agree, seeing it as an opportunity to stay clear of De Cal for the moment.

Brunetti had never been good at giving false assurances to people, but he wanted to give her at least some comfort. 'I'll see what they tell me,' he said. 'People tend to say things they don't mean, especially when they're angry, or when they've had too much to drink.' He remembered De Cal's face and asked, 'Does your father drink more than he should?'

She sighed again. 'A glass of wine is more than he should

drink,' she said. 'He's a diabetic and shouldn't drink at all, and certainly not as much as he does.'

'Does this happen often?'

'You know how it is, especially with workmen,' she said with the resignation of long familiarity. '*Un'ombra* at eleven, and then wine with lunch, then a couple of beers to get through the afternoon, especially in the summer when it's hot, and then a couple more *ombre* before dinner, and more wine with the meal, and then maybe a grappa before bed. And then the next day you start all over again.'

It sounded like the kind of drinking he was used to seeing in men of his father's generation: they'd drunk like this most of their adult lives, yet he had never seen one of them behave in a way that would suggest drunkenness. And why on earth should they change just because the professional classes had switched to prosecco and spritz?

'Has he always been like this?' he asked, then clarified the question by adding, 'I don't mean the drinking: I mean his temper and the violent language.'

She nodded. 'A few years ago, the police had to come and stop a fight.'

'Involving him?'

'Yes.'

'What happened?'

'He was in a bar, and someone said something he didn't like – he never told me about it, so I don't know what it was. I know this only from what other people have told me – and he said something back, and then one of them hit the other – I never learned who. And someone called the police, but by the time they got there, the other men had stopped them, and nothing happened. That is, no one was arrested and no one made a *denuncia*.'

'Anything else?' Brunetti asked.

'Not that I know about. No.' She seemed relieved that she could put an end to his questions.

'Has he ever been violent with you?'

Her mouth fell open. 'What?'

'Has he ever hit you?'

'No,' she said with such force that Brunetti could only believe her. 'He loves me. He'd never hit me. He'd cut off his hand first.' Strangely enough, Brunetti believed this, too.

'I see,' he said, and then added, 'That must make this even more painful for you.'

She smiled when he said that. 'I'm glad you can understand.'

There seemed nothing more to ask her, and so Brunetti thanked her for coming to speak to him and asked if she wanted to tell him anything else.

'Just fix this, please,' she said, sounding decades younger.

'I'll try,' Brunetti said. He asked for her *telefonino* number, wrote it down, then got to his feet.

He walked downstairs with her and out on to the embankment. It was warmer than when he had arrived a few hours before. They shook hands and she turned towards SS Giovanni e Paolo and the boat that would take her to Murano. Brunetti stood on the *riva* for a few minutes, looking across at the garden on the other side and running through his memory for personal connections. He went back into the Questura and up to the officers' room, where he found Pucetti.

The young officer stood when his superior entered. 'Good morning, Commissario,' he said. Was that a tan he saw on Pucetti's face? Brunetti had signed the forms authorizing staff leave during the Easter holiday, but he couldn't recall if Pucetti's name had been on it.

'Pucetti,' he said as he drew near the desk. 'You have family on Murano, don't you?' Brunetti could not remember why this piece of information had lodged in his memory, but he was fairly certain that it had.

'Yes, sir. Aunts and uncles and three cousins.'

'Any of them work at the *fornaci*?'

He watched Pucetti run through the list of his relatives. Finally he said, 'Two.'

'They people you can ask things?' Brunetti asked, not having to specify that the question referred to their discretion more than to the information they might possess.

'One of them is,' Pucetti said.

'Good. I'd like you to ask about Giovanni De Cal. He owns a *fornace* out there.'

'I know it, sir. It's on Sacca Serenella.'

'Do you know him?' Brunetti asked.

'No, sir. I don't. But I've heard about him. Is there anything specific you'd like to know?'

'Yes. He's got a son-in-law he hates and whom he may have threatened. I'd like to know if anyone thinks he'd actually do anything or if it's just talk. And I'd like to know if there's any word that he's thinking of selling his *fornace*.'

Brunetti watched Pucetti suppress the impulse to salute as he said, 'Yes, sir.' Then the younger man asked, 'Is there any hurry? Should I call him now?'

'No, I'd like to keep this as casual as possible. Why don't you go home and change and go out and talk to him? I don't want it to seem like . . .' Brunetti let his voice trail off.

'Seem like it is what it is?' Pucetti asked with a smile.

'Exactly,' Brunetti said, 'though I'm not sure I know what that is.'

7

L'uomo di notte, Brunetti considered, by definition worked nights, which would have him home during the day. It was only a little after eleven, one of the sweetest times of day in springtime, and so Brunetti decided to walk down to Castello to talk to Giorgio Tassini and see if he would be willing to repeat what De Cal had told him. It occurred to Brunetti that he was perhaps engaging in that portmanteau offence, *abuso d'ufficio*, for he was certainly using the powers of his office to look into something that was of interest to him personally and had no official interest to the forces of order. The thought that the alternative to a walk in the sunshine down to Via Garibaldi was to return to his office to begin reading through the personnel files of the officers due for promotion was more than enough to propel Brunetti out on to Riva degli Schiavoni.

He turned left and started down towards Sant'Elena. His strides grew longer as he felt the sun begin to work the winter stiffness out of him. Days like these reminded him of what a filthy climate the city really had: cold and damp in the winter; hot and damp in the summer. He banished this thought as the remains of winter gloom and looked around him, his smile as bright as the day itself.

He turned into Via Garibaldi, leaving the warmth of the sun behind him. According to Assunta, Tassini lived opposite the church of San Francesco di Paola, and he slowed as he saw the church on his left. He found the number he sought, read the names on the three bells and pressed the one at the top with 'Tassini' written below it. When there was no response, he rang the bell again, this time keeping his finger on it long enough to wake the sleeping man. Suddenly he heard a loud squawk from the speaker phone and then the low hiss of a loose connection. Silence. He rang a third time, and this time a low-pitched voice asked what he wanted.

'I'd like to speak to Signor Tassini,' he said, his voice unnaturally loud in an attempt to penetrate the hiss and the static that didn't stop.

'What?' the voice asked through another roar of static.

'Signor Tassini,' he shouted.

'. . . trouble . . . who? . . . enough . . .' the voice said.

Brunetti decided communication was useless, so he pressed his finger against the bell and kept it there until the door snapped open.

He climbed the stairs to the third floor, where he found a white-haired woman standing in a doorway on the top landing. She had the papery skin of a heavy smoker and short, badly permed white hair that fell in a jagged fringe across her eyebrows. Below it, her eyes were deep green and held in a perpetual squint, as though forced into it by decades of rising smoke. She was short, and her squat rotundity spoke of endurance and strength. She did not smile, but her face relaxed, and a thin tracery of wrinkles softened around her eyes and mouth. 'What can I do for you?' she asked in purest Castello, her voice almost as deep as his own.

Brunetti answered in dialect, as seemed only polite. 'I'd like to speak to Signor Tassini if he's here,' he said.

'Signor Tassini is it, now?' she asked with an inquisitive tilt of her chin. 'What could my son-in-law have done that the cops are interested in him?' She seemed curious rather than fearful.

'Is it that obvious, Signora?' Brunetti asked, waving his right hand at his own body. 'Couldn't I be the gasman?'

'As easily as I could be the Queen of Sheba,' she said and laughed from somewhere deep behind her stomach. When she stopped, both of them heard what sounded like the yipping of a puppy from inside the apartment. She turned her head towards it, still speaking to Brunetti as she did so. 'You better come in, then, so you can talk to me. Besides, I've got to keep an eye on them while Sonia does the shopping, isn't it true?'

As he gave her his name and shook her hand, it occurred to Brunetti to wonder how much of what she said would be comprehensible to a person from, say, Bologna. A number of the teeth on the top left side of her mouth were missing, so her speech was slurred, but it was the *Veneziano stretto* that was sure to defeat any ear not born within a hundred kilometres of the *laguna*. Yet how sweet it was to hear that dialect, so much like the one his grandmother had spoken all her life, never bothering to have anything to do with Italian, which she had always dismissed as a foreign language and not worthy of her attention.

The woman, who might have been fifty as easily as sixty, led him into a meticulously clean living room at the end of which stood a bookcase out of which books pretty well did whatever they wanted to do – hung, leaned, fell, tilted. Facing the sofa where the woman must have been sitting was a small television with a hothouse cyclamen in a plastic pot on top of it. On the television, pastel-coloured cartoon creatures danced around silently, for the sound had been turned down or off.

The sofa was draped with a plaid blanket and might once

61

have been white, though it was now the colour of oatmeal. In the middle of the sofa sat a young boy, perhaps two years old. He was the source of the noise, a piping cry of wordless joy with which he kept time to the jumps and steps of the pastel creatures. At the approach of the adults, the little boy smiled at his grandmother and patted the place beside him.

She plumped herself down next to him, grabbed him up and pulled him on to her lap. She bent and kissed the top of his head, provoking ecstatic wriggles. He turned away from the screen, hiked himself up on his feet, and planted a wet kiss on her nose. She looked up at Brunetti, smiled, then put her face up to the little boy's. Then she buried her face in his neck and whispered, 'More, xe beo, xe propio beo.' She looked at Brunetti, face bright, and asked, 'E xe beo, me puteo?'

Brunetti grinned in agreement and praised the boy's sun-like radiance, his obvious superiority to any child he'd ever seen, his remarkable resemblance to his grandmother. Her eyes narrowed momentarily, and she gave Brunetti a long, speculative glance.

'Mine are older now,' he said, 'but I still remember when they were his age. I used to invent some excuse to leave and go home from work just to be with them. I'd say I was going out to question someone, and I'd go home and play with my babies.'

Her smile widened in approval. From the back of the apartment there came a muffled noise, the unmistakable cry of a baby, and Brunetti looked at her in confusion. 'It's Emma,' she said. She bounced the boy on her lap and added, 'His twin sister.' She sized up Brunetti with astute eyes and asked, 'You think you could go and get her? He'll cry if I leave him now, even for a minute.'

Brunetti looked towards the back of the apartment.

'Just follow the noise,' she said and went back to bouncing the boy on her lap.

He did as he was told and went into a bedroom on the right side of the corridor, where he found two cribs that stood head to head. Bright-coloured mobiles floated from the ceiling, and a small zoo of stuffed animals stood behind the bars of the cribs. A little girl lay in one of them, beside her a furry elephant just as big as she. He walked over to her, saying, 'Emma, how are you? Aren't you a pretty girl? Come on, now, we're going out to see your *nonna*, eh?'

He bent and picked her up, surprised to find that she lay limp in his hands, like a frightened animal. Not-quite-forgotten habit slipped into operation and he put her over his shoulder, noticing the insubstantiality of her, patting her warm back with his right hand, saying nonsense things to her all the way back to the living room.

'Just put her here, next to me,' the woman said when he came in. He seated the little girl next to her grandmother, whereupon she tilted to the right and fell over. She made a low noise but did not move.

Before Brunetti could reach down and set her upright, the woman said, 'No, leave her. She can't sit up yet.'

At two, both of his children were walking, even running, and Raffi had declared war on any object within his reach. Brunetti made himself respond as if he found her remark in no way surprising.

'Has she seen a doctor?'

'Ah, doctors,' she said, the way Venetians always spoke of doctors.

She got to her feet, propped the little boy upright next to his sister, stuck a pillow on his other side, and took a packet of Nazionale blu out of the pocket of her apron. 'Would you watch them while I go and have a cigarette?' she asked. 'Sonia and Giorgio don't want me to smoke in the house, so I have to go out on the landing and open the window.' She grinned at this. 'I suppose it's only fair. I did it to Sonia, God knows, for years.' The grin turned into a smile and she added, 'At least, with her, it worked, and she doesn't smoke. I suppose I should be thankful for that.'

Before Brunetti could agree, she walked to the door of the apartment and out on to the landing, leaving the door ajar. He decided to sit on the chair to the left of the sofa, leaving the children as undisturbed as possible. The little boy seemed to forget his grandmother as soon as she was gone and returned his attention to the plump figures on the screen that were now jumping into a river of blue flowers. The little girl lay where she had fallen. Brunetti sat, gazing at the small children, suddenly overcome by a wild uneasiness that something would happen to one of them while their grandmother was out of the room and he would not know how to deal with the situation. He watched the twins, amazed at the difference in their sizes, looked at the half-closed door, and then at the television screen.

After a few minutes, the woman came back into the apartment, trailing the odour of smoke. 'Giorgio never stops telling me how bad it is for me,' she said, patting the cigarettes that appeared to be back in her pocket. 'And I suppose he's right, but I've been smoking since before he was born, so it can't be as bad for me as he says.' She saw Brunetti's reluctant smile and added, 'Whenever he keeps at it, I always tell him that the salad he's eating is probably just as dangerous as my cigarettes.' She raised her shoulders, lowered them, and sighed deeply. 'I suppose we're both right, but you'd think he'd know me well enough by now to leave me alone about it.' Another sigh, another shrug. 'But he wants to believe what he wants to believe. Just like all of us. *Pazienza.*'

She took her seat on the sofa again, but this time she lifted the little girl on to her lap, placed a hand at her waist, and held her upright. The boy, seeing that she was holding his sister, scrambled on to his feet on the sofa and wrapped his grandmother's neck in his embrace, whispering secrets in her ear and laughing.

64

'Oh, look at them,' the woman said, pointing a finger at the screen and using that voice of feigned enthusiasm that seems always to deceive children. 'Look what they're doing now.'

The little boy fell for it and turned his attention away from his grandmother's ear and back to the television. Though he kept one arm draped around her shoulders, he appeared to forget about her. 'What was it you wanted to talk to him about?' she asked Brunetti. The little girl lay inert on her lap.

'Your son-in-law works at the De Cal *fornace*, I believe,' Brunetti said.

'At the factory?' she asked.

'Yes.'

'What do you want to know? He's only the watchman.'

Brunetti was surprised by her reaction to what had seemed an entirely innocuous question.

'There's been talk of threats being made there, and I wanted to speak to your son-in-law about it,' Brunetti said, not thinking it necessary to tell her any more than that.

'Whatever he said, I'm sure it was just talk and he didn't mean it,' she said.

'Do you know Signor De Cal?' Brunetti asked.

Her free hand moved automatically towards her cigarettes and patted them for whatever comfort the packet might provide. 'I've seen him, but I've never spoken to him,' she said. 'People say he's a difficult man to get along with, and there was that fight in the bar a couple of years ago. Everyone on Murano knows about it.'

'So your son-in-law has told you about the threats?' Brunetti asked.

She patted the little boy's bottom, pulled him a bit closer, but his attention was entirely engaged by the figures on the screen and he could not be distracted. Finally she said, 'Yes. But I told you, it was just talk. I'm sure he didn't mean anything.'

65

Then why, Brunetti wondered, mention the fight? 'Did your son-in-law tell you exactly what was said?'

Brunetti thought she looked as though he had trapped her into saying something she should not have said and regretted ever having spoken to him. 'He's always blamed De Cal,' she began, speaking softly. 'I know, I know, even though there's nothing that can prove it, Giorgio still believes it. Just like with the cigarettes: he believes it and that's that. No use talking to him.'

She looked at the little girl and placed her palm on her back, covering it completely. 'I've tried to talk to him. Sonia's tried. The doctors. Nothing. He believes it and that's that.'

Brunetti felt as though he had been looking at one programme on television, and while he was momentarily distracted, someone had pressed the remote control and he was now watching a different programme with no idea of what had happened at the beginning.

'And the threat?' was the only thing he could think to ask.

'I don't know what made him do it. In the past, he's always been careful what he said, never said anything directly. Though I'm sure they know what he thinks: no one keeps any secrets out there, and he's talked to the men he works with.' She raised her hands as if her open palms could summon help from heaven. 'Two weeks ago, he told Sonia he was close to having the final proof. But he's said that so many times,' she went on, her face and her voice growing sadder. 'Besides, we know there's no proof.'

She wrapped her right arm around the boy and pulled him close to her, then used her left hand to wipe her eyes. Suddenly speaking in a voice close to anger, she took her hand from her face and waved it in the direction of the book-case on the opposite wall. 'I should have known when he started reading all that stuff. How long is it? Two years? Three? And all he wants to do is read. So he keeps that job that pays almost nothing so he can read all night. But the children have to eat, we have to eat, and if I didn't own this apartment and couldn't stay home with the children, God knows what would happen to them: Sonia wouldn't work, and they'd starve on what he earns alone.' Her voice tightened with rage and she made a spitting motion with her lips. 'And try to get any help from this government; just try it. With all the proof they've got, with doctors' letters and certificates and tests from the hospital, and what do they give them? Two hundred Euros a month. And nothing for me, even though I have to stay here with them all the time. You try to raise two children on two hundred Euros a month and come and tell me how easy it is.'

The figures disappeared from the screen, and it was as if the little boy had suddenly been released to feel his grandmother's rage. He turned and put his arms around her neck. 'Good *nonna*, good *nonna*,' he said and began to stroke both her cheeks, pressing his face closer to hers.

'See?' she said, looking across at Brunetti. 'See what you've made me do?'

He saw that the woman was emotionally exhausted and was unlikely to answer any more questions, and so he said, 'I'd still like to speak to your son-in-law, Signora.' He pulled out his wallet and handed her one of his cards, then took out a pen and said, 'Could you give me his number so I can get in touch with him?'

'You mean the number of his *telefonino*?' she asked with an abrupt laugh.

Brunetti nodded.

'He doesn't have a *telefonino*,' she said, this time her voice carefully restrained. 'He won't use one because he believes the waves that come out of it are bad for his brain.' From her voice, it was evident how little credence she gave this opinion. 'That's another idea he got from his books,' she said. 'It's not enough that he thinks he's contaminated; he's got to think *telefonini* are dangerous.'

'Can you believe that?' she asked with real curiosity. 'Can you believe they'd let that happen, that rays could come out and hurt you?' She made the spitting motion again, though what emerged was really little more than a puff of disbelief. She gave him the phone number of the house, and Brunetti wrote it down.

The woman's agitation finally registered with the little girl, who began to squirm around on the sofa. She made a noise, but it was nothing like the peeping noise her brother had made in time to the motions of the dancing figures. It was a bleat, a wail, the voice of anguish in a very high register. It started, it went on, and then the woman said, 'You better go now. Once she starts like this, it can go on for hours, and I don't think you want to hear it.'

Brunetti thanked her, did not offer her his hand and did not pat the little boy on the head, as he would have done had the girl not begun to wail. He left the apartment, went down the stairs, and out into the light.

8

As he walked back towards the Questura, Brunetti found himself dwelling on a noise and a confusion. The noise was the one made by the little girl: something prevented him from referring to it as her voice. The other was the strangely parallel conversation he had had with the grandmother: he spoke of threats, and she said they were meaningless, nothing, all the while suggesting that De Cal was a potentially violent man. He tried to remember everything they had said and could come up with only one alternative interpretation: it was Tassini who had made the threats, perhaps provoked into them by De Cal's violence. If not this, then the old woman was talking nonsense, and that was something Brunetti was convinced this particular woman would not do. Lie, perhaps; evade, certainly; but she would always talk sense.

His phone rang, and when he stopped walking to answer it he heard Pucetti's voice asking, 'Commissario?'

'Yes. What is it, Pucetti?'

'You had lunch yet, sir?'

'No,' Brunetti answered, suddenly reminded that he was hungry.

'Would you like to go out to Murano and talk to someone?'

'One of your relatives?' Brunetti asked, pleased that the young man had worked so fast.

'Yes. My uncle.'

'I'd be happy to,' Brunetti said, changing direction and starting back towards Celestia, where he could get a boat to Murano.

'Good. What time do you think you could be there?'

'It shouldn't take me more than half an hour.'

'All right. I'll tell him to meet you at one-thirty.'

'Where?'

'Nanni's,' Pucetti answered. 'It's on Sacca Serenella, the place where all the glass-workers eat. Anyone can tell you where it is.'

'What's your uncle's name?'

'Navarro. Giulio. He'll be there.'

'How will I know him?'

'Oh, don't worry about that, sir. He'll know you.'

'How?' Brunetti asked.

'Are you wearing a suit?'

'Yes.'

Did he hear Pucetti laugh? 'He'll know you, sir', he said and broke the connection.

It took Brunetti more than half an hour because he just missed a boat and had to wait at the Celestia stop for the next and then again at Fondamenta Nuove. As he got off the boat at Sacca Serenella, he stopped a man behind him and asked where the trattoria was.

'You mean Nanni's?' he asked.

'Yes. I've got to meet someone there, but all I know is that it's the place where the workers go.'

'And where you eat well?' the man asked with a smile.

'I wasn't told that,' Brunetti answered, 'but it wouldn't hurt.'

70

'Come with me, then,' the man said, turning off to the right and leading Brunetti along a cement pavement that ran beside the canal towards the entrance to a shipyard. 'It's Wednesday,' the man said. 'So there'll be liver. It's good.'

'With polenta?' Brunetti asked.

'Of course,' the man said, pausing to glance aside at this man who spoke Veneziano yet who had to ask if liver was served with polenta.

The man turned to the left, leaving the water behind them, and led Brunetti along a dirt trail that crossed an abandoned field. At the end, Brunetti saw a low cement building, its walls striped with what looked like dark trails of rust running down from leaking gutters. In front of it, a few rusted metal tables stood around drunkenly, their legs trapped in the dirt or propped up with chunks of cement. The man led Brunetti past the tables and to the door of the building. He pushed it open and held it politely for Brunetti to enter.

Inside, Brunetti found the trattoria of his youth: the tables were covered with sheets of white butcher paper, and on most tables lay four plates and four sets of knives and forks. The glasses had once been clean, perhaps even still were. They were squat things that held little more than two swigs of wine; years of use had scratched and clouded them almost to whiteness. There were paper napkins, and in the centre of each table a metal tray that held suspiciously pale olive oil, some white vinegar, salt, pepper, and individually wrapped packets of toothpicks.

Brunetti was surprised to see Vianello, in jeans and jacket, sitting at one of these tables, accompanied by an older man who bore no resemblance whatsoever to Pucetti. Brunetti thanked the man who had led him there, offered him *un'ombra* which the man refused, and walked over to greet Vianello. The other man stood and held out his hand. 'Navarro,' he said as he took Brunetti's hand. 'Giulio.' He was a thick man, with a bull-like neck and a barrel chest: he looked like he had spent his life lifting weight, rather than lifting weights. His legs were slightly bowed, as if they had slowly given way under decades of heavy burdens. His nose had been broken a few times and badly set, or not set at all, and his right front tooth had been chipped off at a sharp angle. Though Navarro was surely more than sixty, Brunetti had no doubt that he would have no trouble lifting either him or Vianello and tossing them halfway across the room.

Brunetti introduced himself and said, 'Thanks for coming to talk to us', including Vianello, though he had no idea how the Inspector happened to be there.

Navarro looked embarrassed by such easy gratitude. 'I live just around the corner. Really.'

'Your nephew is a good boy,' Brunetti said. 'We're lucky to have him.'

This time, it was praise that made Navarro glance away in embarrassment. When he looked back, his face had softened, even grown sweet. 'He's my sister's boy,' he explained. 'Yes, a good boy.'

'As I suppose he's told you,' Brunetti said as they seated themselves, 'we'd like to ask you about some of the people out here.'

'He told me. You want to know about De Cal?'

Before Brunetti could answer, a waiter came to the table. He had no pen or order pad, rattled off the menu and asked them what they'd like.

Navarro said the men were friends of his, which caused the waiter to recite the menu again, slowly, with comments, even with recommendations.

They ended up asking for spaghetti with *vongole*. The waiter winked to suggest that they had been dredged up, perhaps illegally, but definitely in the *laguna*, the night before. Brunetti had never much liked liver, so he asked for a grilled *rombo*, while Vianello and Navarro both asked for *coda di rospo*.

'*Patate bollite?*' the waiter asked before he walked away.

They all said yes.

Without asking, the waiter was soon back with a litre of mineral water and one of white wine, which he set down on their table before going into the kitchen, where they could hear him shouting out their order.

As if there had been no interruption, Brunetti asked, 'What do you know about him? Do you work for him?'

'No,' Navarro answered, obviously surprised by the question. 'But I know him. Everyone here does. He's a bastard.' Navarro tore open a package of *grissini*. He put one in his mouth and nibbled it right down to the bottom, like a cartoon rabbit eating a carrot.

'You mean in the sense that he's difficult to work with?' Brunetti asked.

'You said it. He's had two *maestri* now for about two years: longest he's ever kept any of them, far as I know.'

'Why is that?' asked Vianello, pouring wine for all of them.

'Because he's a bastard.' Even Navarro sensed the circularity of his argument and so added, 'He'll try on anything to cheat you.'

'Could you give us an example?' Brunetti asked.

This seemed to stump Navarro for a moment, as though a request to supply evidence to support a judgement were a novelty for him. He drank a glass of wine, filled his glass and drank another, then ate two more *grissini*. Finally he said, 'He'll always hire *garzoni* and let them go before they can become *serventi* so he won't have to pay them more. He'll keep them for a year or so, working off the books or working with two-month contracts, but then when it's time for them to move up, and get more money, he fires them. Invents some reason to get rid of them, and hires new ones.'

'How long can he go on doing this?' Vianello asked.

Navarro shrugged. 'So long as there are boys who need jobs, he can probably go on doing it for ever.'

'What else?'

'He argues and fights.'

'With?' Vianello asked.

'Suppliers, workers, the guys on the boats who bring the sand or the guys on the boats who take the glass away. If there's money involved – and there's money involved in all of this – then he'll argue with them.'

'I've heard about a fight in a bar a couple of years ago . . .' Brunetti began and let his voice drop away.

'Oh that,' Navarro said. 'It's probably the one time the old bastard didn't start it. Some guy said something he didn't like and De Cal said something back, and the guy hit him. I wasn't there, but my brother was. Believe me, he hates De Cal more than I do, so if he said the old bastard didn't start it, then he didn't.'

'What about his daughter?' Brunetti asked.

Before Navarro could answer, the waiter brought their pasta and set the plates in front of them. Conversation stopped as the three men dug into the spaghetti. The waiter returned with three empty plates for the shells.

'Peperoncino,' Brunetti said, mouth full.

'Good, eh?' Navarro said.

Brunetti nodded, took a sip of wine, and returned to the spaghetti, which was better than good. He had to remember to tell Paola about the peperoncino, which was more than she used but still good.

When their plates were empty and the other plates full of shells, the waiter came and took them all away, asking if they had eaten well. Brunetti and Vianello said enthusiastic things: Navarro, a regular customer, was not obliged to comment.

Soon the waiter was back with a bowl of potatoes and the fish: Brunetti's was already filleted. Navarro asked for olive oil, and the waiter returned with a bottle of much better oil. All three poured it on their fish but not on the potatoes, which already sat in a pool of it at the bottom of the bowl. None of them spoke for some time.

While Vianello spooned the last of the potatoes from the bowl, Brunetti returned to his questions and asked, 'His daughter, do you know much about her?'

Navarro finished the wine and held up the empty carafe to get the waiter's attention. 'She's a good girl, but she married that engineer.'

Brunetti nodded. 'Do you know him or know anything about him?'

'He's an ecologist,' Navarro said, using the same sort of tone another person might use to identify a pederast or a kleptomaniac. It was meant to end discussion. Brunetti allowed it to pass and decided to play ignorant. 'Does he work here on Murano?' he asked.

'Ah, thank God, no,' Navarro said, taking the litre of white wine from the waiter's hand and filling all of their glasses. 'He works on the mainland somewhere, goes around looking for places where we'll still be allowed to put our garbage.' He drank a half-glass of wine, perhaps thought of Ribetti's professional duties, and finished the glass.

'We've got two perfectly good incinerators here, so why can't we just burn it all? Or if it's dangerous, just bury it somewhere in the countryside or ship it to Africa or China. Those people will let you pay for that. So why not do it? They've got all those open spaces, so just bury it there.'

Brunetti allowed himself a quick glance at Vianello, who was finishing the last of his potatoes. He set his knife and fork down on his plate and, as Brunetti feared he would, opened his mouth to speak to Navarro. 'If we built nuclear plants, then we could do the same thing with the waste from them, and then we wouldn't have to import all that electricity from Switzerland and France, either.' Vianello gave a manly smile, first to Navarro and then to Brunetti.

'Yes,' said Navarro. 'I hadn't thought about that, but it's a good idea.' Smiling, he turned back to Brunetti, 'What else did you want to know about De Cal?'

'I've heard there's talk he wants to sell the *fornace*,' Vianello interrupted, now that Navarro had looked on him with approval.

'Yes. I've heard that, too,' Navarro said, not much interested. 'But there's always talk like that.' He shrugged off such talk, then added, 'Besides, if anyone buys it, it'll be Fasano. He's got the factory right alongside De Cal's, so if he bought it, he'd only have to join the two buildings together and he'd double his production.' Navarro thought about this possibility for a while and nodded.

'Fasano runs the Glassmakers' Association, doesn't he?' Vianello asked as the waiter arrived with another bowl of potatoes. Vianello let the waiter spoon a few on to his plate, but Navarro and Brunetti said no.

In answer to Vianello's question, Navarro smiled at the waiter and said, 'That's what he does now, but who knows what he wants to become?' Hearing this, the waiter nodded and turned away.

Brunetti feared the conversation was veering away from De Cal, so he interrupted to say, 'I've heard there's been talk that De Cal's been threatening his son-in-law.'

'You mean that he says he's going to kill him?'

'Yes,' Brunetti said.

'He's said it in the bars, but he was usually drunk when he said it. Drinks too much, the old bastard,' Navarro said, filling his glass again. 'He's got diabetes and shouldn't drink, but . . .' Navarro paused and considered something for a moment, then said, 'That's funny. You know, in the last couple of months he's started to look worse, like the disease is really getting to him.'

Brunetti, who had seen the old man only once some weeks before, had no point of comparison: he had seen an old man weakened and perhaps fuddled by years of drink.

'I'm not sure this is a legitimate question, Signor Navarro,' Brunetti began, taking a sip of wine he did not want. 'You think there's any real threat?'

'You mean that he'd really kill him?'

'Yes.'

Navarro finished his wine and put the glass on the table. He made no move to help himself to more and called to the waiter for three coffees. After he had given the order, he returned to Brunetti's question and at last said, 'I think I'd rather not answer that, Commissario.'

The waiter cleared away their plates. Both Brunetti and Vianello said that the meal had been excellent, and Navarro seemed more pleased than the waiter to hear them say it. When the coffee came, he put two packets of sugar into his cup, stirred it, looked at his watch, and said, 'I've got to get back to work, gentlemen.' He stood and shook hands with both of them, called over to the waiter that the bill was his and that he'd pay it the next day. Brunetti started to object, but Vianello stood and put out his hand again and thanked the older man. Brunetti did the same.

Navarro smiled one last time and said, 'Take good care of my sister's boy for me, all right?' He went over to the door, opened it, and was gone.

Brunetti and Vianello sat back down. Brunetti drank the last of his coffee, looked over at Vianello, and asked, 'Did Pucetti call you?'

'Yes.'

'What did he say?'

'That you were coming out here and maybe I should join you.'

Undecided as to whether he liked it or not, Brunetti finally said, 'I liked that about the nuclear waste.'

'I'm sure it's a feeling in which you are joined by count- less people in the government,' Vianello said.

9

'Oh my, oh my, oh my,' Vianello said, directing his attention to the entrance of the trattoria. Brunetti, curious, started to turn around, but Vianello put a hand on his arm and said, 'No, don't look.' When Brunetti was facing him again, Vianello said, unable to disguise his surprise, 'What Navarro said about De Cal is true: he looks much worse than he did the last time.'

'Where is he?'

'He just came in and he's standing at the bar, having a drink.'

'Alone or with someone?'

'He's with someone,' Vianello answered. 'And that's what's interesting.'

'Why?'

'Because he's with Gianluca Fasano.'

An involuntary 'ah' escaped Brunetti and then he said, 'Not only President of the Glassmakers of Murano, but, as I've heard a few times and as even Navarro seems to know, a man who might be very interested in becoming our next mayor.'

'Right on both counts,' Vianello said, raising his glass in Brunetti's direction but not taking a sip. *'Complimenti.'* He kept his eyes on Brunetti's face, but occasionally shifted his head to one side and cast his attention towards the two men standing at the bar. If the men looked in their direction, Brunetti realized, they would see two men at a table, one with his back to them. The only time De Cal had seen Vianello, he had been in uniform: without it, he could be anyone. Vianello nodded in the direction of the two men and said, 'Be interesting to know what they're saying, wouldn't it?'

'De Cal's a glassmaker, and Fasano's their leader,' Brunetti said. 'I don't see much of a mystery there.'

'There are more than a hundred *fornaci*,' Vianello said. 'De Cal's is one of the smallest.'

'He's got a *fornace* to sell,' Brunetti argued.

'He's got a daughter to inherit,' Vianello countered. The Inspector reached into the pocket of his jacket and pulled out five Euros. 'At least we can tip,' he said, putting the bill on the table.

'Probably give the waiter in a place like this a seizure,' Brunetti said. He saw Vianello shift in his chair and asked, 'Are they still there?'

'De Cal's paying.' After a minute, Vianello got quickly to his feet, saying, 'I want to see where they go.'

Brunetti doubted that De Cal, who had been beside himself with anger the one time they met, would remember him, but he stayed at the table and let Vianello go outside by himself.

After a few minutes, Vianello came back; Brunetti got to his feet and went over to join him at the door. 'Well?' he asked.

'They walked down to the water and turned left, down to a dirt path and turned left again. Then they went back to some buildings on the other side of an empty field.'

'Do you have your *telefonino*?' Brunetti asked.

Vianello took his phone from the pocket of his jacket and held it up.

'Why don't you call that classmate of yours who told you the love story about Assunta and ask him where De Cal's factory is?'

Vianello flipped the phone open, found the number and called. Brunetti heard him ask the question, then explain that they were at Nanni's. He watched as Vianello nodded his way through his friend's explanation, thanked him and hung up. 'That's where De Cal's place is: down at the end of that path, the buildings on the right. Just beside Fasano's.'

'You think that's important?' Brunetti asked.

Vianello shrugged. 'I don't know, not really. I'm interested because of what I've read in the papers – that Fasano's suddenly discovered ecology, or suddenly discovered his commitment to it.'

Brunetti had a vague memory of having read something along these lines, some months ago, and of having had a similarly cynical response, but he simply asked, 'That's the way it happens to most people, though, isn't it?' Brunetti left it to Vianello to realize, or not, that it was precisely what had happened to him.

'Yes,' Vianello admitted, though reluctantly. 'Maybe it's because of his interest in politics. Once someone says they're thinking about public office, I start to get suspicious of anything they do or say.'

Though he had taken a few steps, Brunetti was not yet this far along the road to total cynicism, and so he said, 'It's other people who are saying it about him, if I remember correctly.'

'It's one of the things politicians love the most: popular acclamation,' Vianello replied.

'Come on, Lorenzo,' Brunetti said, unwilling to continue with this subject. Remembering the other thing he could usefully do while he was on Murano, he explained about Assunta's visit and said he wanted to go and talk to one of the men who had heard her father threaten Ribetti. He told Vianello he would see him back at the Questura. They walked out to the *riva*, and Vianello went down to the Sacca Serenella stop to wait for the 41.

Assunta had told him Bovo lived just on the other side of the bridge, in Calle drio i Orti, and he found the *calle* with little trouble. He walked as far as Calle Leonarducci without finding the house and turned to go back and check more closely. This time he found the number and Bovo's name among those on the doorbells. He rang and waited, then rang again. He heard a window open above him, stepped back, and looked up. A child, from this vantage point its age and sex unclear, stuck its head out of a third-floor window and called, '*Sì?*'

'I'm looking for your father,' Brunetti called up.

'He's down at the bar,' the child called back in a voice so high it could have belonged to either a boy or a girl.

'Which one?'

A tiny hand stuck out the window, pointing to Brunetti's left. 'Down there,' the voice called, and then the child disappeared.

The window remained open, so Brunetti called his thanks up to it and turned to return to Calle Leonarducci. At the corner he came to a window covered to chest height with curtains that had begun life as a red-and-white check but had moved into a wrinkled, hepatic middle age. He opened the door and walked into a room more filled with smoke than any he could remember having entered in years. He went to the bar and ordered a coffee. He displayed no interest in the barman's tattoos, a pattern of intertwined serpents that encircled both wrists with their tails and ran up his arms until they disappeared under the sleeves of his T-shirt. When the coffee came, Brunetti said, 'I'm looking for Paolo Bovo. His kid told me he was here.'

'Paolo,' the barman called towards a table at the back,

where three men sat around a bottle of red wine, talking, 'the cop wants to talk to you.'

Brunetti smiled and asked, 'How come everyone always knows?'

The barman's smile was equal in warmth to Brunetti's, though not in the number of teeth exposed. 'Anyone who talks as good as you do has to be a cop.'

'A lot of people talk as well as I do,' Brunetti said.

'Not the ones who want to see Paolo,' he answered, wiping at the counter with an unusually clean cloth.

Brunetti sensed movement to his left and turned to meet a man of his own height, who appeared to have lost not only all of his hair but at least twenty of the kilos Brunetti was carrying. From this distance, Brunetti could see that he had lost his eyebrows and eyelashes as well, which explained the pale greasiness of his skin.

Brunetti extended his hand and said, 'Signor Bovo?' At the man's nod, Brunetti asked, 'May I offer you something to drink?'

Bovo declined with a shake of his head. In a deep voice presumably left over from his former body, he said, 'I've got some wine back with my friends.' He shook Brunetti's hand and Brunetti read on his face the effort it cost him to make his grip firm. He spoke in Veneziano, with a Muranese accent of the sort that Brunetti and his friends used to imitate for comic effect.

'What do you want?' Bovo asked. He rested one elbow on the bar, succeeding in making the gesture look casual rather than necessary. Before his illness, Brunetti realized, this situation would have been charged with aggression, perhaps even danger: now the best the man could manage was gruffness.

'You know Giovanni De Cal,' Brunetti said and stopped.

Bovo said nothing for some time. He looked at the barman, who was pretending to take no interest in their conversation;

then he glanced back at the men he had left at the table. Brunetti watched him weighing the chances that, reduced to no power except words, he could still impress his friends with his toughness. 'The bastard wouldn't give me a job.'

'When was that?'

'When that bastard at the other *fornace* fired me,' he said but offered no further information.

'Why did he fire you?' Brunetti asked.

Brunetti watched his question register with Bovo, saw in his eyes the confusion it caused him, as if he had never given the matter any thought.

Finally Bovo said, 'Because I couldn't lift things any more.'

'What sort of things?'

'Bags of sand, the chemicals, the barrels we have to move. How was I supposed to lift them if I couldn't even bend down to tie my shoes?'

Brunetti said, 'I don't know.' He waited some time before asking, 'And then what happened?'

'Then I left. What else could I do?' Bovo moved a bit closer to the bar and put his other elbow on it, shifting his weight as he changed arms.

This conversation seemed not to be going anywhere, so Brunetti decided to return to his original point. 'I'd like to know what you heard De Cal say about Ribetti and if you could tell me the circumstances.'

Bovo called the barman over and asked for a glass of mineral water. When it came, he lifted it to salute Brunetti and drank some of it. He put the glass back on the bar and said, 'He was in here one night after work. He usually doesn't come in here: got his own bar he goes to, down towards Colonna, but they were closed or something, so he came in here.' He looked at Brunetti to see that he was following, and Brunetti nodded.

'So he was sitting there, in the back, when I came in. He was being the big man with his friends, drinking and talking about how many orders he had, and how people always wanted his glass pieces, and how someone from the museum asked if they could have a piece for a show.' He looked at Brunetti and pursed his lips, as if to ask him if he had ever heard anything so ridiculous.

'Did he see you?'

'Of course he saw me,' Bovo said. 'This was six months ago.' He said it with pride, as though boasting of some other person whose every entrance was sure to be noted by everyone in the place.

'What happened?'

'Some friends of mine were at another table, so I went back to have a drink with them. No, we weren't close: there was a table between us. I sat down and I guess he sort of forgot about me. And after a while he started to talk about his son-in-law: the usual shit he always says, that he's crazy and married Assunta for her money and doesn't know anything and just cares about animals. We've all heard it a thousand times, ever since Assunta married him.'

'Do you know Ribetti?' Brunetti asked.

'Yeah, sort of,' Bovo answered. It appeared he was going to leave it at that, but as Brunetti started to ask for an explanation Bovo went on. 'She's a good person, Assunta, and it's obvious the guy loves her. Younger than she is, and he's an engineer, but he's still a good enough guy.'

'What was it that De Cal said about him?' Brunetti asked.

'That he'd like to open the *Gazzettino* one morning and read that he'd been killed in an accident. On the road, at work, in his house: the old bastard didn't care, just so long as he was dead.'

Brunetti waited to see if this was all, then said, 'I'm not sure that's a threat, Signor Bovo.' He added a smile to soften his observation.

'You going to let me finish?' Bovo asked.

'Sorry.'

'Then he said that if he didn't die in an accident, he might have to kill him himself.'

'Do you think he was serious?' Brunetti asked, when it seemed that Bovo had indeed finished.

'I don't know. It's the sort of thing you say, isn't it?' Bovo asked, and Brunetti nodded. The sort of thing you say.

'But I had the feeling he'd really do it, the old bastard.' He took a few more small sips of the water. 'He can't stand it that Assunta's happy.'

'Is that the reason he hates Ribetti so much?'

'I suppose. And that he'll have a say in the *fornace* when the old bastard dies. I think that's what makes him crazy. He keeps saying Ribetti will ruin everything.'

'You mean if he leaves it to his daughter?'

'Who else can he leave it to?' Bovo asked.

Brunetti paused to acknowledge the truth of that and then said, 'She knows the business. And Ribetti's an engineer; besides, they've been married long enough for him to have learned something about running the place.'

Bovo gave him a long look. 'Maybe that's why the old man thinks he'll ruin everything.'

'I don't understand,' Brunetti confessed.

'If she inherits it, then he'll want to take over, won't he?' Bovo asked. Brunetti maintained a neutral expression and waited for an answer. 'She's a woman, isn't she?' Bovo asked. 'So she'll let him.'

Brunetti smiled. 'I hadn't thought of that,' he said.

Bovo looked satisfied at having successfully explained things to the policeman. 'I'm sorry for Assunta,' he said.

'Why?'

'She's a good person.'

'Is she a friend of yours?' Brunetti asked, curious as to whether there might have been some history between them. They were of an age, and he must once have been a very impressive man.

'No, no, nothing like that,' Bovo said. 'It's that she tried to keep that other bastard from firing me. And when he did, she tried to give me a job, but her father wouldn't let her.' He finished the water and put the glass on the counter. 'So now I don't have a job. My wife does – she goes out and cleans houses – and I'm supposed to stay home with the kids.'

Brunetti thanked him, put two Euros on the counter, and held out his hand. He shook Bovo's hand carefully, thanked him again, and left.

Deciding it would be quicker, Brunetti walked down to the Faro stop and took the 41 back to Fondamenta Nuove, then switched to the 42 that would take him down to the hospital stop. From there, it was a quick walk back to the Questura.

As he walked inside, Brunetti was forced to accept the fact that he had spent almost an entire working day on something that could in no way be justified as a legitimate use of his time. Further, he had involved both an inspector and a junior officer, and some days ago he had commandeered both a police launch and a police car in the same matter. In the absence of a crime, it could not be called an investigation: it was nothing more than indulgence in the sort of curiosity he should have abandoned years before.

Conscious of this, he went to Signorina Elettra's office and was happy to find her at her desk, wrapped in spring. A pink scarf was tied around her head, gypsy fashion, and she wore a green shirt and severe black slacks. Her lipstick matched the scarf, prompting Brunetti to wonder when it would start matching the shirt.

'Are you very busy, Signorina?' he asked after they had exchanged greetings.

'No more so than usual,' she said. 'What can I do for you?'

'I'd like you to take a look and see what you can find about two men,' he began and saw her slide a notebook closer. 'Giovanni De Cal, who owns a *fornace* on Murano, and Giorgio Tassini, the night-watchman at De Cal's factory.'

'Everything?' she asked.

'Whatever you can find, please.'

Idly, driven only by the same sort of curiosity Brunetti felt propelling him, she asked, 'Is this for anything?'

'No, not really,' Brunetti had to admit. He was about to leave, when he added, 'And Marco Ribetti, who works for a French company, but is Venetian. An engineer. His speciality is garbage disposal, I think, or building garbage dumps.'

'I'll see what I can find.'

He thought of adding Fasano's name but stopped himself. It was only a fishing expedition, not an investigation, and she had better things to do. He thanked her and left.

10

A day passed, and then another. Brunetti heard nothing from Assunta De Cal and gave her little thought, nor did he spend time thinking about Murano and the threats made by a drunken old man. He had young men, instead, to keep him occupied, young men – though legally they were still children – who were repeatedly arrested, processed, then identified and collected by people claiming to be their parents or guardians, though because they were gypsies, few of them had documents which could prove this.

And then came the shock story in one of the weekly newspaper inserts about the fate of such young boys in more than one South American city, where they were reportedly being executed by squads of off-duty policemen. 'Well, we aren't there yet,' Brunetti muttered to himself as he finished reading the article. There were many qualities in his fellow citizens that Brunetti, as a policeman, abhorred: their willingness to accommodate crime; their failure to trust the law; their lack of rage at the inefficiency of the legal system. But we don't shoot children in the street because they steal oranges, he said, though he was not at all sure if this was sufficient reason for civic pride.

Like an epileptic sensing the imminence of a seizure, Brunetti knew he was best advised to use work to distract himself from these thoughts. He took out his notebook and found the phone number Tassini's mother-in-law had given him. A man answered.

'Signor Tassini?' Brunetti asked.

'*Sì.*'

'This is Commissario Guido Brunetti, Signore.' He paused, waiting for Tassini's question, but the man said nothing, and so Brunetti continued. 'I wonder if I could trouble you for some of your time, Signor Tassini. I'd like to speak to you.'

'Are you the one who was here?' Tassini asked, making no attempt to hide his suspicion.

'Yes, I am,' Brunetti answered easily. 'I spoke to your mother-in-law, but she could give me very little information.'

'What about?' Tassini asked neutrally.

'About the place where you work, Signore,' he said and again waited for Tassini to respond.

'What about it?'

'It has to do with your employer, Giovanni De Cal. That's why I chose to contact you away from your place of work. We would prefer that your employer not learn that we're taking an interest in him.' This was true enough, and it was similarly true that De Cal could cause considerable trouble if he were to learn that Brunetti was in essence running a private investigation.

'Is it about my complaint?' Tassini asked, curiosity getting the better of his distrust.

'It's about that, of course,' Brunetti lied effortlessly, 'as well as about Signor De Cal and a report we've had about him.'

'A report from whom?' Tassini asked.

'I'm afraid I'm not at liberty to reveal that, Signor Tassini. I'm sure you understand that everything we're told, we're told in confidence.' He waited to see if Tassini would swallow this, and when his silence suggested that he had, Brunetti asked, 'Would it be possible to speak to you?'

After some hesitation, Tassini asked, 'When?'

'Whenever it's convenient for you, Signore.'

Tassini's voice, when he answered, was less easy than it had been a moment before. 'How did you get this number?'

'Your mother-in-law gave it to me,' Brunetti said. Softening his voice and putting into it a note of near-embarrassment, he added 'Your mother-in-law told me you have no *telefonino*, Signor Tassini. Speaking personally, I'd like to compliment you on the wisdom of that decision.' He ended with a half-laugh.

'You think they're dangerous, too?' Tassini asked eagerly.

'From what I've read, I'd say there's good reason to believe it,' Brunetti said. From what he had read, there was also good reason to believe that automobiles, central heating and aeroplanes were dangerous, but this was a sentiment he chose not to reveal to Signor Tassini.

'When do you want to meet?' Tassini asked.

'If you could possibly spare me the time right now, I could be there in about fifteen minutes.'

The line sang emptily for a long time, but Brunetti resisted the impulse to speak. 'All right,' Tassini said, 'but not here at the house. There's a bar opposite San Francesco di Paola.'

'On the corner before the park?' Brunetti asked.

'Yes.'

'I know it, the place that draws the little hearts on the cappuccino *schiuma*, no?'

'Yes,' said Tassini in a gentler tone.

'I'll be there in fifteen minutes,' said Brunetti and put down the phone.

When Brunetti entered the bar, he looked around for a man who might be the night-watchman in a glass factory. There was one man at the bar, drinking a coffee and talking to the barman. Another pair stood farther along, two coffees in front of them, one man with a briefcase propped against his leg. Another man with a large nose and a peculiarly small head stood at the end of the bar, feeding one-Euro coins into a video poker machine. His gestures were rhythmic: feed a coin, punch a button, wait to see the flashing results, punch more buttons, wait again to see the results, quick double sip at a glass of red wine, then another coin.

Brunetti excluded them all, as he did a young man next to the poker player, who was drinking what looked like a *gingerino*. There were four tables against the back wall: at one of them sat three women, each with a cup and a pot of tea. They were handing around photographs and exclaiming in enthusiasm that sounded genuine enough for it to be a baby and not a vacation. At the last table, in the angle behind the bar, sat a man who glanced in Brunetti's direction. He had a glass of water in front of him, and as Brunetti moved towards him, the man raised the glass in his left hand and saluted him with it.

The man got to his feet and extended his hand. 'Tassini,' he said. He was tall, perhaps in his mid-thirties, with large dark eyes set wide apart and a nose that seemed too small to fill the space left for it. He had an untrimmed beard with some grey in it that covered, though it did not hide, the hollowness of his cheeks. Brunetti had seen that face on count-less icons: the suffering Christ. 'Commissario Brunetti?' Tassini asked.

Brunetti took his hand and thanked him for agreeing to speak to him. 'What would you like to drink?' Tassini asked when Brunetti was seated, raising his hand to catch the attention of the barman.

'Since I'm here,' Brunetti said with a smile, 'I should have a cappuccino, don't you think?' He sat, and Tassini called the order to the barman. For some time, neither man spoke.

Brunetti finally said, 'Signor Tassini, as I told you on the phone, we'd like to speak to you about Giovanni De Cal, your employer.' Before Tassini could ask, Brunetti added, using his gravest voice, 'And, of course, about your complaint.'

'So you're beginning to believe me, eh?' Tassini asked, using the plural.

'We're certainly interested in listening to what you have to say,' Brunetti said. He was spared the need to elaborate by the arrival of the barman with his cappuccino. As he anticipated, the foam had been poured in a swirling motion that created a heart on the surface. He tore open a packet of sugar and poured it in. He stirred the coffee around, and broke its heart.

'What about my letters, then?' Tassini asked.

'That's certainly part of the reason I'm here, Signor Tassini,' Brunetti said and took a sip of his coffee. It was still too hot to drink, so he set the cup back in the saucer to let it cool.

'Did you read them?'

Brunetti gave him his most direct look. 'Ordinarily, if this were part of an official investigation, I'm afraid I'd lie here and say I had,' he said, trying to sound faintly embarrassed by the confession. 'But in this case, let me deal frankly, right from the start.' Before Tassini could reply, he went on. 'They're in a file held by another division. But I've been told about them by people who have read them, and some excerpts have been passed on to us.'

'But they were addressed to you,' Tassini insisted. 'That is, to the police.'

'Yes,' Brunetti acknowledged with a nod, 'but we're detectives, and such things don't get sent on to us automatically. The letters were given to the complaints department and a file was opened. But before those files are processed and passed on to the people who actually will conduct an investigation, months can pass.' He saw the anguished look on Tassini's face, saw him open his mouth to protest, and added, lowering his face in feigned embarrassment again, 'or even longer.'

'But you know about them?'

'I've been told about them, as I've said, but it's come to me third hand.' Brunetti looked across at Tassini and opened his eyes wider as if to suggest that some new possibility had suddenly occurred to him. 'Would you be willing to tell me, in your own words, so that I'd finally understand what's in them? That might help things move more quickly.'

At the sight of Tassini's dawning relief, Brunetti felt faintly soiled by what he had just done: it was too simple, too effortless: human need was just too easy to take advantage of. He picked up his cappuccino and took a few sips.

'It's about the factory,' Tassini began. 'You know at least that much?'

'Of course,' Brunetti said with a little deceitful bow of his head.

'It's a death trap,' Tassini said. 'All sorts of things: potassium, nitric acid and fluoric acid, cadmium, even arsenic. We work around this stuff; we breathe it in; we probably even eat it.'

Brunetti nodded. Any Venetian knew this much, but even Vianello had never suggested there existed any significant risk for the workers on Murano. And if anyone would know, it was Vianello.

'That's why it happened,' Tassini said.

'Why what happened, Signor Tassini?'

Tassini's eyes contracted in a look replete with what Brunetti knew was suspicion. But still he said, 'My daughter.'

'Emma?' Brunetti supplied seamlessly. And then, filled with something close to disgust at himself, he said, 'Poor little girl.'

That did it: Tassini was his. He watched as all reservation, all suspicion, all discretion fled from Tassini's face. 'That's why it happened,' Tassini said, voice hot with

93

conviction. 'All those things. I've been working there for years, breathing them, touching them, spilling them on me.' He drew his hands together in tight fists. 'That's why I keep writing those letters, even when no one will pay attention to what I say.' He looked up at Brunetti with a face made soft by hope, or love, or some emotion Brunetti chose not to identify. 'You're the first one who's paid any attention to me.'

'Tell me about it,' Brunetti forced himself to say.

'I've read a lot,' Tassini began. 'I read all the time. I've got a computer and I read things on the Internet, and I've read books about chemistry and genetics. And it's all there, it's all there.' He rapped his left fist three times on the table as he repeated, 'It's all there.'

'Go on.'

'These things, especially the minerals, can damage the genetic structure. And once the genes are affected, then we can pass the damage on to our children. Damaged genes. You know about the letters, so you know what I've described. When you see the medical reports, you'll know what the doctors say is wrong with her.' He looked at Brunetti. 'Have you seen the photos?'

Even though Brunetti had seen the child so could have continued to lie, he could not bring himself to do so: all the rest, but not this. 'No.'

'Well,' Tassini said. 'Maybe that's better. Besides, you know what's wrong, so there's no need for you to see them.'

'And the doctors? What do they say?'

Tassini's enthusiasm disappeared abruptly; apparently mention of the doctors took him back into the land of the unbelievers. 'They don't want to get involved.'

'Why's that?' Brunetti asked.

'You've seen what's happened at Marghera, with the protests and people wanting to shut it all down. Imagine if it became public, what's going on on Murano.'

Brunetti nodded.

'So you see why they have to lie,' Tassini said with growing heat. 'I've tried to talk to the people at the hospital, tried to get them to test Emma. To test me. I know what's wrong. I know why she's the way she is. All they have to do is find the right test, find the right thing that's in me and in her, and then they'd know what happened. If they admitted what happened to Emma, then they'd have to look at all the other damage, all the other people who are sick, all the people who have died.' He spoke with conviction and urgency, willing Brunetti to understand, and agree.

Brunetti was suddenly aware that, though he had known how to get himself into this one, he had no idea how to get out.

'And your employer?'

'De Cal?'

'Do you think he knows?'

Tassini's face changed again and he moved his mouth into something that resembled a smile but was not. 'Yes, he knows. They both do, but they have to cover it all up, don't they?' he asked, and Brunetti wondered in what way Assunta could be involved in this.

'But you have proof?' Brunetti asked.

Tassini gave a sly smile. 'I've started a file, and I keep everything in there. The new job gives me the time to find the final proofs. I'm close. I'm very close.' He glanced across at Brunetti, his eyes filled with the illumination of one who has discovered the truth. 'I put it all in there. I read a lot, and it helps me understand things. I keep track of everything.' With a sly glance he added, 'But we'll have to wait and see, won't we?'

'Why?'

Brunetti was not sure Tassini had heard his question, for by way of answer he said, 'Our greatest men knew about these things long before we did, and so now I do, too.' Ever

95

since his daughter had been mentioned, Tassini had become increasingly agitated. When he started to talk of his file and the information he kept there, a bemused Brunetti decided it was time to deflect him back to the subject of De Cal.

He lowered his head in a gesture that suggested deep thought, then looked across at Tassini and said, 'I'll have a look at our file as soon as I get back to the Questura.' He shifted his cup to one side to indicate a change of subject and went on, 'I'd like to ask you some questions about your employer, Giovanni De Cal.'

His question brought Tassini up short, and the man could not disguise his surprise and disappointment, just when he had begun to talk about the great men who agreed with him. He took a not very clean handkerchief out of his left-hand pocket and blew his nose. He stuffed it back in his pocket and asked, 'What do you want to know?'

'It's been reported to us that Signor De Cal has threatened the life of his son-in-law. Do you know anything about this?'

'Well, it makes sense, doesn't it?' Tassini asked.

Brunetti gave a smile of mild confusion and said, 'I'm not sure I follow your reasoning.' He smiled again to emphasize his belief that there was some thread of reasoning here, although he in fact suspected there might be none.

'To keep him from inheriting the *fornace*.'

'But isn't it his daughter who would inherit?' Brunetti inquired.

'Yes. But then Ribetti would be free to go there,' Tassini said, as if this were something so obvious it hardly needed mentioning.

'Doesn't he go there now?' Behind them, a telephone rang; not a *telefonino*, a real telephone.

Tassini laughed. 'I heard the old bastard talk about killing him once. That was just talk, but if he saw him at the *fornace*, he'd probably try.'

Just as Brunetti started to ask Tassini to explain this remark, the barman called, 'Giorgio, it's your wife. She wants to talk to you.'

Panic crossed Tassini's face and he scrambled to his feet. He walked quickly to the bar and took the receiver the barman handed to him. He turned his back on both the barman and Brunetti and hunched over the phone.

As Brunetti watched, Tassini's body relaxed, but only minimally. He listened for some time, spoke again, and then listened for an even longer time. As the conversation progressed, he gradually stood more and more upright until he reached his normal height. He said something and put the phone down, then turned and thanked the barman. He took a few coins out of his pocket and put them on the bar.

He came back to Brunetti and said, 'I have to go.' From the look on his face, he was already gone; he had already forgotten Brunetti or dismissed him as insignificant.

Brunetti pushed his chair back and started to get to his feet, but by the time he was standing, Tassini had already turned and was walking towards the door. He opened it, slipped through it, and shut it behind him.

11

The conversation, interrogation, whatever it was, with Tassini left Brunetti uneasy. He felt cheapened by the way he had deceived the man and by the way he had induced him to speak of his daughter. Who knew what the poor devil suffered because of her? And who knew the effect of the presence of the healthy child: a sense of relief that at least one of them was not afflicted? Or was his health and vitality but part of the daily flagellation that the profundity of the other child's condition caused the father?

Brunetti was neither a religious nor a superstitious man, though if he could have thought of the proper deity, he would have given thanks for the health and safety of his own children. As it was, he was left with a vague sense of unease at their continued good fortune and never ceased to worry about them. Sometimes he viewed this quality in himself with favour and thought of it as feminine; other times he saw it as a form of cowardice and chided himself with being womanly. Paola, not much given to sparing him the rough edge of her tongue, never joked with him about this tendency, certainly an indication that she saw it as central to his being and thus unapproachable.

He carried these unhappy thoughts back to the Questura and, to divert himself from them, went directly to Signorina Elettra's office. Perhaps the Vice-Questore had come up with some new directive suggesting a strategy for dealing with the recidivist adolescents.

She smiled when he came in and asked, 'Did Vianello tell you?'

'Tell me what?'

'To come and see me after you spoke to Signor Tassini.'

'No. Nothing. What have you got?'

She picked up a sheaf of papers and waved them, then set them on the desk and started to leaf through them, identifying each as she did: 'The non-arrest report for Signor De Cal; Ribetti's driver's licence application and driving record – it was the only thing about him in our files; Bovo's real arrest record, for assault, though it was six years ago; and copies of the letters Tassini has been sending for more than a year, as well as the medical records for his wife and child.'

There were still a number of papers on the desk when she finished, and he asked, 'And those?'

She looked up with an embarrassed grin and said, 'Copies of De Cal's tax statements for the last six years. Once I start looking for things, it's hard for me to stop.' She smiled with what a less astute person might have mistaken for sincerity.

He nodded to suggest that he, too, understood the frenzy of the hunt, and she said, 'The most interesting are the medical records, especially if you read them in conjunction with Tassini's letters.'

'Do you want to tell me,' he asked seriously, 'or do you want me to read them and then come back and talk about them to see if I find them interesting in the same way you do?'

'I think that would be the best thing,' she said and handed

him the papers. 'But I'll come up when you want to look at them together. I'm not sure the Vice-Questore would be pleased, if he should come in and find us discussing documents from a non-case.'

He thanked her, accepted the papers, and went up to his office to read them. Though he trusted her judgement that the first papers were not likely to prove of great interest, he read through them anyway, only to come to the same conclusion. The police report exonerated De Cal from any aggression; Bovo's case was quite the opposite, but things ended when the other man refused to press charges; and Ribetti was revealed to have a blameless driving record.

He turned to the medical records and noticed a few notations and, above the first of them, in Signorina Elettra's hand, 'Barbara checked through these.' Her sister, a doctor, should certainly be able to interpret a medical record, and judging from the pencilled notes in the margin, she had paid close attention.

The story told by the records was a grim one. It began with a pregnant woman who had decided, with her husband, to have her child at home. Even when they were told that the child they were expecting was two children, thus increasing the danger of home delivery, they persisted in their decision. The record of obstetrical visits had a pencilled *'tutto normale'* in the margin. Two weeks before the estimated date of delivery, there was an unscheduled obstetrical visit. The record contained a recommendation for a Caesarean, followed by, 'Refused by patient.' The margin contained a lone exclamation point.

There was a gap of two weeks, and when Brunetti turned the page he found himself with two babies, though their mother and one of the babies were in the *sala di rianimazione*. A marginal note read: 'Attached 118 report of original phone call at 3.17 AM', and sent him to the last sheet of paper, where he found a brief description of the call for medical help and the 3.21 departure time of the emergency ambulance boat. When the crew arrived at the Murano address, seventeen minutes later, they found Signora Sonia Tassini already delivered of one baby, while the other was trapped in the birth canal. The ambulance arrived at the Ospedale Civile at 4.16, which was astonishing, given the fact that they had had to go out to Murano.

Brunetti flipped back to the medical record. The second delivery, by Caesarean, was difficult, both for the mother and for the baby, who appeared to have been cut off from the oxygen supply during the final minutes of the procedure.

Sara Tassini remained in the hospital for more than two weeks, though she was released as a patient on the fifth day. The second child, a girl to be named Emma, had remained in *rianimazione* for four more days, and then had been put in a room with her mother and her brother, where they all remained for another week. When they were released, her mother was instructed to bring the child back every two weeks for tests to monitor her development, both physical and neurological.

For the first six months, the Tassinis brought the child to the hospital, but they failed to cooperate with the various social agencies which existed to help people in similar circumstances. When he read the phrase, 'similar circumstances', Brunetti whispered '*Gesù Bambino*' and turned the page. The child was described as being smaller than other children her age, and likely to remain so for however long she lived. Though the full extent of her handicaps would become evident only with time, there was no doubt in the minds of any of the doctors who examined her that the damage was the result of the lack of oxygen to her brain during her birth, and was irreversible.

Because of the demands of caring for the child, the Tassinis moved, when the children were six months old, to the home of Signora Tassini's mother, a widow who lived in Castello. At this point, Signora Tassini ceased to take the child to the hospital, and this was also the point when Tassini's letters started arriving at the police and at various other city offices. Some months later, Signora Tassini had begun treatment for depression at Palazzo Boldù. She was oppressed, she said, by a sense of guilt at having gone along with her husband's insistence that the children be born at home.

Attached was a report from Palazzo Boldù, chronicling her gradual ascent out of depression. Though she still felt guilt, the report stated, it was no longer crippling her life. However, Signora Tassini stated that her husband was still very much afflicted with it, though it manifested itself in his trying to find another explanation for the child's condition. For a time, she said, he claimed it was a result of the environmental contamination of their vegetarian diet, of medical incompetence, and then of some defect in their genes. 'Classic,' was pencilled in the margin. During her many conversations with her doctor, she never mentioned the letters her husband was writing, making Brunetti wonder if she even knew about them.

Brunetti turned almost with relief to Tassini's letters. They chronicled the changing targets his wife had mentioned but also referred to the negligence of the boat crew and the delivery room staff. And then on to genes and genetic disturbance, which he claimed had been exacerbated by the electric transformer one street from their home in Murano. Tassini also blamed his daughter's condition on the air that drifted over to the city from Marghera, but then he began to maintain that it resulted from his employment in a glass factory on Murano. What struck Brunetti was the apparent lucidity of the early letters, the clear, cogent style, with frequent reference to specific reports and scientific papers which presented evidence in support of his various and everchanging contentions.

The villain responsible for the Tassinis' plight was chameleon-like, changing and changing again as Tassini read more, explored farther with his reading and Internet researches. But the guilty party was always at one remove, was always other, never his own ideas or behaviour. Brunetti didn't know whether to weep for the man or take him by the shoulders and shake him until he admitted what he had done.

The most recent letter was dated more than three weeks before and made mention of new information that Tassini was in the process of acquiring, more evidence he would soon be able to produce to prove that he had been the unknowing victim of the criminal behaviour of two people. He said that he was now in a position to prove his assertions and had but to perform what he called two more 'examinations' in order to confirm his suspicions.

Brunetti read through the letters again and reinforced the sense he had the first time he read them, that the style had deteriorated over time, that they ceased to present their case clearly or cogently and came ever more to resemble the sort of vague accusatory letters the police were all too familiar with. The conjunction Signorina Elettra identified was no doubt that of the growing misery of the child's condition with the mounting confusion of Tassini's letters.

He finished reading the letters for a second time and let them fall on to his desk. Paola had once told him about a medieval Russian epic she had read about while at university, named after its hero: *Misery Luckless Plight*. Indeed.

The content of the papers had made him forget Signorina Elettra's admonition that they discuss them in his office, not hers; absent-mindedly, he picked them up and started down to her. If she seemed surprised to see him or to see him with the papers, she gave no sign of it and said only, 'Terrible, eh?'

'I've seen the little girl,' he said.

Her answering nod could either have been in acknowledgement that she knew he had seen her or that he was telling her now.

'Poor, desperate people,' she said.

103

He allowed a long silence to pass before he asked, 'The letters?'

'He's got to blame somebody else, hasn't he?'

'The wife doesn't seem to feel the same need,' Brunetti said with some asperity. 'That is, she realizes they were responsible for what happened.'

'Women have . . .' she started to say and then stopped.

Brunetti waited a moment and at her continued silence, prodded, 'Have what?'

Her glance put him on the scales and weighed him, and then she said, 'Less trouble accepting reality, I think.'

'Possibly,' he answered, hearing in his own voice that tone of half-doubt with which the unwilling greet the expression of good sense. He corrected himself to 'Probably', and her expression softened.

'What now?' she asked.

'I think I have no choice but to wait until he contacts me and gives me this evidence he keeps talking about.'

'You don't sound very persuaded,' she said.

With a wry look, Brunetti asked, 'Would you be?'

'I didn't talk to him, remember. So I don't have a real sense of him, as a person. Just the letters, and they . . . they don't suggest great reliability. At least not the ones he's writing now. In the beginning, perhaps.' She stopped and then could do nothing more than repeat, after a long pause, 'Poor, desperate people.'

'Which people?' Patta asked from behind Brunetti.

Neither of them had heard the Vice-Questore approach, but it was Signorina Elettra who recovered more quickly. Without missing a beat, she answered, 'The *extracomunitari* who apply for residence permits and then never hear anything more about them.'

'I beg your pardon,' Patta said, pausing just outside his door. He looked at Signorina Elettra but pointed a finger at Brunetti and then at the door to his office. 'If they apply, then they have to be patient. Just like everyone else who deals with a bureaucracy.'

'Three years?' she inquired.

That stopped him. 'No, not three years.' He made to continue into his office but then stopped on the threshold and turned back to her. 'Who's had to wait three years?'

'The woman who cleans my father's apartment, sir.'

'Three years?'

She nodded.

'Why has it taken so long?'

Brunetti wondered if she would make the obvious response and say that this was exactly what she wanted to know, but she opted for moderation and instead answered, 'I've no idea, sir. She applied three years ago, paid the application fee, and then she heard nothing. She thought that her case would come under the amnesty, but she never heard anything further. So she asked me if I thought she should begin the whole process again and reapply. And pay the fee again.'

'What did you tell her?'

'I don't have an answer to give her, Vice-Questore. It's a lot of money for her – it's a lot of money for anyone – and she doesn't want to go to the expense of applying again if there's any hope that the original application will be successful. That's why I was telling the Commissario that she and her husband were poor, desperate people.'

'I see,' Patta said, turning from her. He waved the waiting Brunetti ahead of him, then turned to Signorina Elettra and said, 'Give me her name and, if you can, her file number and I'll see what I can find out about it.'

'You're very kind, sir,' she said, sounding like she meant it.

Inside, Patta wasted no time: turning to Brunetti, he asked, 'What's all this business of your going out to Murano?'

Deny that he had? Ask how Patta knew? Repeat the question to give himself more time to think of an answer? De Cal? Fasano? Who on Murano had told Patta?

105

Brunetti opted to tell Patta the truth about what he was doing. 'A woman I know on Murano,' he began – suggesting that she was a woman he had known for some time and thus showing himself how incapable he was of telling Patta the real truth about anything – 'told me her father has been threatening her husband, well, making threatening statements about him. Not to him. She wanted me to see if I thought there was any real reason to fear that her father would do something.'

Brunetti watched Patta weigh this, wondering what his superior's response would be to this uncharacteristic frankness. The habit of suspicion, as Brunetti feared, triumphed. 'I suppose this explains why you went out to Murano for some sort of secret meeting in a trattoria, eh?' Patta asked, unable to disguise his satisfaction at the sight of Brunetti's surprise.

Having begun with the truth, not that it seemed to have helped, Brunetti continued that way. 'He's someone who knows the man who's been making the threats,' Brunetti explained, relieved that Patta appeared to know nothing of Navarro's relationship to Pucetti and even more relieved that his superior had made no mention of Vianello's presence at the meeting. 'I asked him if he thought there was any real basis in them.'

'And? What did he say?'

'He chose not to answer my question.'

'Have you spoken to anyone else?' Patta demanded.

Since telling the truth to Patta had failed as a strategy, Brunetti decided to return to the tried and true path of deceit and said, 'No.'

Patta's information had come from someone who had seen them in the restaurant, so perhaps he knew nothing about Brunetti's visits to Bovo and Tassini.

'So there's no threat?' Patta demanded.

'I'd say no. The man, Giovanni De Cal, is violent, but I think it's language and nothing more.'

106

'And so?' Patta asked.

'And so I go back to seeing what's to be done about the gypsies,' Brunetti answered, trying to sound contrite.

'*Rom,*' Patta corrected him.

'Exactly,' said Brunetti in acknowledgement of Patta's concession to the language of political correctness, and left his office.

12

Brunetti called Paola, after one, told her he would not be home for lunch and was hurt when she accepted the news with equanimity. When, however, she went on to observe that, since he said he was calling from his office, and he had not called until now, she had already come to that sad conclusion, he felt himself strangely heartened by her disappointment, however sarcastically she might choose to express it.

He dialled the number of Assunta De Cal's *telefonino* and told her he would like to come out to Murano to speak to her. No, he assured her, she had nothing to fear from her father's threats: he believed there was little danger in them. But he would still like to speak to her if that were possible.

She asked him how long it would take him to get there. He asked her to hold on a moment, went to the window and saw Foa standing on the *riva*, talking to another officer. He went back to the phone and told her it would not take him more then twenty minutes, heard her say she would wait for him at the *fornace*, and hung up.

When he emerged from the main entrance of the Questura five minutes later there was no sign of Foa, nor of his boat. He asked the man at the door where the pilot was, only to be told he had taken the Vice-Questore to a meeting. This left Brunetti with no choice but to head back to Fondamenta Nuove and the 41.

Thus it took him more than forty minutes to get to the De Cal factory. When he tried the office, Assunta was not there, nor was there any response when he knocked on the door to what a sign indicated was her father's office. Brunetti left that part of the building and went across the courtyard to the entrance to the *fornace*, hoping to find her there.

The sliding metal doors to the immense brick building had been rolled back sufficiently to allow room for a man to slip in or out. Brunetti stepped inside and found himself in darkness. It took his eyes a moment to adjust, and when they did they were captured by what, for an instant, he thought was an enormous Caravaggio at the other end of the dim room. Six men stood poised for an instant at the doors of a round furnace, half illuminated by the natural daylight that filtered in through the skylights in the roof and by the light that streamed from the furnace. They moved, and the painting fell apart into the intricate motions that lay deep in Brunetti's memory.

Two rectangular ovens stood against the right wall, but the *forno di lavoro* stood free at the center of the room. There appeared to be only two *piazze* at work, for he saw only two men twirling the blobs of molten glass at the ends of their *canne*. One seemed to be working on what would become a platter, for as he spun the *canna*, centrifugal force transformed the blob first into a saucer and then into a pizza. Memory took Brunetti back to the factory where his father had worked – not as a *maestro* but as a *servente* – decades ago. As he watched, this *maestro* became the *maestro* for whom his father had worked. And as Brunetti continued to watch, he became

109

every *maestro* who had worked the glass for more than a thousand years. Except for his jeans and his Nike trainers, he could have stepped out of any of the centuries when such men had done this work.

Ballet was not an art for which Brunetti had much affection, but in the motions of these men he saw the beauty others saw in dance. Still spinning the *canna*, the *maestro* glided over to the door of the furnace. He turned to keep his left side towards it, and Brunetti noticed the thick glove and the sleeve protector he wore against the savage heat. In went the *canna*, one side of the platter passing no more than a centimetre from the solid edge of the door.

Brunetti drew closer and looked beyond him and into the flame, where he saw the inferno of his youth, the Hell to which the good sisters had assured him and all his classmates they would be consigned for any infraction, no matter how minor. He saw white, yellow, red, and in the midst of it he saw the plate spinning, changing colour, growing.

The *maestro* pulled it out, again missing the side by a hair, and this time went back and sat at his *banco* and resumed spinning the plate. Without needing to look for them, he picked up an enormous pair of pincers, nor did he seem to have to look at the platter as he pressed the point of one blade up to its surface and, spinning, spinning, still spinning, cut a groove in the surface of one side. A sliver of wet glass peeled off the plate and slithered to the floor.

The *servente* responded to a signal too subtle for Brunetti to see and came over and carried the *canna* to the furnace while the *maestro* picked up a bottle that stood under his chair and took a long drink. He set it down one second before the *servente* came back and passed him the *canna* with the freshly heated plate suspended from the end. Their motions were as liquid as the glass itself.

Brunetti heard his name and turned to see Assunta standing at the door. He realized that his shirt was stuck to

110

his body and his face beaded with sweat. He had no idea how long he had stood, transfixed by the beauty of the men at work.

He walked towards her, conscious of the sudden chill of the perspiration on his back. 'I was delayed,' Brunetti said, offering no explanation. 'So I came to look for you in here.'

She smiled and waved this aside. 'It's all right. I was down at the dock. Today's the day they collect the acid and the mud, and I like to be there to see that the numbers and weights are right.'

Brunetti's confusion was no doubt apparent – he had never heard of such things in his father's time – for she explained: 'The laws are clear about what we can use and what we must do with it after we use it. They have to be.' Her smile grew softer and she added, 'I know I must sound like Marco when I say these things, but he's right about them.'

'What acid?' Brunetti asked.

'Nitric and fluoric,' she said. She saw that Brunetti was no less confused and so went on. 'When we make beads, we drill a copper wire through the centre to make the hole, then the copper has to be dissolved in nitric acid. Every now and then, we have to change the acid.' Brunetti did not want to know what had been done with the acid in the past.

'Same with the fluoric. We need it to smooth the surfaces on the big pieces. Well, it's the same in that we have to pay to get rid of it.'

'And mud, did you say?' he asked.

'From the grinding, when they do the final polishing,' she said, then asked, 'Would you like to see?'

'My father worked out here, but that was decades ago,' Brunetti said, in an attempt not to appear completely ignorant. 'Things have changed, I suppose.'

'Less than you'd think,' she answered. She stepped past him and waved an arm at the men who continued undisturbed in their ritual movements in front of the furnaces. 'It's

111

one of the things I love about this,' she said, her voice warmer. 'No one's found a better way to do what we've been doing for hundreds of years.'

She leaned towards Brunetti and put her hand on his arm to capture his attention fully. 'See what he's doing?' she asked, pointing to the second of the *maestri*, who was just returning from the furnace. He took his place behind a small wooden bucket on the floor. As they watched, he blew into one end of the iron *canna*, inflating the blob of glass at the other end. Quickly, with the grace of a baton twirler, he swung the glowing mass until it was just above the bucket and squeezed it carefully into the cylindrical tub, moving it up and down and slipping it around until it slid inside. He blew repeatedly into the end of the pipe, each puff forcing a halo of sparks to fly from the top of the tub.

When he pulled the *canna* out, the blob was a perfect cylinder, now recognizable as the flat-bottomed vase it would become. 'Same raw materials, same tools, same technique as we were using here centuries ago,' she said.

He glanced aside at her and their smiles met, reflecting one another. 'It's wonderful, isn't it, something so permanent?' Brunetti said, not quite certain if that last word was the one he sought, but she nodded, understanding him.

'The only change we've made is to switch to gas,' she said. 'Aside from that, nothing's changed.'

'Except these laws Marco supports?' Brunetti asked.

Her expression changed and became serious. 'Is that meant as a joke?'

He had not intended to offend her. 'No, not at all,' he protested quickly. 'I assure you. I don't know what laws you mean, but what I know about your husband tells me they're probably ecological laws, in which case I'm sure they were necessary and well past time.'

'Marco says it's too little, too late,' she said, but she said it quietly.

This was not the place for a conversation like this, Brunetti knew, so he took a step away from her and closer to the workers, hoping to break the mood created by her last words. He pointed at the men near the furnaces and turned back to ask her, 'How many workers do you have here?'

She seemed relieved by the change of subject and began to count them off on her fingers. 'Two *piazze*, that's six; then the two men down at the dock and who do the packing and delivery; then three who do the final *molatura*, that's eleven, and then *l'uomo di notte*: that makes twelve, I think.'

He watched her tally the men again on her fingers. 'Yes, twelve, and my father and I.'

'Tassini's the *uomo di notte*, isn't he?'

'You spoke to him?'

'Yes, and he thought there would be no danger unless your husband were to come to the *fornace*,' Brunetti said, and then at her look of fear, he added, 'But he never comes here, does he?'

'No, not at all,' she said, voice rich with disappointment. Brunetti could well understand this. He had observed her passion for her work and for her husband. To have one excluded from the other, either by choice or decree, was understandably a difficult thing for her to bear.

'Did he once?' he asked.

'Before we were married, yes. He's an engineer, remember, so he's interested in the process of mixing and making glass and working it, everything about it.' As if to remind herself of one of those passions, she looked over at the men, the rhythm of whose work continued undisturbed by their talk: the first one was already working on an entirely different piece. Brunetti looked at them and saw the *servente* to the first *maestro* touch a pendulant drop of red glass onto one side of the top of what appeared to be a vase. The *maestro*'s pliers smoothed the tip of the drop on to the vase, then pulled it, as though it were a piece of chewing gum, and attached the

113

other end lower down on the vase. A quick snip, smooth the sides, and the first handle was made.

'They make it look so easy,' Brunetti said, his wonder audible.

'For them, I suppose it is. After all, Gianni's been working glass all his life. He could probably make some pieces in his sleep by now.'

'Do you ever get tired of it?' Brunetti asked.

She turned and looked at him, trying to assess how serious a question this was. Apparently she concluded that Brunetti meant it, for she said, 'Not of watching it. No. Never. But the paper part of it, if I can call it that, yes, I'm tired of that, tired of the endless laws and taxes and regulations.'

'Which laws do you mean?' Brunetti asked, wondering if she would refer again to the ecological laws her husband seemed so to favour.

'The ones that specify how many copies of each receipt I have to make and who I have to send them to, and the ones about the forms I have to fill in for every kilo of raw material we buy.' She shrugged them off. 'And that's not even to mention the taxes.'

If he had known her better, Brunetti would have said that she must still manage to evade a great deal, but their friendship had not advanced to the stage of having the taxman as a common enemy, at least not as an openly declared one, so he contented himself with saying, 'I hope you find someone to do the paper part so you can keep the part you like for yourself.'

'Yes,' she said absently, 'that would be nice.' Then, shaking off whatever the effect of his words had been, she asked, 'Would you like to see the rest?'

'Yes,' he admitted with a smile. 'I'd like to see how much it's changed since I was a kid.'

'How old were you when you first came out?'

Brunetti had to think about this for a while, running the

years and paging through the list of the jobs his father had held in the last decade of his life. 'I must have been about twelve.'

She laughed and said, 'That's the perfect age for you to have become a *garzon*.'

Brunetti laughed outright. 'That's all I wanted to be,' he said. 'And to grow up and become a *maestro* and make those beautiful things.'

'But?' she asked, turning towards the main doors.

Though she could not see him, Brunetti shrugged as he said, 'But it didn't happen.'

Something in his tone must have sounded in a particular way, for she stopped and turned towards him. 'Are you sorry?'

He smiled and shook his head. 'I don't think that way,' he said. 'Besides, I like the way things went.'

She smiled in response and said, 'How pleasant to hear someone say that.' She led him through the doors and out into the courtyard, then immediately towards a door on the right. Inside, he found the *molatura*, where a low wooden trough ran along one entire wall, numerous taps lined up above it. Two young men with rubber aprons stood at the trough, each holding a piece of glass, one a bowl and one a plate that looked very much like the one the *maestro* had been making a little earlier.

As Brunetti watched, they turned the objects, holding first one surface, then another, to the grinding wheels in front of them. Streams of water flowed down from the taps over the grinding wheels and then over the pieces of glass: Brunetti remembered that the water would keep the temperature down and prevent the heat shattering the glass as well as prevent the glass particles from filling the air and the lungs of the worker. Water splashed down the aprons and over the boots of the workers on to the floor, but the bulk of it was washed into the trough and flowed to the end, where,

115

grey with glass dust, it disappeared down a pipe.

Just inside the door Brunetti saw vases, cups, platters, and statues standing on a wooden table, waiting their turn at the wheels. He could see the marks left by the clippers and by the straight edges used to fuse two colours of glass together: the grinding would quickly erase all imperfections, he knew.

Raising his voice over the noise of the wheel and running water, Brunetti said, 'It's not as exciting as the other.'

She nodded but said, 'But it's just as necessary.'

'I know.'

He looked over at the two workers, back at Assunta, and asked, 'Masks?'

This time she shrugged but said nothing until she had led him out of the room and back into the courtyard. 'They're given two fresh masks every day: that's what the law says. But it doesn't tell me how to make them wear them.' Before Brunetti could comment, she said, 'If I could, I would. But they see it as some compromise of their masculinity, and they won't wear them.'

'The men who worked with my father never did, either,' Brunetti said.

She tossed her hands up in the air and walked away from him towards the front of the building. Brunetti joined her there and asked, 'I didn't see your father in his office. Isn't he here today?'

'He had a doctor's appointment,' she explained. 'But I hope he'll be back before the end of the afternoon.'

'Nothing serious, I hope,' Brunetti said, making a note to ask Signorina Elettra to see what she could find out about De Cal's health.

She nodded her thanks for his wishes but said nothing.

'Well,' Brunetti said, 'I'll go back now. Thanks for the tour. It brings back a lot of memories.'

'And thank you for going to the trouble of coming out here to tell me.'

116

'Don't worry,' he said. 'Your father's not likely to do anything rash.'

'I hope not,' she said, shaking his hand and turning back towards the office and her world.

13

The following morning, Brunetti arrived at the Questura after nine and went into Signorina Elettra's office, having forgotten that this was the day when she did not come in until after lunch. He started to write her a message, asking her if she could find De Cal's hospital records, but the thought that either Patta or Scarpa could read anything left on her desk made him change it to a simple request that she call him in his office when she could.

Upstairs, he read through the reports on his desk, had a look at the list of proposed promotions, and then started to read his way through a thick folder of papers from the Ministry of the Interior relating to new laws regarding the arrest and detention of suspected terrorists. National law did not accord with European law, it seemed, and that in its turn failed to conform to international law. Brunetti read with mounting interest as the confusions and contradictions became increasingly evident.

The section on interrogation was brief, as though the person commissioned to write it wanted to get through the assignment as quickly as possible without taking a stand of any sort. The document repeated something Brunetti had read elsewhere, that some foreign authorities – left unnamed – believed that the infliction of pain during interrogation was permissible up 'to the level of serious illness'. Brunetti turned from these words to a consideration of the doors of his wardrobe. 'Diabetes or bone cancer?' he asked the doors, but they made no response.

He read the report until the end, closed it, and pushed it to one side of his desk. During his early years as a policeman, he remembered, people still argued about whether it was right or wrong to use force during an interrogation, and he had heard all of the arguments from both sides. Now they argued about how much pain they could inflict.

Euclid came to mind: was it he who had claimed that, given a lever long enough, he could move the Earth itself? Brunetti's experience and his reading of history had led him to believe that, given the right pressure, almost anyone could be moved to confess to anything. So it had always seemed to him that the important question to be asked about interrogation was not how far the subject had to be pushed in order to confess, so much as how far the questioner was willing to go in order to get the inevitable confession.

These melancholy thoughts remained with him for some time, after which he decided to go downstairs to see if Vianello was in. As he went down the stairs, he encountered Lieutenant Scarpa, coming up them. They nodded but did not speak as they registered one another's presence. But Brunetti was brought up short when Scarpa moved to the left, effectively blocking his descent.

'Yes, Lieutenant?'

Without introduction, Scarpa asked, 'This Hungarian, Mary Dox, is she your doing?'

'I beg your pardon, Lieutenant?'

Scarpa held up a folder, as if the sight of it would make

119

things clear to Brunetti. 'Is she yours?' the lieutenant asked again, his voice neutral.

'I'm afraid I don't know what you're talking about, Lieutenant,' Brunetti said.

In an intentionally melodramatic gesture, Scarpa raised the hand with the folder in the air between them, as if he had suddenly decided to auction it off, and asked, 'You don't know what I'm talking about? You don't know anything about Mary Dox?'

'No.'

Just as Assunta De Cal had done when confronted with evidence of knuckle-headed masculinity, Scarpa threw his hands up in the air, then stepped to the right and continued on up the stairs without saying anything further.

Brunetti went to the officers' room in search of Vianello. He found, instead, Pucetti, hunched over his desk and deeply engrossed in what looked like the same report Brunetti had just finished. The young officer was so engrossed in what he was reading that he did not hear Brunetti approach.

'Pucetti,' Brunetti said as he reached the desk, 'have you seen Vianello?'

At the sound of his name, Pucetti looked up from the papers, but it took him a few seconds to tear his attention away from them; he pushed his chair back and got to his feet. 'Excuse me, Commissario, I didn't hear you,' he said. His right hand still grasped the papers, so he was prevented from saluting. To compensate, he stood as straight as he could.

'Vianello,' Brunetti said and smiled. 'I'm looking for him.'

He watched Pucetti's eyes and saw him force himself to recall who Vianello was. Then Pucetti said, 'He was here before.' He looked around the office, as if curious to discover where he found himself. 'But he must have gone out.'

Brunetti let almost a full minute pass, and during that time he watched Pucetti return from the land where interrogation techniques were discussed with cold dispassion – if, in fact, that was the subject that had so fully captured the attention of the young man.

When he had Pucetti's full attention, Brunetti said, 'Lieutenant Scarpa asked me about a folder he had, dealing with a Hungarian woman named Mary Dox. Do you have any idea what this is about?'

Pucetti's face registered comprehension and he said, 'He came in here this morning, sir, asking about the same woman. He wanted to know if any of us knew about her case.'

'And?'

'And no one did.'

Aware of the uniformed staff's opinion of the lieutenant, Brunetti asked, 'No one did or no one said they did?'

'No one did, sir. We talked about it after he left, and no one knew what he was talking about.'

'Is this where Vianello's gone?'

'I don't think so. He didn't know anything, either. My guess is that he's just gone down to get a coffee.'

Brunetti thanked him and told him to continue with his reading, to which Pucetti did not respond.

At the bar near Ponte dei Greci, Brunetti found Vianello at the counter, a glass of wine in front of him as he leafed through that day's paper.

'What did Scarpa want?' Brunetti asked as he came in. He asked the barman for a coffee.

Vianello folded the newspaper and moved it to one side of the bar. 'I've no idea,' he answered. 'Whatever it is, or whoever she is, it's trouble. I've never seen him so angry.'

'No idea?' Brunetti asked, nodding his thanks to the barman as he set down the coffee.

'None,' Vianello answered.

Brunetti stirred in sugar and drank half the coffee, then finished it. 'You read these regulations from the Ministry of the Interior?' he asked Vianello.

'I never read their directives,' Vianello said and took a sip of his wine. 'I used to, but I don't care about them any more.'

'Why?'

'They never say anything much: just words, words all tortured so as to sound good while justifying the fact that they really don't want to achieve anything.'

'Anything about what?' Brunetti asked.

'You ever been sent to ask one of the Chinese where the cash came from to buy his bar? You ever been asked to check the work permits of the people who work in those bars? You ever been sent out to close down a factory that got caught dumping its garbage in a national forest?'

What struck Brunetti was not the subject of Vianello's questions – questions that floated around the Questura like lint in a shirt factory – but the cool dispassion with which he asked them. 'You don't sound like you care much,' he observed.

'About this woman Scarpa wants to know about?' Vianello asked. 'No, I don't.'

That made quite a list of things Vianello didn't care much about this morning. 'I'll see you after lunch,' Brunetti said and left, heading home.

On the kitchen table, he found a note from Paola, saying she had to meet one of the students whose doctoral work she was overseeing but that there was lasagne in the oven. The kids would not be home, and a salad was in the refrigerator: all he had to do was add oil and vinegar. Just as Brunetti was preparing to start grumbling his way through lunch – having come halfway across the city, only to be deprived of the company of his family, forced to eat heated-up things from the oven, probably made with some sort of pre-packaged whatever and that disgusting orange American cheese for all he knew – he saw the last line of Paola's note: 'Stop sulking. It's your mother's recipe and you love it.'

Left to eat alone, Brunetti's first concern was to find the right thing to read. A magazine would be right, but he had already finished that week's *Espresso*. A newspaper took up too much space on the table. A paperback book could never be forced to stay open, not without breaking the binding completely, which would later cause the pages to fall out. Art books, which were surely big enough, suffered from oil stains. He compromised by going into the bedroom and taking from his bedside Gibbon, whose style forced him to read in translation.

He took out the lasagne, cut it and put a chunk on a plate. He poured a glass of Pinot grigio then opened Gibbon to his place and propped it up against two books Paola had left on the table. He employed a cutting board and a serving spoon to hold the pages open on both sides. Satisfied with the arrangement, he sat down and started to eat.

Brunetti found himself back in the court of the Emperor Heliogabalus, one of his favorite monsters. Ah, the excess of it, the violence, the utter corruption of everything and everyone. The lasagne had layers of ham and thin slices of artichoke hearts interleaved with layers of pasta that he suspected might have been home made. He would have preferred more artichokes. He shared his table with decapitated senators, evil counsellors, barbarians bent on the destruction of the empire. He took a sip of wine and ate another bite of lasagne.

The Emperor appeared, arrayed like the sun itself. All hailed him, his glory, and his graciousness. The court was splendid and excessive, a place where, as Gibbon observed, 'a capricious prodigality supplied the want of taste and elegance'. Brunetti set his fork down, the better to savour both the lasagne and Gibbon's description.

He got up and took the salad, poured in oil and vinegar and sprinkled in some salt. He ate from the bowl, as Heliogabalus died under the swords of his guards.

On the way back to the Questura, Brunetti stopped for a coffee and pastry at Ballarin, then arrived just in time to meet

123

Signorina Elettra at the front entrance.

After they exchanged greetings, Brunetti said, 'There's something I'd like you to try and check for me, Signorina.'

'Of course,' she said encouragingly, 'if I can.'

'De Cal's medical records,' he said. 'His daughter said he had a doctor's appointment this afternoon, and a number of people have commented on his health. I wondered if there's reason for, well, for preoccupation.'

'That shouldn't be at all difficult, sir,' she said, pausing at the beginning of the second flight of steps. 'Anything else?'

If anyone could find out, it was she. 'Yes, there's one thing. Lieutenant Scarpa has been asking if anyone knows anything about a foreign woman, and I wondered if he's spoken to you.'

She looked frankly puzzled and said, 'No. He hasn't said a word. Who's the poor person?'

'A Hungarian woman,' Brunetti said. 'Mary Dox.'

'What?' she demanded sharply, coming to a halt. 'What did you say?'

'Mary Dox,' explained a puzzled Brunetti. 'He asked me, and it seems he went into the officers' room this morning to ask them if they knew anything about her.'

'Did he say what he wanted?' she asked, her voice calmer.

'No, not that I know of. When I saw him, he had a folder in his hand.' As he talked, the memory surfaced and he said, 'It looked like one of our files.' He hoped she would volunteer whatever information she had, but when she remained silent, he asked, 'Do you know her?'

After a pause he could describe only as speculative, she said, 'Yes, I do.' Her eyes shifted into long focus, as if the reason for Scarpa's curiosity might be found on the far wall. 'She's my father's cleaning woman.'

'The one you spoke to the Vice-Questore about?'

'Yes.'

'Did you give him her name?' Brunetti asked.

'Yes, I did, and the file number.'

'You think he could have passed them on to Scarpa and asked him to find out about her?'

'Possibly,' she said. 'But I left the information on his desk, so anyone could have seen it.'

'But why would Scarpa start asking about her unless Patta told him to do so?'

'I've no idea,' she said. She smiled and tried to dismiss the unease provoked by the idea that Scarpa was involved in something that concerned her, however tangentially. 'I'll ask the Vice-Questore if he needs any other information about her.'

'I'm sure that's what it is,' Brunetti – who wasn't – said.

'Yes, thank you,' she answered. 'I'll go and have a look for the medical records, shall I?'

'Yes,' Brunetti said, leaving her, and went back to his office, his mind a jumble of Scarpa, Heliogabalus, and the mysterious Mary Dox.

14

Most people dread middle of the night phone calls for their presage of loss or violence or death. The certainty that one's family is sleeping peacefully nearby in no way diminishes the alarm; it merely directs it towards other people. Thus Brunetti's fear was no less sharp when his phone rang a little after five the following morning.

'Commissario Brunetti?' inquired a voice he recognized as Alvise's. Had the call reached him at home at any other time of day, Brunetti would have asked the officer what man he expected to find answering the phone at his home, but it was too early for sarcasm: it was always too early for anything other than the literal with Alvise.

'Yes. What is it?'

'We just had a call from someone on Murano.' Alvise stopped, as if to suggest that this information was sufficient.

'What about, Alvise?'

'He found a dead man, sir.'

'Who?'

'He didn't say who he was, sir, just that he was calling from Murano.'

'Did he say who the dead man was, Alvise?' Brunetti asked as sleepiness retreated, to be supplanted by the careful, plodding patience one had always to use with Alvise.

'No, sir.'

'Did he say where he was?' Brunetti asked.

'Where he works, sir.'

'Where is that, Alvise?'

'At a *fornace*, sir.'

'Which one?'

'I think he said De Cal, sir. I didn't have a pen. Anyway, it's on Sacca Serenella.'

Brunetti pushed back the covers and sat up. He got out of bed and looked at Paola, who had one eye open and was looking at him. 'I'll be at the end of the *calle* in twenty minutes,' Brunetti said. 'Send a launch.' Before Alvise could begin to explain why this would be difficult, Brunetti cut him off by saying, 'If we don't have one, call the *Carabinieri*, and if they can't come, call me a taxi.' He replaced the phone.

'Dead man?' Paola asked.

'On Murano,' he said, glancing out the window to see what sort of promise the day might hold.

When he looked back at her, her eyes were closed, and the thought struck him that she had fallen asleep. But before disappointment could register, she opened her eyes again and said, 'God, what a terrible job you do, Guido.'

He ignored the remark and went into the bathroom.

When he emerged, shaved and showered, the bed was empty, and he smelled fresh coffee. He dressed, remembering to put on heavy shoes in case he was going to spend time in the *fornace*, then went down to the kitchen and found her seated at the table, a small cup of coffee in front of her and a large cup of coffee with milk ready for him.

127

'There's sugar in it already,' she said as he reached for it. He studied his wife of more than twenty years, conscious that something was wrong with her but unable to recognize what it was. He studied her and she looked back at him, smiling quizzically.

'What's wrong?' Paola asked.

The fact that she had heard him say someone was dead should have been enough, but he continued to study her, trying to figure it out. Finally he saw it and blurted out, 'You're not reading.' There was no book, no newspaper, no magazine in front of her: she simply sat there, drinking her coffee and, it seemed, waiting for him.

'I'll make more coffee when you're gone and go back to bed and read until the kids are up,' she said. Order returned to Brunetti's universe. He finished his coffee, kissed Paola, and said he had no idea when he'd be home but would call when he knew.

When he turned into the *calle* that led to the canal, the silence told him that the boat had not arrived. If he had given the order to anyone but Alvise, Brunetti would have thought this nothing but a short delay; as it was, he wondered if he would end up having to call a taxi. Occupied with these thoughts, he reached the edge of the canal and looked to the right. And saw what he had seen only in photos taken in the early part of the last century: the mirror-smooth waters of the Grand Canal. Not a ripple stirred the surface, no boats passed, not a puff of wind, no gulls paddled around. He stood transfixed and looked on what his ancestors had seen: the same light, the same façades, the same windows and plants, and the same vital silence. And, as far as he could distinguish the reflections, it all existed in double.

He heard the drone of the boat's approaching motor, and then it swept around the curve in front of the university and headed towards him. As it came, it destroyed the stillness ahead of it and left in its wake those many wavelets that, minutes after it passed, would still be splashing against the steps of the *palazzi* on both sides of the canal.

Brunetti saw Foa at the wheel and raised a hand in greeting. The pilot slid the launch towards the twin pilings, slipped the motor into reverse, and glided up to the dock with a touch as gentle as a kiss. Brunetti stepped aboard, wished the pilot good morning, and asked him to take him to the De Cal factory on Sacca Serenella.

Foa, like most pilots, had the grace of silence and did nothing more than nod to acknowledge Brunetti's request. He seemed to feel no need to fill up the journey with words. By the time they reached Rialto, the broad-beamed boats that hauled produce to the market had turned the stillness into memory. Foa swung into Rio dei SS Apostoli and directly past the *palazzo* in which some distant ancestor of Paola's had lived before being beheaded for treason. They shot out into the *laguna* where the first thing Brunetti saw, off to the right, were the walls of the cemetery and, behind it, banks of clouds scuttling towards the city.

He turned away deliberately and faced Murano, stood with the warmth of spring on his body; the boat swung past the island then slipped around to the right and into the Serenella Canal. Brunetti glanced at his watch and saw that it was barely six o'clock. Foa made another silk-smooth landing, and Brunetti stepped up on to the ACTV *embarcadero*.

'You can go back,' he told the pilot. 'And thanks.'

'Do you mind if I try to find a coffee and then come back and wait for you, Commissario?' Foa asked. He did not explain his reluctance to return to the Questura; somehow, Brunetti suspected it had nothing to do with not wanting to work.

'What you could do,' Brunetti said, 'is call Vianello at home and then go and get him and bring him here.' Brunetti had been too dulled by sleep and then distracted by the inevitable irritation of having to deal with Alvise to have thought of calling Vianello, but he would prefer to have the Inspector here with him.

Foa raised his hand minimally and smiled. Brunetti barely saw the pilot's hands move, but the boat swung away from the dock in a tight U, and then Foa gunned the motor, forcing the prow up above the water as he sped away in a straight line towards the city.

Brunetti turned into the field and followed the cement path towards the factory in the background. It came to him then that he had not thought to tell Alvise to send the crime squad. *'Maria Vergine,'* he exclaimed aloud, taking out his *telefonino.* He dialled the central number of the Questura and spent a few minutes learning that, yes, a crime scene team had been requested: they were waiting for the photographer and would leave as soon as he arrived.

Brunetti hung up, wondering how long it would take them to get out to Murano. He continued towards the building and as he drew close, he saw two men standing outside the sliding metal doors. They stood side by side, but they were not talking, nor did it seem they had broken off conversation when they saw him approach.

He recognized one of them as the *maestro* he had seen making the vase – had it been only two days before? Close to him, Brunetti only now noticed the deep acne scars on both his cheeks. The other man might have been any of the ones who had been working with or around him.

They glanced over at Brunetti and kept their eyes on him as he approached. Neither gave any sign that they had seen him before. As he drew up to them, Brunetti said, 'I'm Commissario Brunetti, from the police. Someone called to report finding a dead man.' He raised his voice at the end of this, turning it into a question.

The *maestro* turned and looked at the other man, who gave Brunetti an agonized glance and then looked at the ground, exposing the top of his head. Brunetti saw how sparse his hair was and how shiny the scalp beneath it.

'Was it you who found him, Signore?' he asked the top of the man's head.

The *maestro* held up an admonitory hand to catch Brunetti's attention. He raised one finger and waved it back and forth to silence Brunetti, then shook his head in the same rhythm, pointing at the other man. Before Brunetti could speak, the *maestro* placed his hand on the other man's sleeve and pulled him gently aside. Together they walked a metre or two away from Brunetti.

After a moment, the *maestro* came back. 'Don't ask him,' he said in a barely audible voice. 'He can't go back in there again.'

Brunetti wondered if the other man's guilt was preventing him from returning to the scene of the crime, but then he sensed the real fear and compassion that led the *maestro* to try to protect his friend. In the face of Brunetti's continuing silence, the *maestro* said, 'Really, Commissario, he can't. You can't do that to him.'

In what he hoped was a reasonable voice, Brunetti said, 'I won't force him to do anything. But I need him to tell me what happened.'

'But that's what I'm telling you,' the *maestro* said. 'He can't.'

Brunetti walked over and extended his hand to touch the arm of the silent man, hoping to give a sign of understanding or sympathy. He spoke to the *maestro*, as though he had become his companion's translator. 'I need to know what happened here. I need to know about the dead man.'

At those words, the man who had not spoken clapped his hand over his mouth and turned away. He gagged and took two steps on to the grass, brushing past Brunetti. He doubled over and retched again and again, though nothing came up but thin yellow bile. Spasms tore his body until he was forced to lean over and brace himself with his hands on his knees.

131

Another wave struck him, and he fell to one knee, his head bent over, one hand on the earth. More bile came up.

Brunetti stood by helplessly. It was the *maestro* who finally intervened and helped the other man to his feet. 'Come on, Giuliano. I think you better go home. Come on, now.' Neither man so much as glanced at Brunetti, who stepped back and let them pass in front of him. He watched them until they reached the pavement running along the canal, where they turned to the left and disappeared in the direction of the bridge that crossed to the main part of the island. The men seemed to take some of the light with them, for just as they disappeared, clouds rolled in and blotted out some of the day.

Brunetti looked around and saw no one. He heard a boat pass on the canal; the tide was low, so all he saw was a man's head pass smoothly by, just above the height of the embankment. The man noticed Brunetti and smiled, and Brunetti thought of the Cheshire Cat.

He waited a minute, a minute more, as the boat's motor faded and nothing replaced it. He turned and approached the *fornace*; the metal doors had been pushed partly back. He slipped inside and paused a moment to allow his eyes to adjust to the dimness.

He had noticed the last time just how dirty the windows and skylights were, but because it had been full day, there had been enough light to work by. This morning, however, with the clouds darkening the sky, little light penetrated. He looked around for a light switch, but the sight of the closed doors of the two furnaces against the wall made him fear what turning the wrong switch might do to them. He knew that their temperature had to diminish gradually during the night, so as not to risk cracking the pieces that slept their way to solidity inside them.

He took a few steps deeper into the factory, drawn by the light that emerged from the open door of the farthest furnace. It illuminated the area directly in front of it and a bit to either side, but the rest of the enormous shed remained shadowy and dim.

He took another step, and it was then that Brunetti first became aware of a strange odour in the air; something sweet mixed with something foul and sour. Though it was spring-time and trees and plants were already stirring into bloom, there was nothing floral about this scent. Nor was it like the rich fecund smell of the earth as busy plants renewed them-selves and began to grow, though it was more the second than the first.

Brunetti looked around, wondering if something, some chemical or colourant, could have been spilled, but it was not exactly chemical, that smell. He approached the first furnace and, as he drew closer, felt the sudden increase of tempera-ture, even through the closed door. The wave of heat drove him to the left, to the space between the first and second furnaces. The temperature dropped suddenly, and he felt almost chilled by the contrast with the searing heat in the radius of the first furnace.

As he drew closer to the second furnace, the heat leaped out at him again, stroking at the side of his arm and leg, warm at his face, offering to set him afire. Instinctively he held his hand up to protect his face and passed into the cooler zone beyond it.

The door to the free-standing furnace lured Brunetti. He was helpless to prevent himself from glancing towards the infernal depths. He squinted as the heat dried his eyes, blinking repeatedly. He stepped back, into a cooler zone farther from the door, glad of the sudden drop in tempera-ture. The smell was much stronger here.

He looked around him, to left and right, but still he saw nothing untoward. He turned his attention back to the open door of the furnace, where the flames roared and hurled their heat at him. It had grown lighter while he was inside the building: perhaps the clouds had lifted or been blown away.

The sun must just then have risen above the rooftops, for the first direct rays to come through the east-facing windows brought a sudden burst of illumination.

Brunetti noticed a shadow on the floor, just in front of the furnace, little more than two metres from him. He held his hand up again, this time to block the too-bright light from the open furnace, hoping that he would be able to make it out, whatever it was. But the radiance flooded around his outspread palm, forcing him to raise his other hand to create a broader shield. And he saw it, then, in the early light of the day. A man, a tall man, lay on the floor in front of the third furnace. Brunetti looked away and found himself facing the row of thermometers on the wall. *Forno* III had a temperature of 1342 degrees centigrade while the temperatures of the other two were less than half of that. He had to step back from the heat, for even here it assailed and seared him.

The smell. The smell. Brunetti fell forward to his knees like an ox felled by an axe. He braced his palms on the burning floor and brought up bile and more bile as he felt the sweet odour on him, on his clothing, in his hair.

The *maestro* found him like that a few minutes later. He bent over Brunetti, helped him to his feet, and steadied him as they walked out of the factory. The *maestro* led Brunetti a few metres away from the door, then released his arm and stepped away as Brunetti bent over again. The *maestro* turned towards the canal and paid careful attention to a boat that was going by.

Brunetti dragged out his handkerchief and wiped at his mouth, then tried to stand up straight. It took him a full minute before he could look at the other man.

'Was it you who found him?' Brunetti asked weakly.

'No, that was Colussi, my *servetto*. He usually comes in about five to check the *fornaci* and anything we left cooling there.'

Brunetti nodded. The other man went on. 'He called me,

but I couldn't make much sense of what he was saying. He kept telling me, "Tassini's dead, Tassini's dead." So I told him to go outside and wait for me, and I called the police and then came over here.' When Brunetti said nothing, the other man said, as if he felt the need to justify himself, 'You saw him. I had to take him home.'

'Where can we get something to drink?' Brunetti asked.

The *maestro* looked at his watch and said, 'On the other side of the bridge. Franco's usually open by now.'

It surprised Brunetti to find how unsteady he still was when he walked, but he fought against it and followed the other man. At the foot of the bridge was an old AMAV garbage tin, and Brunetti stepped aside to thrust his handkerchief deep into it.

On the other side of the bridge, the *maestro* led Brunetti to the left along the *riva*, then quickly turned right into a narrow *calle*. Halfway along, he stepped into a bar that smelled of coffee and fresh pastries. Just inside the door, the man stopped and offered his hand to Brunetti. 'Grassi,' he said. 'Luca.' Brunetti returned the handshake and brought his other hand up to pat the man on the arm by way of thanks.

Grassi turned away and walked to the bar. '*Caffè coretto*,' he said to the barman, then gave Brunetti an interrogative glance.

'A grappa and a glass of *acqua minerale non gassata*,' Brunetti said, those being the only things he could think of that his body might accept.

'Give him the good grappa, Franco,' Grassi called after the barman. When the coffee and drinks came, Grassi picked up his glass and indicated one of the tables, but Brunetti shook his head, saying, 'A boat's coming out. I have to get back.'

Grassi spooned in three sugars, then stirred the coffee around a few times. Brunetti picked up the grappa, swirled it around in rhythm with Grassi's spoon, and drank it quickly. Almost before the taste registered, he drank down half of the water and stood quietly, waiting to see what happened. After a moment, he finished the water and set the glass on the counter, and nodded for another.

Brunetti had not recognized the dead man. 'How did he know it was Tassini?'

'I don't know,' Grassi answered with a tired shake of his head. 'When I saw him outside, all he said was that it was Tassini.'

It was difficult for Brunetti to articulate the next question for to do so was to recall what he had seen inside the factory. 'Did you see him?' He held up his empty glass to the barman.

'No,' Grassi answered. 'When I came in for you, I didn't look at him.' He shrugged at this admission. 'And when I got there after Giuliano called, he was standing outside, crying.' He gave Brunetti a quick glance. 'Don't tell him I told you that, all right?' Brunetti nodded. 'He told me Tassini was inside and he was dead. I tried to go in to see, but Giuliano grabbed my arm and pulled me back. He wouldn't let me go inside and he wouldn't tell me why.' He finished his coffee and set the cup down. 'So we stood outside and waited for someone to come. It must have been half an hour. He threw up a couple of times, but he still wouldn't tell me anything about it, just asked me to wait with him until you – the police – got there.'

'I see,' Brunetti said and picked up the second glass of water. He took a small sip, and his body told him that was enough for the moment. He set the glass on the counter.

'Why did you come inside?' Brunetti asked.

Grassi moved the empty cup to the side and said, 'When I got back and you weren't there, I thought something might have happened to you, so I went in to see if you were all right. But I didn't look at him.' He paused for some time. 'Giuliano told me about it, when I was taking him home, so I didn't want to see.' He shoved the cup to the other side of the counter and said, 'Poor stupid devil.'

Brunetti's attention was arrested by the second word: he

was not certain whom the other man was talking about. 'Tassini?'

'Yes,' he said, his tone a mixture of dismay and affection. 'He was always falling over things, getting in the way, tripping over his feet. He told De Cal once that he wanted to work the glass, but none of us would have him. We'd seen him drop things for years: imagine what he'd do if he tried to work with us.' Grassi seemed to realize he had switched into the present tense and stopped. 'I mean, he was a good man: honest. And he did his job. But he's not a glassmaker, never could be one.'

'What did he do, exactly?' Brunetti asked, picking up his water and risking another small sip.

'He had to keep the places clean and take care of the *fornaci* at night.'

Brunetti waved a hand and said, 'I'm not sure I understand what that means, Signore. Aside from sweeping the floors, that is.'

Grassi smiled in return and said, 'That was part of it: sweeping, both our place and Fasano's. Well, after he started working for him, as well, that is. And making sure that the bags of sand didn't leak after they were opened.' He paused, as if he had never considered what the duties of *l'uomo di notte* might be.

'And he had to keep an eye on the temperature and the *miscela* during the night,' he continued. 'But he also had to see that the bags didn't tip over and get mixed up.' Grassi asked the barman for another coffee, and while he waited for it, he asked, 'You know about the *miscela*, don't you?'

Brunetti certainly remembered the word, but little more than that. 'Only that it's made of sand and other things,' he said.

The coffee came and Grassi stirred in three more sugars. 'Sand, yes,' he said, 'then the minerals for the right *miscela*. If the colour we want is amethyst, then we mix in manganese,

137

or cadmium for red. Some of the bags look alike, so they have to be kept separate and upright. The stuff can't spill on the floor or we have an awful mess and have to throw it all away.' He looked at Brunetti, who nodded to show he was following.

'Starting when the rest of us get off work, *l'uomo di notte* shovels the *miscela* into the *crogiolo*, adding it according to the formula and stirring it, and then it heats all night long, so it's ready and we can start working at seven, when we come in.'

'What else did he have to do?'

Again, Grassi paused to try to remember what the dead man's duties would have been. 'Check the filters and maybe shift the barrels around.'

'What filters?' Brunetti asked.

'From the grinding wheels. It all gets filtered, the water they use when they're grinding, and then the gunk that's collected gets put in barrels. It's filtered a couple of times,' Grassi said without interest. 'I don't know about that stuff, really, only about glass.'

Grassi gave Brunetti a speculative look, as if weighing his audience, and then said, 'It's crazy, isn't it? They let Marghera pump any crap it wants to into the air or the *laguna*: cadmium, dioxin, petro this and petro that, and no one says a word about it. But if we let a cupful of powdered glass drain into the *laguna*, they're all over us with inspectors and fines. Some of them are so big it would put you out of business.' He considered what he had said and then added, 'No wonder De Cal's thinking about selling the place.'

Brunetti set this remark aside for future reference and returned to Tassini. 'Were these the sort of things Tassini said? About the environment?'

Grassi rolled his eyes. 'It's all he'd talk about. All you had to do was start him talking about these things and he was off, sometimes until we had to tell him to shut up. Poison this and poison that, and not only at Marghera. Even here, and it was poisoning us all.' He delved into memory, then said, 'I tried to talk to him a couple of times. But he wouldn't listen.' He leaned towards Brunetti and put a hand on his arm. 'I've seen the numbers, and I know we don't die the way they do in Marghera: they die like flies over there.' He moved back and removed his hand. 'Maybe it's the currents: maybe they take things away from here. I don't know. I tried to tell Giorgio this, but he wouldn't listen. He had his mind made up that we were all being poisoned, and that's what he was going to believe, no matter what anyone said.'

Grassi stopped talking for a moment, then added, with a note of real sadness in his voice. 'He had to believe it, didn't he? Because of the little girl.' He shook his head, at the thought of the child or at the thought of human frailty, Brunetti had no idea. Grassi spoke with a complete absence of disapproval; in fact, Brunetti could hear little but affection in his voice, the sort one has for a person who always manages to get everything wrong yet who never manages to alienate anyone in the process.

'I think your boat's coming,' Grassi said.

Brunetti's question was no more than a tilting of his head.

'I don't recognize the engine, and it's coming fast, out from the city,' the *maestro* said. He pulled some money from his pocket and left it on the counter; Brunetti thanked him and they headed for the door.

When they reached the canal, Grassi was right: the police boat was pulling up to the ACTV *embarcadero*. On board were Bocchese and the crime team.

15

Brunetti waved to them from his side of the canal and crossed the bridge to meet them. Apart from Bocchese, there were two photographers and two technicians, all with the usual amount of equipment, which the men were busy unloading from the boat.

Brunetti introduced Bocchese to Grassi and explained to the technician that Grassi was one of the *maestri* who worked at the *fornace* where the dead man was. Bocchese and Grassi shook hands and then Bocchese turned and said something to one of his crew, who waved a lazy hand in acknowledgement. Boxes and bags piled up on the dock; Brunetti waited until it seemed everything had been unloaded and then led them down the dirt path towards the metal doors of the factory. He was surprised to see two men standing outside, one of them a man in police uniform – he recognized Lazzari from the Murano squad – and the other De Cal, who was waving his arms and speaking loudly.

De Cal saw Brunetti and stormed towards him, shouting,

'What the hell is it now? First you let that bastard out of jail, and now I can't even go into my own factory.'

More familiar with De Cal than the others, Grassi stepped forward and, gesturing at the technicians, who were now struggling into their disposable scene-of-crime suits, said, 'I think they want to go in there alone, sir.'

'Remember who you work for, Grassi,' De Cal spat with effulgent rage. 'For me. Not for the police. I give the orders here, not the police.' He put his face close to Grassi's. Brunetti could see that the tendons of his neck were swollen. 'You understand that?'

Brunetti moved up beside Grassi. 'Your factory is the scene of a death, Signor De Cal,' he said, noticing that Lazzari seemed relieved by his having taken over. 'The technical crew will be here for a few hours, and then the scene will be opened and your men can go back to work.'

De Cal came suddenly closer, forcing Brunetti to move back one step. 'I can't afford a few hours.' De Cal noticed, as if for the first time, the technicians and their equipment. 'These fools will be in there all day. How can my men work with them there?'

'If you prefer, Signore,' Brunetti said with his most official voice, 'we can get an order from a judge and sequester the site for a week or two.' He smiled. Grassi, he noticed, had taken the opportunity to disappear.

De Cal opened his mouth, then closed it and backed away, muttering. Brunetti heard 'bastard' a few times, and worse, but he chose to ignore the old man.

The technicians, who had set down their bags while all this was going on, now picked them up and moved towards the doors. Brunetti held up a hand to stop them. Turning to Bocchese, he said, 'If you have masks, you better use them.' The men set their bags down again and one of them hunted around until he found a stack of cellophane-wrapped surgical masks, which he passed out to the other men. Brunetti put

141

out his hand and accepted one, ripped it open, and pulled the elastics over his ears. He adjusted the mask over his nose and mouth, then took a pair of plastic gloves from the same man and slipped them on.

One of the crew humped a long bag on to his shoulder: lights and tripods. He went in first and started looking around for an electrical socket. To no one in particular, Brunetti said, 'He's down by the free-standing furnace', and then joined the technicians entering the building.

His eyes had barely adjusted to the dimmer light when he heard his name called from the entrance and turned to see Vianello, wearing gloves but no mask. Brunetti held up a hand to Vianello and went over to the technician to ask for another mask. He took it over to the Inspector and said, 'You'll need this.'

Side by side, Brunetti fortified by the other man's presence, they went towards the third furnace but stopped a few metres from it and waited for the photographer to finish. Brunetti glanced at the gauges and saw that *Forno* III had risen to 1348 degrees. He had no idea what the temperature just outside and below the door would be.

The photographer finished taking photos of the floor and moved in to take photographs of the dead man from all angles.

'Which doctor's coming?' Brunetti asked.

'Venturi,' Vianello answered with a marked lack of enthusiasm.

To Brunetti's right stood a row of the iron tools the glass-blowers used: rods and pipes of all lengths and diameters. The work desk of the *maestro* was covered with clippers and pincers and straight-edged tools: none of them showed any signs of traces of blood. On the wall hung posters of naked women with enormous breasts, casting looks of sexual invitation at the dead man and the men who moved silently around him.

Brunetti stood to one side and studied Tassini's bearded face. He looked away, not wanting to see any more of the soiled body than he had to. The flash of the photographer drew his eyes back, and he saw that the end of one of the metal rods was trapped under Tassini's body.

He heard a noise behind him and turned to see Dottor Venturi, who had just set his leather case on top of the tools on the *maestro*'s workbench. A pair of pliers fell to the ground. Brunetti walked over, bent down, and replaced them, saying nothing to Venturi. The doctor opened his bag, took out a pair of gloves and put them on. He glanced at the dead man, sniffed, and made a face rich with disgust. Brunetti noticed that the lapels of his overcoat were hand-stitched. His black shoes reflected the light from the furnace.

'That him?' the young doctor asked, pointing at the dead man. No one answered him. He reached back into his bag and pulled out a gauze mask, then extracted a bottle of 4711 toilet water, opened it, and sprinkled it liberally on the gauze. He replaced the cap on the bottle and slipped it into place in his bag. He put the mask to his face and slipped the elastics behind his ears.

There was a dark green sweater folded over the back of the *maestro*'s chair; Venturi picked it up and carried it over to the dead man and let it drop on to the floor beside him. He hiked up the left knee of his trousers and lowered himself beside the body, careful to place his knee on the sweater. He picked up the dead man's wrist, held it for a second, and then let it fall back to the ground. 'Not cooked yet, I'd say,' Venturi muttered, not under his breath, but at the volume a student might use to say something about the teacher during class.

He got to his feet and turned to Brunetti. Stripping off his gloves, he dropped them beside his bag on the *maestro*'s workbench. 'He's dead,' Venturi said. He snapped his bag closed and picked it up by the handle. He turned towards the door.

143

'Excuse me,' Venturi said, then added, 'gentlemen.'

'You forgot the sweater,' Brunetti said, and then, after an even longer pause, added, '*Dottore.*'

'What?' Venturi demanded, his voice unusually loud, even in here, with the fierce competition of the howling furnaces.

'The sweater,' Brunetti repeated. 'You forgot to pick up the sweater.' While he was saying this, Brunetti sensed Bocchese move to stand at his right, Vianello to his left.

Venturi ran his eyes across their faces, saw the sweat on Vianello's, Bocchese's narrowed eyes. He stepped back and reached down for the sweater. He picked it up by one sleeve and made as if to drop it in the centre of the workbench, but Vianello shifted his weight. The doctor leaned to his right and draped it across the back of the *maestro*'s chair. He picked up his bag.

None of the three men moved. Venturi took two steps to the left and walked around Bocchese. None of them bothered to watch him leave, so none of them saw him tear off his mask and drop it on the floor.

Bocchese called over to the photographers. 'You guys got it all?'

'Yes.'

Brunetti did not want to do it, and he was sure that neither Bocchese nor Vianello wanted any part of it. But the sooner they had some idea of what might have happened to Tassini, the sooner they could . . . they could what? Ask him more questions? Bring him back to life?

Brunetti banished these thoughts. 'You don't have to,' he said to the two men and walked over to Tassini's soiled body. He knelt down. The smell of urine and faeces grew stronger. Vianello walked over to the other side and Bocchese knelt beside the Inspector. Together, the three men put their hands under the body. It was hot under there, and Brunetti had the feeling that what he touched was slippery. He tasted the grappa in his mouth.

They turned the man over slowly. His face was swollen, and Brunetti saw a mark on the side of his forehead, just where his hair began. His left arm had been trapped under his body, and when they turned him over, it fell free and slapped to the ground, the sound muffled by the thick heat-resistant glove and arm protector he wore. Vianello and Bocchese got to their feet and walked towards the door. Brunetti willed himself to go through all of Tassini's pockets, took one more look at him, and abandoned the idea. Outside, he found Vianello leaning his back against the wall of the building. Bocchese stood on the edge of the grass, leaning over and bracing his hands on his knees. Neither man wore a mask.

Brunetti stripped off his mask. 'There's a bar on the other side of the canal,' he said in what he hoped was a normal voice. He led the way, along the canal, up and down the bridge, and then towards the bar. By the time they got there, Vianello's face had returned to its normal colour and Bocchese had his hands in his pockets.

The lingering aftertaste of the grappa warned Brunetti against another one, so he asked for a camomile tea. Bocchese and Vianello exchanged a glance and then asked for the same. They remained silent until the three small pots of tea were set on the bar in front of them, when they each spooned sugar directly into the pots and took them and their cups over to a table by the window.

'Could be anything,' Bocchese finally broke the silence by suggesting.

Vianello poured out his tea and blew softly on the surface a few times and then said, 'He hit his head.'

'Or his head was hit,' said Brunetti.

'He could have stumbled on that rod,' Bocchese suggested.

Brunetti remembered the precision with which the factory implements were ordered. 'Not unless he was using it. The place is too neat: nothing else was left lying around, and there

145

was glass at the end of it,' Brunetti said. 'So he was using it to make something. Or was just beginning.' He recalled what Grassi had said about Tassini, that he did not have the talent to be a glass-blower. But that might not have stopped him from trying.

'Maybe he did it to try to keep himself awake,' Bocchese suggested. 'Worked the glass.'

'He read,' Brunetti said. Both men gave him strange looks.

Bocchese finished his cup of tea and refilled it from the pot. 'That's not how you learn to make glass, playing with it alone in a factory at night.'

Brunetti looked at his watch and saw that it was after nine; he took out his *telefonino* and dialled the hospital number of Dottor Rizzardi. He recognized the doctor's voice when he answered.

'It's me, Ettore. I'm out on Murano. Yes, a dead man.' He listened for a while and then said, 'Venturi.' There was an even longer silence, this time on both sides. Finally Brunetti said, 'I'd appreciate it if you could arrange to do it.'

Vianello and Bocchese heard the murmur of Rizzardi's voice, but all they could distinguish clearly was that of Brunetti, who said, 'In a glass factory. He was in front of one of the furnaces.' Another silence, and then Brunetti said, 'I don't know. Maybe all night.'

Brunetti glanced at the posters at the end of the bar, fixing his attention on the Costiera Amalfitana to keep it away from the words he had just spoken. Houses pitty-patted down the cliffs, holding on to whatever they could, and colours did whatever they pleased, never giving a thought to harmony. The sun glistened on the sea, and sailboats swept away to what the viewer knew were even more beautiful places.

'Thanks, Ettore,' Brunetti said and ended the call. He got to his feet, went over and put a ten-Euro bill on the counter, and the three men left.

When they got back to the factory, the ambulance boat from

the hospital was just pulling away from the dock. There was no sign of De Cal, though three or four workmen stood outside the door, smoking and talking in low voices. Inside the building, the paper-clad technicians were busy packing up their equipment. Brunetti noticed that one of the long iron rods stood against the wall, its surface covered with grey powder. The floor was very clean: had Tassini swept it before he died?

Bocchese spoke to two of his men, then came back to Vianello and Brunetti. 'Some prints on that rod,' he said, 'and lots of smudges.' He allowed a moment to pass and added, 'Means he could have fallen on it.'

'On anything else?' Brunetti asked.

Before Bocchese could answer, one of his men pulled something out of his bag and walked over to the rod. The object he held proved to be a long, thin plastic bag, much like one used to wrap a baguette, though it was considerably longer. He slipped it over the top of the rod and pulled it down to the ground. He went back to his bag and got a roll of tape and used it to seal the bottom of what now looked like a plastic sheath. He twisted the tape to create handles on either end, turning it into a package that could be carried by two men without disturbing the surface where the fingerprints were.

'Might as well take a closer look,' Bocchese said, and Brunetti thought of the mark on Tassini's forehead.

As the technician turned away, Brunetti said, 'Let me know, will you?'

Bocchese answered with a noise and a sideways motion of his hand, and then he and the technicians filed out. A few minutes later, two of them came back and used the handles to take the iron rod out of the factory.

'Let's have a look around,' Brunetti said. Knowing the technicians had checked the floor and surfaces, Brunetti walked towards the back of the factory and a table with its surface covered with glass pieces.

147

They saw the lines of porpoises and the toreador in his shiny black pants and red jacket.

'*De gustibus,*' Vianello said, moving along the line of objects. A door led to a cell-like room in which stood a chair and a camp-bed. A copy of the previous day's *Gazzettino* lay open, spread across the chair, as though it had been placed there in haste. At the head of the bed a pillow stood propped against the wall, what looked like the indentation made by a head visible in it.

Brunetti took the newspaper by the two upper corners and lifted the pages on to the bed. Below it on the chair lay two books: *Industrial Illness, the Curse of Our Millennium* and Dante's *Inferno*, a paper-covered school edition whose worn look suggested it had been often read. Ignoring the first, Brunetti picked up the second book. The corners of many pages were torn and darkened with frequent handling; as he flipped through the pages, he found copious notes in the margins. Tassini had signed the book in red ink on the inside of the front cover, a mannered signature with unnecessary horizontal lines trailing around and away from the dot on the final i. The edition had been published more than twenty years before. Brunetti flipped through the pages again and noticed that there were notes in red and black but that the black handwriting appeared to have grown smaller and less attention-grabbing.

Vianello had moved over to look through a small window that stood behind the head of the bed. It gave a clear view back towards the glaring flames of the open furnaces. 'What is it?' he asked, nodding at the book in Brunetti's hands.

'*Inferno.*'

'Perfect place for it, I'd say,' the Inspector replied.

16

Brunetti took Tassini's books; he and Vianello left the little bedroom and walked back through the factory. Since one book was a paperback edition and the other a small schoolbook, he slipped them easily into the pockets of his jacket. He had just done this when De Cal catapulted himself through the main doors and directly towards them.

'I spend two thousand Euros a week on gas for the furnaces, for God's sake,' he began, quite as if he were reaching the end of a long explanation they had been resisting. 'Two thousand Euros. If I lose a day of production, who's going to pay me for the gas? It's not like these furnaces can be turned on and off like a radio, you know,' he said, waving distractedly towards the three furnaces, all of them open now.

'And I still have to pay the workers. I'm paying for them now. Your men are gone, and all you're doing is standing around, doing nothing. Which is exactly what the workers are doing, only I'm paying them to do it.'

Vianello and Brunetti approached him and stopped. De Cal continued. 'I saw them leave,' he said, pointing in the direction of the canal. 'I saw their boat go back to the city. I want to open my factory and get my men back to work. I don't want to pay them to stand around and talk while the gas burns and I have nothing to show for it.'

Brunetti could not prevent himself from saying, 'A man died here this morning.'

With apparent difficulty, De Cal prevented himself from spitting. 'He died this morning. He died yesterday. He died two days ago. What difference does it make? He's not here any more.' As he spoke, De Cal's voice grew increasingly out of control. 'It costs me *money*,' he shouted, the emphasis heavy on the last word, 'to keep my furnaces burning, and I pay my workers whether they're in here, working, or whether they're standing outside, convincing themselves what a nice fellow Tassini really was, after all.' He moved closer and stared up at Brunetti's face, then at Vianello's, as if searching for the reason they could not understand something so simple. 'I'm losing money.'

Neither Vianello nor Brunetti looked at the other. Finally Brunetti said, 'Your workers can come back in, Signor De Cal.'

Without bothering to thank him, De Cal wheeled around and went out the door. From inside, they could hear him calling to the workers, telling one of them to go and summon some others. Time to go back to work. Business as usual. Life goes on.

Suddenly Brunetti realized what he would have to do now, and was taken aback to think that he had so successfully ignored it. Tassini's wife, Tassini's family: someone had to go and tell them that things would never be the same again. Someone would have to go and tell them that their life, as they knew it, was over, that an event had come hurtling at them and destroyed it. He fought the urge to call the Questura and ask them to send a woman officer. He did not know the widow, had spoken only once with the mother-in-law, and his meeting with Tassini had lasted no more than a quarter of an hour, yet there was nothing for it but for him to go.

He turned to Vianello and explained what he was going to do and asked him to stay and talk to the workers and, if he could manage it, to De Cal. Had Tassini any enemies? Who else might have come to the factory at night? Was Tassini as clumsy as Grassi said?

Saying that he would see Vianello back at the Questura, Brunetti went out to the *riva* and headed for the police launch. Foa was in the cabin, one of the wooden doors to the control panel open as he wrapped electrical tape around a wire. When he heard Brunetti's steps on the dock, the pilot looked up and nodded a greeting, shoved the wire into place and closed the panel. He switched on the engine.

'I'd like to go to the Arsenale stop,' Brunetti said. He started to go down into the cabin, but as the boat swung out into the canal, he was stopped by the feel of the morning's softness on his face and decided to remain on deck. Though he tried to keep his mind blank, he was conscious of the way the breeze, and then the wind as they picked up speed, tugged at his jacket, at all his clothing, blowing away whatever still clung to him.

'We in a hurry, Commissario?' Foa asked as they approached Fondamenta Nuove.

Brunetti wanted this trip to last as long as possible; he wanted never to have to deliver this news. But he answered, 'Yes.'

'I'll ask if we can go through the Arsenale, then,' Foa said, taking out his *telefonino*. He found a number programmed into the phone and spoke for no more than a moment. He put the phone in his pocket and cut hard to the left, and then arched around to the right, under the footbridge and straight through the centre of the Arsenale.

How many years had it been since the Number Five did this every ten minutes? Brunetti asked himself. Ordinarily

Brunetti would have enjoyed the sight of the shipyard that had fuelled Venice's greatness, but at this moment he could think of little save the cleansing wind.

Foa pulled into one of the taxi slots beside the Arsenale stop and paused long enough for Brunetti to leap on to the dock. Brunetti waved his thanks to the pilot but said nothing about what Foa should do now: return to the Questura, go fishing – it was all the same to Brunetti.

He walked up Via Garibaldi, resisting, as he passed every bar, the desire to go in and have a coffee, a glass of water. He rang the doorbell to Tassini's home, saw that it was almost eleven, and rang again. 'Who . . .' he heard what he thought was a woman's voice ask, but then it was obliterated by a blast of static from the loose wires. 'Giorgio?' the same voice asked, ending on the rising note of hope.

He rang again and the door snapped open.

As he climbed the stairs, he heard quick footsteps above him, and when he turned into the last flight a woman appeared on the steps above him. She was taller than her mother and had the same green eyes. Her hair came down below her shoulders: there was a great deal of grey in it, and it aged her beyond her years. She wore a brown skirt and flat shoes, held a beige cardigan closed with her hands, as much for protection as for warmth.

'What is it?' she asked when she saw him on the stairs. 'What's wrong?' Her voice broke off, as if the sight of him – or, for one horrified moment Brunetti wondered, the smell of him – were enough to crucify hope.

He continued up the stairs, trying to banish pity from his face. 'Signora Tassini,' he began.

'What's happened to him?' she asked, her voice breaking on the last word.

From behind her, Brunetti heard what he did not immediately recognize as a familiar voice. 'What's wrong?' it called, then became familiar when she said, 'Sonia, come back up.'

A moment passed, and the older woman's voice became more urgent. 'Sonia, Emma's crying.'

Caught between the perceived threat of Brunetti's presence and the real threat of her mother's warning, she turned and hurried up the stairs. Before she reached the door, she glanced back at Brunetti twice before disappearing into the apartment.

Her mother waited for him outside the door. 'What's wrong?' she demanded when she saw him.

'There was an accident at the factory,' he thought it best to say, though he no more believed in an accident than he believed in the Second Coming.

Those green eyes pierced him, and he wondered at how he had underestimated the intelligence in them. 'He's dead, isn't he?' she asked.

Brunetti nodded. From behind the woman came the sound of her daughter's voice, words mixed with noises as she crooned to her own daughter.

'What happened?' the older woman asked in a softer voice.

'We don't know yet,' he answered, seeing no reason to lie to her. 'He collapsed in the factory and wasn't found until this morning.' It was not a lie, though it was hardly the truth.

'What was it?' she asked.

'We don't know yet, Signora,' Brunetti said. 'That will be established by the autopsy, I hope.' He spoke of it as though it were a normal procedure.

'*Maria santissima,*' she said and pulled out her battered packet of Nazionale blu. Brunetti had time only to read the enormous letters that promised death before she had a cigarette lit and the packet back in her pocket. 'Go inside,' she said. 'I'll come when I've finished this.'

Brunetti moved around her and went into the apartment. Tassini's wife sat on the stained sofa, the whimpering child cradled in her arms. She smiled and bent down to kiss the little girl's face. There was no sign of the boy, though he heard a semi-singing from the back of the apartment.

153

He went to the window and pushed aside the curtain to look out at the house across the *calle*. He saw bricks and windows and thought of nothing.

The first sign of the older woman's return was her voice, saying, 'I think you better tell her, Commissario.' When Brunetti turned back to the room, she was sitting on the sofa beside her daughter.

'I'm sorry, Signora,' he began. 'But I have bad news. The worst news.' The woman looked up from her child but said nothing. She sat, looking at him, and waited for this worst of news, though she must have known what it was.

'Your husband,' he began, unsure of how to phrase it. 'Your husband was found in the factory this morning by one of the other workmen when he went in to work. He was dead.'

Before he could read her expression, she looked down at the baby, who had calmed and seemed to have drifted off to sleep. She looked back at Brunetti and asked, 'What happened?'

'We don't know that yet, Signora,' he said. Brunetti had no idea how to comfort this woman and wished her mother would do something or say something, but neither of them spoke or moved.

The baby gurgled, and the woman placed a hand on her chest. Speaking as much to the child as to Brunetti, she said, 'He knew.'

'Knew what, Signora?'

'Knew that something would happen.' She looked at Brunetti after she said this.

'What did he tell you, Signora?' She did not answer, so he said, 'That something like this would happen to him?'

She shook her head. 'No, only that he knew things and that they were dangerous things to know.' Beside her, her mother nodded in agreement, at least in agreement that she had heard him say these things.

'Did he tell you what he thought the danger was, Signora?

154

Or did he tell you what it was he knew?' In the face of their silence, he asked, 'Or did he tell you what the source of the danger was?'

The older woman turned her eyes to her daughter to see how great had been her burden of knowledge, but Tassini's wife said, 'No. Nothing. Just that he knew things and it was dangerous for him to know them.'

Brunetti thought of the information Tassini had talked about when they met. 'When I spoke to him . . .' he began, wondering if she would display surprise. When she did not, he went on, 'your husband said he had a file where he kept the information he found. He said he had papers that were important.' Her glance was steady: the file was no surprise to her.

'I'd like to see if the file can help us understand what might have happened.'

'What's happened is that Giorgio's dead!' the older woman exploded. 'So there's no way his papers are going to help.'

Brunetti made no attempt to oppose her. 'They might help me,' he said.

Signora Tassini turned to her mother and placed the sleeping child in her lap. She got up and went into the back of the apartment, as if she was simply going to check on the other child.

From the other room, he heard her voice, soothing and calm, as she spoke to her son. In a few minutes she was back, carrying a manila folder. She handed it to him, saying, 'I think this is all I want to do for you, and I'd like you to leave now.'

Without thanking either of them, Brunetti stood, took the folder from her outstretched hand, and left the apartment.

17

As soon as he got outside, Brunetti opened the file. He had no idea what he had expected to find, but certainly something more than three sheets of paper with numbers on them. At the top of the first were the letters VR and DC, the second an obvious reference to De Cal. Lower down were two numbers: 200973962, and 100982915: amounts of money written without the commas? Bank codes of some sort? Phone numbers? The second sheet bore four numbers: the first part of each was written in Roman numerals, separated by a slash from a number written in Arabic numbers. At first he thought they might be dates, the month and then the day, but one of the second numbers was greater than 31, eliminating that possibility. The third page had six pairs of numbers. The first pair read 45° 27.60, and 12° 20.90; the other pairs were almost the same, with slightly different final numbers. His first thought, because of the degree sign, was that this was a way to list the high and low temperatures of one of the furnaces, or perhaps each of them, but surely the temperatures were far too low.

Brunetti had never been good at crossword puzzles; quizzes and mental teasers had always bored him. He walked back towards the Questura and stopped at the bottom of Ponte dei Grechi, suddenly aware that he was lost in time. He saw that it was half-past twelve and called Paola to explain that he would not be home before the evening. She reacted to his tone more than to his message and told him only to eat something and to try to get home at a reasonable hour.

He went into the bar, where he had a panino and a glass of mineral water, then another panino when his body discovered how hungry he was. When he was finished – not satisfied but finished – he went down the *riva* and into the Questura. Foa's boat was moored in front, but there was no sign of the pilot.

Inside, the officer at the door told him that Vianello was still not back. Brunetti left word for the Inspector to come up when he returned and went to find Bocchese in his lab.

The technician looked up when he saw Brunetti come in, then returned his attention to the table in front of him. At the end of his long work table was the iron rod, raised ten centimetres above the surface on a pair of wooden blocks, one beneath either end.

'Anything?' Brunetti asked, gesturing with his chin towards the rod.

Bocchese looked up from the pair of scissors he was sharpening and said, 'The dead man's prints were all up and down the near end. There are partials under his, but he was using it for so long that his prints smeared or covered anything else.'

Brunetti looked at the rod, as if he might be able to discern some sign with his naked eye. The end near them held a blob of material that could have been a turtle: flat on the bottom, rounded at the top. 'What might have happened?' Brunetti asked, wise enough not to ask Bocchese what he thought had happened. Bocchese never answered questions like that: perhaps he refused to think in such terms.

Bocchese pointed to the turtle with the scissors and said, 'He might have been trying to make something out of glass. The furnace he was in front of was much hotter than the others: it was preparing glass for the next day. He was alone in the place, so he might have tried to make something. If he dropped the rod, the molten glass would be flattened on the bottom like this.'

'Could something have happened to him?' Brunetti repeated.

Bocchese looked up from the scissors and said, 'Guido, I can tell you what the evidence looks like. You have to figure out how it got to be that way.'

Ignoring this, Brunetti asked, 'You have a chance to look at the body?'

'There was a mark on his head. It could have happened when he fell. Hit his head against the door, maybe.'

'Any sign on the door?'

Bocchese took a sheet of the *Gazzettino* that covered his table, held it up in the air, and cut it in half with six sudden clips of the scissors. As one piece fluttered on to the table, he said, 'The temperature in the heart of the furnace was almost 1400 all night, at the door a bit less. No physical evidence can survive that temperature.'

'On the floor?' Brunetti asked. 'On him?'

Bocchese shook his head. 'Nothing. The place had been swept clean.' He took another swipe at the remaining piece of *Gazzettino*. 'Part of his job, I'm told: sweeping.'

'You don't like it, do you?' Brunetti asked.

Bocchese shrugged. 'I measure and I tabulate. You do the liking, Guido.'

Brunetti held up a hand in acknowledgement, thanked him, and turned to go. From behind him, he heard Bocchese say, 'But no, I don't like it.'

Back in his office, Brunetti spread the three sheets of paper on his desk, propped his chin in his hands, and stared at the numbers. Twenty minutes later, he got to his feet and went to the window, but the change in position brought him no closer to understanding.

He cast his memory back to his meeting with Tassini. The more he thought about it, the stranger Tassini's behaviour seemed. He had been both secretive and protective about what he knew, yet his behaviour had suggested that his information was of great import. He had said he read a lot and kept a record of his conclusions and that great men had helped him understand, but he had not explained what it was he understood. Nor had he made clear why De Cal so strongly wanted to keep his son-in-law from the *fornace*.

Tassini had said he was close to finding the final proof, but Brunetti had no idea what he had meant by that. What happened was that Tassini died, and his wife said he had been afraid of something.

Brunetti went back to his desk and stared at the numbers again.

Signorina Elettra found him like that some time later when she came in with a single sheet of paper in her hand. 'Commissario,' she said when he looked at her with troubled eyes, 'what's the matter?' When he failed to answer, she said, her voice softer, 'I heard about that poor man. I'm sorry.'

'He was too young,' Brunetti surprised himself by saying. After a moment, he said, 'I'm trying to puzzle something out.' Seeing her confused glance, he redirected his attention back to her and asked, 'What is it?'

'I've been looking around, and I thought you might be interested to see what I've found: it's the *Carabinieri* report.' Seeing his momentary confusion, she added, 'Of a visit Tassini made.'

Brunetti asked her to take a seat. She sat down, placed the sheet of paper on his desk, and said, 'This is a copy of their

159

report, though there's little enough to tell. Then there are some things I learned by speaking to people.'

'All right,' Brunetti said. 'Tell me.'

She pointed towards the sheet of paper. 'A friend of mine sent me a copy of their file. Tassini went in there a year ago to file a *denuncia* against his employer for operating an unsafe workplace. The record shows that the *maresciallo* there – over by Riva degli Schiavoni – told him he didn't have enough evidence and suggested he go and see a lawyer and try to bring a civil suit. That is, if Tassini wanted to persist in the complaint. They refused to let him file it officially.'

'Did he do that?' Brunetti asked: 'find a lawyer?'

'I don't know. There's nothing else in their records, and he never came to us. I don't know whether I should check further.'

Brunetti shook his head at this. Tassini was beyond lawyers now. 'Anything else?' he asked.

'The De Cal factory, sir. I asked around and the word is he's very close to selling it.'

'Who did you ask?'

'A friend,' she answered, and that was that, Elettra as reluctant as he to reveal a source when it was not necessary to do so.

'Is there talk about who might want to buy it?'

'Since the Chinese haven't discovered glass yet,' she began, using the ironic tone she usually reserved for the acquisitive habits of Venice's Chinese, 'at least not Venetian glass, the only name that's been mentioned is Gianluca Fasano's. He owns the factory next door. My friend said De Cal's furnaces are much newer than his are.'

'He wants to continue running a glass factory?' Brunetti asked, thinking of the rumours about Fasano's political aspirations.

'What's more Venetian than Murano glass?' she asked, and it surprised him to realize that she was serious. 'It would be

160

proof that he really does want to help the city come back to life.' Usually Signorina Elettra was incapable of speaking such words except in tones of mock solemnity, but this was hardly the case here. 'Well,' she added, 'for us, that is. For Venetians.'

'You believe him, then?' Brunetti asked, adding, 'even if he wants to become a politician?'

Sensitive to his scepticism, she tempered her enthusiasm and said only, 'He's the chairman of the glassmakers' organization: that's hardly a political position.'

'It's a very good jumping-off point,' Brunetti said, his voice calm and objective. 'He could start on Murano and then move to Venice. You said it yourself: what's more Venetian than Murano glass?' He took her silence as assent and asked, 'How else does he propose to bring the city back to life?'

'He says that no more apartments should be sold to non-Venetians –' and before he could object or quote European law, she added – 'unless they're made to pay a substantial non-residents' tax.' When Brunetti did not respond, she added, 'He says that, if they want to live here, then they should pay to do so.'

'Anything else?' Brunetti asked neutrally.

'Because the city always claims it has no money, he's suggested that the finances of the Casinò be made public, so people can see how much is spent on salaries, and who gets them, and how much rent is paid by the people who run the restaurants and bars there. And who those concessions are rented to.' This sounded like sovereign good sense to Brunetti, who nodded to encourage her to continue. 'He wants the city or the region to go back to paying forty per cent of the cost of gas for the furnaces on Murano. Or else a lot of people are going to be out of work in a few years' time.'

When Brunetti made no comment, she added, 'And he's concerned about the risk to the *laguna* from Marghera. He asks why so few fines have been paid.'

161

'Penalize big business?' Brunetti asked, and immediately regretted the words.

'Or save the *laguna*,' she said, 'whichever you choose to call it.'

'Does he have any political backing?' Brunetti asked.

'The Greens like him, though he's not their candidate. I suppose he's hoping to do what Di Pietro did, start his own party. But I really don't know that.'

'Not with similar results, I trust,' Brunetti said, thinking of Di Pietro's failed campaign.

'The report's here, sir,' she said, pushing the page a bit farther across the desk. Not for the first time, Signorina Elettra's sudden change of subject made it clear that politics was something about which she preferred not to enter into discussion. But then she surprised him by adding, 'I'm not sure we see eye to eye on the need to protect the *laguna*, sir.' She got to her feet and walked over to the door.

'Thank you,' he said, reaching across to the paper. Because of the sudden shadow of formality, even reprimand, that had fallen, Brunetti decided not to show her the three sheets of paper from Tassini's file, and she did not linger to ask if there was anything else she might do for him.

18

After Signorina Elettra left, Brunetti asked himself, as would someone from the Disease Control Centre, in which direction the arc of ecological infection was now likely to be passing: whether from her to Vianello or from the Inspector to her. His imagination was seized for a moment by this image, and he found himself wondering what risk of contagion he experienced by working in such proximity to them and when he might begin to feel the first symptoms.

Brunetti believed that his concern for the environment and for the ecological future was stronger than that of the average citizen – only a statue could have resisted the constant harassment of his children – but he obviously must have been judged to have failed to live up to the standards established by his two colleagues. Given the sincerity of their beliefs, why then did Vianello and Signorina Elettra work for the police force, when they could be working for some sort of environmental protection office?

For that matter, why did any of them continue to work for the police? Brunetti wondered. He and Vianello had most reason, for it was a job they had done for decades. But what about someone like Pucetti? He was young, bright, ambitious. So why would he opt to wear a uniform, walk the streets of the city at all hours, and dedicate himself to the maintenance of public order? Even more confusing and enigmatic, however, was Signorina Elettra. Over the years, Brunetti had stopped discussing her with Paola, not so much because of any response he had observed in Paola as because of the way it registered in his own ears to hear himself praise or display such curiosity about a woman other than his wife. She had been at the Questura how long? Five years? Six? Brunetti had to confess he knew little more about her than he had when she first started working there: knew little more, that is, than that he could trust both her abilities and her discretion and that her mask of wry amusement at human foibles was just that, a mask.

He lifted his feet on to the desk, folded his hands behind his head, and leaned back in his chair. He studied the middle distance as he considered everything that had happened since Vianello asked him to go out to Mestre. He ran the events through his mind like the beads of a rosary, each one a separate entity but each leading to and from another, until they led to Tassini's body lying in front of the burning furnace.

He had eaten nothing all day save two panini and now regretted it. The sandwiches had done little more than remind him about food without satisfying his desire for it, and it was now too late to get anything to eat at a restaurant while it was still too early to go home.

He leaned forward and picked up the three sheets of paper and looked at them, then let them float, one by one, back to the surface of his desk. He felt his left knee growing stiff, so he crossed his feet, which allowed him to bend the knee. As he turned in the chair to do so, he felt one of the books in his pockets strike against the back of his chair, reminding him of their presence.

164

He pulled them out, looked at the ecological frightener and tossed it on to the desk. That left him with Dante, an old friend he had heard nothing from for more than a year. By nature an optimist, Brunetti would have preferred to find *Purgatorio*, the only book in which hope was a possibility, but given the fact that the alternative was *Industrial Illness*, he chose the black misery of Hell.

As he had fallen into the habit of doing in recent decades, he opened the book at random, thinking that this might well be the way other people read religious texts: letting fate lead them to some new illumination.

He dipped in just as Dante, still new to Hell and still capable of pity, tried to leave a message for Cavalcante that his son was still alive, then followed his Guide deeper into the abyss, already sickened by the stench. He flipped quickly on and found Vanni Fucci's obscene gesture to God, and flipped on again. He read of Dante's violence toward Bocca Degli Abbati and felt a moment's pleasure that such a traitor was so viciously treated.

He turned back and found himself reading one of the passages bordered by the notes Tassini had made in red. Canto XIV, the burning sand and horrid stream and fiery rain, that whole grotesque parody of nature that Dante thought so well suited to those who sinned against it: the usurers and sodomites. Brunetti followed them as, beneath the flaming snow that fell all around them, Dante and Virgil moved deeper into Hell. There appeared the company of shades, one of whom Brunetti recognized, or remembered, as Brunetto Latini, Dante's respected teacher. Though Brunetti had never much liked the passages that followed – the praise of Dante's genius that he puts into Ser Brunetto's mouth and the outing of public figures – he read on to the end of the next canto. He flipped back to Tassini's heavy red lines under '. . . the plain whose soil rejects all roots . . . The wood itself is ringed with the red stream.' In the margin,

165

Tassini had written, 'No roots. No life. Nothing.' In black ink, he had written 'The *grey* stream.'

Brunetti flipped forward and came upon the hypocrites. He recognized them, with their voluminous cloaks, like the Benedictines of Cluny, all dazzle and golden and fair on the outside, leaden and heavy and dull on the inside, the perfect physical manifestation of their deceit, doomed to carry it and measure out their steps until the end of time.

The lines describing their cloaks were circled in green and linked by a line to the text on the facing page, Virgil saying, 'Were I a pane of leaden glass, I could no more instantly imitate your look.'

The phone rang, dragging Brunetti away from Hell. He let his chair fall forward and answered with his name.

'I thought I'd call,' Elio Pelusso said. An old classmate of Brunetti's, Pelusso now worked on the newsdesk of the *Gazzettino* and had in the past been both informative and helpful. Brunetti had no idea why Pelusso would call him, which meant he could not figure out what sort of favour Pelusso would be after.

'Indeed,' Brunetti said. 'It's good to hear your voice.'

Pelusso laughed outright. 'Have they been making you all take sensitivity classes so you'll know how to deal with the press?' he asked.

'It's that obvious, eh?' Brunetti asked.

'To hear a policeman saying he's glad to hear my voice gives me goose-flesh.'

'And if a friend says it?' Brunetti asked, making himself sound offended.

'Then it's different,' Pelusso said in a warmer tone. 'Do you want me to call again and we can start over?'

Brunetti laughed. 'No, Elio, not at all. Just tell me what you'd like to know.'

'This time I'm calling to tell, not to ask.'

Brunetti bit back the remark that he was going to write the

date down so he would be sure to remember it and, instead, asked, 'Tell me what?'

'Someone I spoke to said that your boss has had a bug put in his ear by a certain Gianluca Fasano.'

'What sort of bug?'

'The sort that comes from people who don't like hearing that questions are being asked about their friends.'

'I suppose you wouldn't want to tell me who told you that, would you?' Brunetti asked.

'You're right. I wouldn't.'

'Is he reliable?'

'Yes.'

Brunetti considered this for some time. The waiter, either the waiter or Navarro. 'I was out at the glass factory next to his,' he volunteered to Pelusso.

'De Cal's?' the reporter asked.

'Yes. You know him?'

'Enough to know he's a bastard and enough to know he's a very sick man.'

'How sick?' Brunetti asked. 'And how do you know it?'

'I've met him a few times over the years, but a friend of mine was in a room in the hospital with him, so I saw him there when I went to visit my friend.'

'And?' Brunetti asked.

'You know how it is in oncology,' Pelusso said. 'No one ever tells anyone what they think they don't want to hear. But my friend heard the word "pancreas" enough times to suspect it didn't make any difference what else they said.'

'How long ago was this?'

'About a month. De Cal was in there for tests. Not treatment, but they still kept him in for two days – long enough for my friend to come to hate him as much as he seems to hate his son-in-law,' the reporter said. Then, perhaps because he felt he had given enough information and had no return on his investment, he asked, 'Why are you interested in Fasano?'

167

'I didn't know I was,' Brunetti said. 'But now maybe I am.'

'And De Cal?'

'He's threatened the husband of someone I know.'

'Sounds like something he'd do,' Pelusso said.

'Anything else?' Brunetti asked, though he knew it was greedy to do so.

'No.'

'Thanks for calling,' Brunetti said. 'I have to think about this for a while.'

'It's my single hope in life, to be of help to the forces of order,' Pelusso said in his most unctuous voice, waited for Brunetti's answering laugh, and when he heard it, hung up.

Inferno open in his lap, Brunetti wondered where Dante would have placed someone like De Cal. With the thieves? No, Brunetti had no reason to suspect he had ever stolen anything, save what the ordinary businessman was obliged to steal from the taxman in order to survive, and that was hardly to be considered a sin. Among the grafters? But how else to run a business? Brunetti remembered the man, his face red with anger, and realized that he would be among the wrathful and be torn limb from limb, like Filippo Argenti, by his fellow sinners. Yet if De Cal knew himself to be a dying man but still bent his mind to profit, then Dante might have put him among the hoarders and condemned him to push his heavy stone, for all eternity, against the stones of other men like himself.

Brunetti had once read in the science column of *La Repubblica* a report on experiments done with people suffering from Alzheimer's. Many of them lost the use of the brain mechanism that told them when they were hungry or full, and if given food repeatedly, would eat again and again, unconscious of the fact that they had just eaten and should no longer be hungry. He sometimes thought it was the same with people afflicted with the disease of greed:

the concept of 'enough' had been eliminated from their minds.

He folded the papers in three and slipped them into the pocket of his jacket. Downstairs he left a note on Vianello's desk, telling the Inspector he had left for the day but would like to talk to him the following morning. Outside the Questura he gave himself over to what was left of the day. He went out to Riva degli Schiavoni and took the Number One to Salute, then headed west with no destination in mind, turning that decision over to his memory and his mood. He cut through the underpass by the abbey, down past building site after building site then left, down towards the Incurabili. Only a fragment of Bobo's fresco remained, glassed in now in order to save what was left from the elements. Had it been warmer, he would have had his first ice-cream of the year, not at Nico's but at the little place down by Ai Schiavi. He passed the Giustinian, crossed over to Fondamenta Foscarini and then went down to Tonolo for a coffee and a pastry. Because he had had no lunch to speak of, he had two: a cream-filled swan and a tiny chocolate éclair as light as silk.

In the window of a shop where he had once bought a grey sweater, he saw what might be its twin, but in green. The size was his and soon, without his bothering to try it on, so was the sweater. As he stepped out into the *calle*, he realized how happy he was, much in the way he had been as a boy to be out of school when the others were still inside, and no one to know where he was or what he was doing.

He went into a wine shop not far from San Pantalon and bought a bottle of Nebbiolo, a Sangiovese, and a very young Barbera. By then it was almost seven, and he decided to go home. As he turned into the *calle*, he noticed Raffi opening the front door of their building and called out to him, but his son didn't hear him and closed the door. Brunetti shifted packages, looking for his keys, and by the time he got inside it was too late to shout up the steps after his son.

As he turned into the final flight of stairs, he heard Raffi's voice, though he had seen him come in alone. This confusion was resolved halfway up the steps, when he saw Raffi, slouched against the wall outside the door, *telefonino* in hand. 'No, not tonight. I've got that calculus to do. You know how much homework he gives us.'

Brunetti smiled at his son, who held up a hand and, in a gesture of unmistakable male solidarity, rolled his eyes toward the ceiling, saying, 'Of course I want to see you.'

Brunetti let himself into the apartment, abandoning Raffi to what he assumed were the tender solicitations of Sara Paganuzzi. Inside, he found himself surrounded by the aroma of artichokes. The scent floated down the hallway from the kitchen, filling the house. The penetrating odour sent Brunetti's mind flashing back to the stench that had surrounded him twelve hours before. He set the packages on the floor and went down the corridor, away from the kitchen, and into the bathroom.

Twenty minutes later, showered, his hair still wet, and wearing a pair of light cotton pants and a T-shirt, he went back down the hallway to get his sweater. Both packages were gone. He went down to the kitchen, where he saw the three bottles lined up on the counter, Paola at the stove, and Chiara setting the table.

Paola turned and made a kissing gesture towards him; Chiara said hello and smiled. 'Aren't you cold?' Paola asked.

'No,' Brunetti answered, turning back towards Raffi's room. As he walked down the corridor, his righteous indignation mounted: it was *his* sweater; he'd worked to pay for it; the colour was perfect for these slacks. He stopped outside Raffi's door, preparing himself for the sight of his son wearing his sweater, knocked on the door and entered when he heard Raffi's voice.

'*Ciao, Papà*,' Raffi said, looking up from the papers scattered over his desk. A textbook was in front of him, propped open by the ceramic frog Chiara had given him for Christmas. Brunetti said hello and gave what he thought was a quite thoroughly professional glance around the room.

'I put it on your bed,' Raffi said and went back to his homework.

'Oh, good,' Brunetti said. 'Thanks.'

He wore it to dinner, earning compliments from Paola and from Chiara, though she complained that men always got to wear the best sweaters and jackets and girls always had to wear pink angora and horrible things like that. Girls, however, did get first crack, it seemed, at fried artichoke bottoms and then at pork ribs with polenta. Not at all disturbed by the fact that it had just been carried home, Paola had opened the Sangiovese, and Brunetti found it perfect.

Because he had eaten the two pastries, Brunetti declined a baked pear, to the considerable surprise of the others at the table. No one asked after his health, but he did notice that Paola was particularly solicitous in asking him if he would like a grappa, perhaps with coffee in the living room while the kids did the dishes?

She came in a little later, carrying a tray with two coffees and two ample glasses of grappa. She placed it on the table and sat beside him. 'Why did you take a shower?' she asked.

He spooned sugar into his coffee and stirred it, saying, 'I went for a walk, and it was colder than I expected, so I thought it would warm me up.'

'Did it?' she asked, sipping at her own coffee.

'Uh huh,' he said, finishing his coffee, and picked up his grappa.

She set her cup down, picked up her glass and moved back in the sofa. 'Nice day for a walk.'

'Uh huh,' was the best Brunetti could do. Then he said, 'I'll tell you another time, all right?'

She moved minimally closer to him, until her shoulder

171

touched his, and said, 'Of course.'

'You're good at crossword puzzles and things like that, aren't you?' he asked.

'I suppose.'

'I have something I'd like you to look at,' he said, getting to his feet. Without waiting for her answer, he went out to the hallway to get the three sheets of paper from his jacket, and took them back into the living room.

He unfolded them, sat back down beside her, and handed them over. 'I found these in the room of someone who worked on Murano. I think he was killed.'

She took the papers and held them at some distance from her. Brunetti got up again, went down to her study, and came back with her glasses. After she put them on, she looked more closely at the papers, studying them. She tried to hold them in line with one another, but gave that up, leaned forward and spread them out on the table, pushing the tray to one side to make enough room for them.

Brunetti offered, 'I thought of bank codes, but that doesn't make any sense. He didn't have any money. I don't think he was very interested in it, either.'

Paola put her head down again and studied the papers. 'You excluded dates, too?' she asked, and he grunted in assent.

After some time, she said, 'The first number on the first page is almost twice as big as the second one.'

'Does that mean anything to you?' he asked.

'No,' she said with a quick shake of her head. She said nothing about the numbers on the second and third pages.

So they sat, for another ten minutes, staring with futile attention at the papers. Chiara, on her way back to her room to continue her Latin homework, found them that way and flopped down on the arm of the sofa next to Brunetti. 'What's that?' she asked.

'Puzzles,' Brunetti answered. 'Neither of us can make any

sense of them.'

'You mean the coordinates?' Chiara asked, pointing at the numbers that appeared on the third page.

'Coordinates?' asked an astonished Brunetti.

'Sure,' Chiara said in her most offhand manner. 'What else could they be? See,' she said, pointing at the degree sign after the first number, 'this is the degree, the minute, and the second.' She pulled the paper a bit closer and said, 'This one is the latitude – that's always given first – and that one's the longitude.' She looked at the numbers a moment more and said, 'The second set is for a place that's got to be very near to the first, slightly to the south-east. And the third is to the south-west. You want to know where they are?'

'Where what are?' Brunetti asked, still slightly stunned.

'The places,' Chiara said, tapping her finger on the paper. 'Do you want to know where they are?'

'Yes,' Paola said.

'OK,' Chiara said and got to her feet. In less than a minute, she was back with the giant atlas she had requested for Christmas, the best Brunetti could find, more than 500 pages and published in England, its page spread almost as large as the *Gazzettino*'s.

Chiara thumped it down on the table, covering the papers, then pulled them out by their corners. She had to use both hands to open the book to the middle, then started to page through it, occasionally glancing at the numbers, then at the book. With a snort of irritation, she turned back to the opening pages, ran her finger across the numbers at the top of a map of Europe, then down the right side of the page.

Carefully she turned the pages by their top corners until she found the page she was looking for, opened the book and let it fall flat, and they all found themselves looking at the *laguna* of Venezia.

'Looks like they're on Murano,' Chiara said, 'but you'd need a more detailed map – probably a nautical chart of the *laguna* – to find the exact places.'

Neither of her parents said anything; both were staring at the map. Chiara got to her feet again, saying, 'I've got to get back to the Gallic Wars', and went to her room.

19

'Did she learn all that from reading those Patrick O'Brian books?' Brunetti asked when Chiara was gone.

He had intended the question as a joke, at least as a semi-joke, but Paola took it seriously and answered, 'They probably used the same notation for writing latitude and longitude in the nineteenth century: she's got the advantage of better maps.'

'I'll never say another word against those books,' Brunetti promised.

'But you still won't try again to read them?' she asked.

Ignoring the question, Brunetti said, 'Do we still have those nautical charts?'

'They'd be in the box,' Paola answered, leaving it to Brunetti to go and hunt out the battered old wooden box in which the family kept their maps.

He was back with it in a few minutes, handed her half of the pile and started sorting through the others. After a few minutes Paola said, holding it up, 'Here's the big one of the *laguna*.'

It was a relic of the summer they had spent exploring the *laguna* in a battered old boat a friend had let them use. It must have been more than twenty years ago, before either of the kids was born. He remembered one star-scattered night when they had been trapped in a canal by the withdrawing tide.

'Those mosquitoes,' Paola said, her memory, too, drawn to that night and what they had done after spreading insect repellent on one another.

Brunetti dropped the maps he held on the floor and spread hers across the table. Unasked, she read him out the latitudinal coordinate of the first number while he ran his finger down the side of the map, stopping when he found the proper place. With his knees he pushed the table back to allow the entire map to fit flat on it. She read out the longitude, and he brought his finger slowly across the top of the map until he found that number, as well. He ran his left index finger down one of the vertical lines on the map; then the right followed a horizontal line until his fingers met at the point of intersection. The second point appeared to be little more than a few metres from the first.

'They're all on Sacca Serenella,' he said.

'You don't sound surprised.'

'I'm not.'

'Why?'

It took Brunetti almost half an hour to tell her, glossing over the precise circumstances of Tassini's death, to arrive at their search of the dead man's room, a room located not far from the point where those lines intersected, and then the grim meeting with his wife and mother-in-law.

When he finished, Paola went into the kitchen and returned holding the bottle of grappa. She handed it to Brunetti and sat next to him, then folded the map and dropped it on top of the others on the floor. She took back the bottle and poured them each another small glass.

'Did he really believe all that about having been contaminated and passing it on to his daughter?' Paola asked.

'I think so, yes.'

'Even in the face of the medical evidence?' Paola asked.

Brunetti shrugged, as if to show how unimportant medical evidence was to a person who chose not to believe it. 'It's what he thought happened.'

'But how would he be contaminated?' she asked. 'I'd believe it if he worked at Marghera, but I've never heard any talk that Murano is at risk, well, that the people who work there are.'

Brunetti thought back to his conversation with Tassini. 'He believed that there was a conspiracy to prevent him from getting accurate test results, so there would never be sufficient genetic evidence.' He read her scepticism and said, 'He believed it.'

'But *what* did he believe?' Paola demanded.

Brunetti opened his hands in a gesture of futility. 'That's what I couldn't get him to tell me: what he thought his problem was or how it would have affected the baby. All he'd tell me was that De Cal wasn't the only person involved in whatever was going on,' and before she could ask again, he added, 'and no, he didn't say what that was.'

'You think he was crazy?' Paola asked in a softer voice.

'I don't know about things like that,' Brunetti answered after considering the question. 'He believed in something for which there seems to be no evidence and for which he appeared to have no proof. I'm not ready to call that crazy.'

He waited to see if Paola would remark that he had just described religious belief, but she was taking no easy shots that evening, it seemed, and said only, 'But he believed it enough to write down these numbers, whatever they are.'

'Yes,' Brunetti admitted. 'Doesn't mean that what he believed is true, just because he wrote some numbers down.'

'What about these other numbers?' she said, taking the

177

other two sheets from the floor and placing them on the table.

'No idea,' Brunetti said. 'I've been staring at them all afternoon and they don't make any sense to me.'

'No clues?' she asked. 'Wasn't there anything else in his room?'

'No, nothing,' Brunetti said, and then he remembered the books. 'Just industrial illness and Dante.'

'Don't be cute, Guido,' she snapped.

He got up and went over to his jacket again; this time he brought back the two books.

Her reaction to *Industrial Illness* was the same as his, though she tossed it on the floor, not on the table. 'Dante,' she said, reaching for the book. He handed it to her and watched as she examined it: she opened to the title page, then turned to the publication information, then opened it in the middle and flipped through to the end.

'It's his school text, isn't it?' she said. 'Was he a reader?'

'There were a lot of books in his house.'

'What sort of books?' Like Brunetti, she believed that books served as a mirror of the person who accumulated them.

'I don't know,' he said. 'They were in a shelf against the back wall, and I never got close enough to read the titles.' He hadn't been conscious of examining them at the time, but now, recalling the room, he saw the rows of books, the backs of some of what might well have been the standard editions of the poets, and the gold-ribbed backs of the same editions of the great novelists Paola had in her study.

'He was a real reader, though,' Brunetti finally said.

Paola had the Dante open and was already lost in it. He watched her for a few minutes, until she turned a page, looked across at him with an expression of blank astonishment, and asked, 'How is it that I forget how perfect he is?'

Brunetti picked up the maps and put them back in the box. He closed it and left it on the floor.

Suddenly the accumulated weight of the day's events bore down on him. 'I think I have to go to bed,' he said, offering no explanation. She acknowledged his words with a nod and plunged back into Hell.

Brunetti sank immediately into a heavy sleep and was not aware of Paola when she came to bed. If she turned on the light, if she made any noise, if she stayed awake reading: Brunetti had no idea. But as the bells of San Marco rolled past their window at five the following morning, he woke up, saying, 'Laws.'

He turned on the light, raised himself on to his shoulder to see if he had woken Paola, and saw that he had not. He pushed back the covers and went out into the hallway, one side of which was lined with the books he thought of as his: the Greek and Roman historians as well as those who had followed them for the next two thousand years. On the other side were art books and travel books and, on the top shelf, some of the textbooks he had used at university as well as some current volumes on civil and criminal law.

In the living room he found Tassini's papers still on the table alongside *Industrial Illness*. He had a degree in law, had spent years reading and memorizing them: why had he not recognized the notation? If the first six digits were read as a date, the first came out as 20 September 1973 and the second as 10 September 1982. The last three numbers would then be the number of the law. He knew he had the volumes of the *Gazzetta Ufficiale* in his office and not here, but still he looked for them. His feet got cold so he took the papers and Tassini's book with him to the bedroom.

He climbed into bed, slapped his pillow into submission behind him, but then cursed under his breath and went back into the living room to get his glasses. Coming back into the room, he grabbed his new sweater and tied it around his shoulders, and got into bed again.

He let the sheets of paper drift into the valley between

himself and his apparently comatose wife and opened *Industrial Illness* at the index.

He read until nearly six, when he set down the book and went into the kitchen, made himself caffè latte, and took it back into the bedroom. He sat, sipping at his coffee and watching the light on the paintings on the far wall.

'Paola,' he said soon after the bells had rung seven. And then again, 'Paola.'

She must have responded to something in his voice rather than to her name, for she replied in an entirely natural voice. 'If you bring me coffee, I'll listen to you.'

For the fourth time, he got out of bed. He made a larger pot of coffee and brought two cups back to the bedroom with him. He found her sitting up, her glasses slipped down to the end of her nose, Tassini's book open on her knees.

He handed her a cup. She took it, sipped, and smiled her thanks. She patted the bed beside her and he sat. They drank some coffee. After a time, she pushed her glasses up on to her head. She said, 'I have no idea what you're doing, Guido. Reading something like this half the night.' With her free hand, she shut the book and tossed it on to the bed.

'I think I know what the numbers mean,' he said. 'He knew the laws that deal with pollution and he listed them in the proper legal way, only without the spaces between the dates and numbers.'

He expected Paola to ask what the laws were, but she surprised him by saying, 'How would he know the numbers of the laws?' In her tone, he detected more than a little of the scorn the educated reserve for those who aspire to their knowledge.

'I have no idea,' Brunetti confessed.

'Did he study law?'

'I don't know,' Brunetti said, realizing how little he knew about Tassini's past; the man had passed too quickly from suspect to victim.

'His mother-in-law said he wanted to be a night-watchman so he could sit there and read all night,' he told Paola.

With a smile, she said, 'I wouldn't be surprised if there was a time when my mother might have said the same thing about you, Guido,' but she leaned over and squeezed his hand to show she was only kidding. He hoped.

He got to his feet and took her empty cup. 'I think I'll go to the Questura,' he said, thinking that he would pick up the newspapers on the way and see how the story was being reported.

She nodded and reached for the book she kept on her night table. She put on her glasses and opened it. Brunetti picked up Tassini's book and went back out to the kitchen to put their cups in the sink.

On his way to the Questura, Brunetti bought the *Corriere* and the *Gazzettino* and unfolded them on his desk as soon as he got to his office. The death had taken place early enough the previous day for reporters to have had a full day to sniff around the factory, the hospital, and then around Tassini's home. There was a photo of Tassini, taken years ago, and one of the De Cal factory with three *carabinieri* standing in front of it: Brunetti had no idea that they had become involved. According to the accounts in both papers, Tassini's body had been discovered by a co-worker when he arrived at the factory to adjust the temperature of the new *gettate* that had spent the night in the furnaces. The man's body was lying in front of one of the furnaces, in a temperature estimated to be in excess of one hundred degrees.

The police had questioned Tassini's co-workers and family, but an official investigation would begin only after the results of the autopsy. Tassini, who was thirty-six, had worked at De Cal's factory for six years and left a wife and two children.

As soon as Brunetti finished reading the article, he dialled

181

the *telefonino* of the *medico legale*, Ettore Rizzardi. The doctor answered with a laconic *'Sì.'*

'It's Guido,' Brunetti began.

Before he could continue, Rizzardi said, 'You are not going to believe this, but he died of a heart attack.'

'What? He wasn't forty yet.'

'Well, it wasn't that kind of a heart attack,' Rizzardi said, surprising Brunetti, who had not known there was more than one type.

'Then what kind was it?'

'From dehydration,' Rizzardi said and went on, 'He was lying there most of the night. The temperature did it. That idiot Venturi didn't bother to measure it, but the men at the *fornace* told me when I called. That is, they told me what it would have been if the temperature inside was about 1400 and the door was open.'

'How much is that?' Brunetti asked.

'One hundred and fifty-seven,' Rizzardi answered, 'but that's just outside the door. Down on the floor, it wouldn't be as hot, but still hot enough to kill him.'

'What happens?'

'You sweat. It's worse than any sauna you can think of, Guido. You sweat and sweat until there's no more sweat to come out. And while it's coming out, it takes all the minerals with it. And once there are no more minerals, especially sodium and potassium, the heart goes into arrhythmia, and then you have a heart attack.'

'And then you die,' Brunetti completed.

'That's right. And then you die.'

'Any signs of violence?' Brunetti asked.

'There was a mark on his head, a bruise. The skin was broken, but there was no dirt in it and no traces of what he might have hit.'

'Or of what might have hit him?' Brunetti suggested.

'Or of what he came into contact with, Guido,' Rizzardi

said in a firm voice. 'It bled for a while, until he died.'

Brunetti had already had Bocchese tell him that any sign of human tissue on the door to the furnace would have been destroyed by the fire, so he did not bother to ask.

'Anything else?' Brunetti asked.

'No,' Rizzardi said, 'nothing that you could think was suspicious.'

'Did you do it?' Brunetti asked, suddenly curious as to why Rizzardi knew so much about the state of Tassini's body.

'I offered to help my colleague, Dottor Venturi, with the autopsy. I told him I was curious because I'd never seen anything like this,' Rizzardi said in his dispassionate, professional voice.

But then his tone changed and he said, 'You know, it's true, Guido. I'd never seen anything like this: just read about it. You should have seen his lungs. I couldn't have imagined. Breathing in that heat: it made them produce so much liquid. I've seen it with smoke, of course, but I had no idea that heat itself could do the same thing.'

'But it was a heart attack?' Brunetti asked, unwilling to hear more of Rizzardi's professional enthusiasm.

'Yes. That's what Venturi put on the death certificate.'

'What would you have put?' Brunetti asked, hoping Rizzardi would confirm his own suspicions.

'Heart attack, Guido. Heart attack. That's what the man died of, a heart attack.'

'One more thing, Ettore: is there a list of what was in his pockets?'

'Wait a minute,' the doctor said. 'I had the list here a minute ago.' Brunetti heard a click as the doctor set the phone down on his desk, then the rustling of papers. A moment later, he was back. 'A set of keys, a wallet with identification and thirty Euros, a handkerchief, and three Euros and eighty-seven cents. That's it.'

Brunetti thanked him and hung up.

20

After his conversation with Rizzardi, Brunetti decided to go down to the Archive and make copies of the laws Tassini's notes had referred to. Back in his office, Brunetti read through them. The 1973 law established limits for waste water that flowed into the *laguna*, the sewers, even the sea. It also established time limits within which the glass manufacturers had to install water purifiers and then established the agency that would inspect those purifiers. The law of 1982 imposed even stricter limits on the water system and addressed the acids that Assunta had mentioned. As Brunetti read of the limits and restrictions, he could not silence the small voice that asked him what had gone on before that and what had flowed into the *laguna* before these laws were passed?

Once he finished reading the laws, good sense urged Brunetti to go down to Patta's office and tell him about the contents of Tassini's file and what some of those numbers meant. He wanted to suggest that some sort of examination be made of the places indicated by the coordinates to see what basis Tassini's suspicions might have had, but long experience of Patta and the way he negotiated the shoals of city bureaucracy told Brunetti just how receptive his superior would be to this suggestion. If Pelusso was telling him the truth – and Brunetti saw no reason not to believe him – then Fasano had enough influence to be able to complain to Patta, and that suggested he was a man of greater influence than Brunetti had previously realized.

As he returned to his chair, one of Tassini's books struck the edge of his desk, once again calling Brunetti's attention to them. Where would Dante have put Patta, Brunetti found himself wondering. Among the hypocrites? The wrathful? Or perhaps he would have been merciful and placed the Vice-Questore outside the gate to Hell, among the opportunists. He opened *Inferno* to the title page and studied it for a moment. Canto I. Canto I. He turned a few pages, and there it was: Canto II, and then Canto III, and then Canto IV. Brunetti took a deep breath, amazed at his own blindness. He had had the book and Tassini's numbers in his hands at the same time and he had not seen it.

He took the copy he had made of Tassini's numbers, found the first, and opened Dante to Canto VII, line 103. '*L'acqua era buia assai più che persa*', 'The water was much darker than persa,' he repeated. 'What the devil is *persa*?' He looked at his watch, saw that Paola was likely still to be home, and dialled their number.

'*Pronto*,' she answered on the fifth ring.

'Paola,' he said, 'what's *persa*?'

'In what context?' she asked, displaying no curiosity as to the reason for his question.

'In Dante,' he said.

'I think it's a colour,' she said, 'but let me get the concordance.' In less than a minute she was back, and he heard her mumbling as she searched for the word, a habit Chiara had picked up from her. Finally she said, '"a colour between purple and black, but black predominates".' She waited for his response, and when he made none, she asked, 'Anything else?'

'Not yet. I'll call.'

Paola hung up.

Brunetti went back to the book. The stream that Dante was following eventually flowed into the Styx, but Tassini's reference was only to line 103, to the black water.

The next was no less grim: *'no green leaves but dark colours, no smooth branches, but gnarled and warped.'*

He continued with Tassini's references: *'the banks were crusted over with a mould from the vapour below that sticks on them and fights with the eyes and nose.'*

And the last: *'do not set your feet upon the burning sand.'*

This was hardly the stuff of a major environmental scandal, but if Signorina Elettra was right and Tassini had the faith of a true believer, he would have interpreted these Dantean descriptions as he pleased and found whatever signs and portents he chose to find.

Brunetti decided to go down and talk to Patta, if only for the perverse desire to prove himself correct in his assessment of the man. Celestine V had renounced the papacy in order to avoid the power of office, had he not? How unlike Patta, who renounced every aspect of his work save for the power and perks of office. Having Patta run naked through a field of worms and maggots, weeping tears and blood, would perhaps be an excessive punishment for his negligence of office, but the contemplation of this image kept Brunetti occupied as he made his way to his superior's office.

Signorina Elettra glanced up from some papers as he came in, and she smiled a peculiar kind of smile. 'I have some information about Signor Fasano, who would appear to be what he claims to be.'

'Good,' he had the presence of mind to say, and, 'thank you.' Then he asked, 'Is the Vice-Questore in?'

'Yes, he is. Would you like to speak to him?' she asked, as if Brunetti might have had some other reason to have come down two flights of stairs to ask if Patta were in. He tried to remember how absent of respect he had been when discussing Fasano with her the previous time: might this be the reason for her formality?

She picked up her phone and pressed a button, asked Dottor Patta if he would see Commissario Brunetti, replaced the phone, and nodded towards the door. Brunetti thanked her and went in without bothering to knock.

'Ah, Brunetti,' Patta said as he entered, 'I was just going to call you.'

'Yes, sir?' Brunetti said, making his way towards Patta's desk.

'Yes, sit down, sit down,' Patta said with a broad wave of his hand.

Brunetti did as he was told, all systems on high alert as they registered Patta's affability.

'I wanted to talk to you about this thing out on Murano,' Patta said.

Brunetti did his best to look mildly interested.

'Yes,' Patta said, 'I wanted to talk to you about this case you seem to be creating.'

'A man died there, sir,' Brunetti said, hoping to surprise Patta into a reconsideration of his own words.

Patta gave him a long look. 'Of a heart attack, Brunetti. The man died of a heart attack.' The affability had disappeared from his voice. When Brunetti said nothing, Patta added, 'I assumed you would have spoken to your friend Rizzardi by now, Commissario.' In the face of Brunetti's refusal to answer him, Patta repeated, 'He died of a heart attack.'

Brunetti sat silently. Apparently Patta had not finished. The Vice-Questore went on, 'I don't know if you've had time to formulate some theory of foul play here, Brunetti, but if you have, I want you to unformulate it. The man collapsed and died of a heart attack while he was at work.'

'He was a watchman, not a glass-blower,' Brunetti said. 'There was no reason for him to be working near the furnace.'

'On the contrary,' Patta said with an equanimity that Brunetti found as puzzling as it was infuriating, 'it's just because he was a watchman that there are any number of reasons he could have been there. There could have been something wrong with the furnace, a sudden rise in temperature that he went to investigate. Someone could have left that rod there for him to trip over, or he could have been doing what a lot of them do out there at night: working a piece of glass for himself.' Patta's smile registered the plausibility of these things, and Brunetti wondered just where the Vice-Questore, a Sicilian, had learned so much about the art of making Murano glass. Scarpa was a possible choice, Scarpa who shared his superior's desire that the city be viewed as free of crime, and what better crime to keep from the records than murder? But Scarpa was no more Venetian than his master. Fasano, then?

Even before he spoke, Brunetti knew it was hopeless, with Patta so contentedly persuaded that the investigation – whatever pale, weak thing that might have been – was over. But still he said, 'I came to speak to you, sir, because of some papers that were in Tassini's possession.'

'How in his possession?'

'They were in his home.'

'And how is it that they happen to be in *your* possession, Commissario?'

'Because I took them away with me when I went to speak to his widow.'

'Have you made a formal report of this?'

'Yes,' Brunetti lied, knowing that Signorina Elettra could easily backdate his report, when he got around to writing it.

Patta did not question this. Instead he asked, 'And what are these papers?'

'Lists of numbers.'

'What sort of numbers?'

'There are references to specific laws and to specific geographic locations. And there are repeated references to *Inferno*. There was a copy of the poem in his room at the factory.'

'And is this book another item in your possession?' Patta asked.

'Yes.'

'Is that all there was, Brunetti? Or was there something other than –' Patta began, using the long-drawn-out enunciation one employs with a wilful or disobedient child – 'references to laws and geographic locations and to *Inferno*?' Patta was unable or unwilling to resist the temptation to repeat Brunetti's words.

As though this had been a request for information rather than an insult, Brunetti said, 'There has to be a reason he was keeping those numbers, sir.'

Patta made a business of shaking his head in feigned confusion. 'Specific laws and specific locations, is it, Brunetti? And what comes next, the winning lottery number for Venice? Or the geographic coordinates of where the extraterrestrials are going to land?' He got up from his chair and took two steps, muttering, 'Dante', as if to calm his troubled spirit. He persuaded himself to return and sit down again. 'Though it might come as a surprise to you, Brunetti, this is a Questura,' he said, leaning across his desk and pointing a finger at the Commissario, 'and we are police officers. It is not a tent in the middle of the desert where people come to you so that you can hold seances and read tarot cards.'

Brunetti glanced at Patta, then shifted his eyes to a spot on the desk between them. 'Do you understand me, Brunetti?' When the Commissario made no attempt to respond, Patta demanded, 'Do you understand me, Brunetti?'

'Yes, sir. I do,' Brunetti said, surprised at just how true this was. He got to his feet.

'And what are you going to do about those numbers, Brunetti?' Patta asked, voice acid with sarcasm and menace.

'I'll keep the references to Dante, sir. It's always good to know where to locate the hypocrites and the opportunists.'

Patta's face went rigid, but he couldn't prevent himself from asking for more. 'And your laws and your coordinates?'

'Oh, I don't know, sir,' Brunetti said, turning and making for the door. 'But it's useful to know what the laws are and exactly where you stand.' He opened the door, said '*Buon giorno*' very quietly, and closed the door behind him.

21

When he emerged from Patta's office, Brunetti paused at Signorina Elettra's desk long enough to take the folder she handed him. He thanked her, checked that he had the paper on which he had written Tassini's coordinates, and went outside the Questura to the dock in front. There was no sign of Foa, whom he finally found down at the bar by the bridge, having a coffee and reading *La Gazzetta dello Sport*.

He smiled when he saw Brunetti come in. 'Would you like a coffee, Commissario?'

'Gladly,' Brunetti said, wishing he knew enough about some sport, any sport, to be able to make some appropriate conversation, but, instead, he could do nothing more than remark on how warm it was.

When the coffee was in front of him, Brunetti asked, 'Have you got one of those location-finding things, Foa?'

'A GPS, sir?'

'Yes.'

'In the boat, sir,' the pilot said. 'You need it?'

'Yes,' Brunetti said, stirring his coffee. 'You doing anything now?'

'Other than reading about these hopeless clowns,' Foa said, slapping the paper with the backs of his fingers, 'nothing. Why, you need to go somewhere?'

'Out to Murano,' Brunetti said. 'Yes.'

As they walked back to the launch, Brunetti explained about the numbers Tassini had written and did nothing to deflect Foa's compliments at having figured out what they were. After they climbed on board, Foa unlocked a panel on the dashboard and took out a glass-faced instrument. He showed Brunetti the GPS, which was little larger than a *telefonino* and served the double function of pointing to true North and giving the exact coordinates of the point where the instrument was. He set it on the ledge in front of him and switched on the engine. He pulled away from the dock and, after a moment, turned into Rio di Santa Giustina and took them quickly out into the *laguna*.

'How does it work?' Brunetti asked, picking it up. Because he had grown up without proximity to cars, he always blamed Venice for his mechanical and technological ineptitude, when he knew the real explanation was simply his lack of interest in the way things, especially gadgets, functioned.

'Satellites,' the pilot said, suddenly deciding to cut across the wake of a 42 on its way to the cemetery. The heavy bouncing of the launch forced Brunetti to grab the railing beside him, but Foa seemed to float and bob with the waves. The pilot took his right hand from the wheel and waved towards the heavens. 'It's full of them, circling around, registering, recording, keeping an eye on matters.' Foa waited a moment, and then added, 'Probably taking photos of what we eat for breakfast, too.'

Brunetti opted to ignore this opening, and Foa returned to more prosaic things. 'The satellite sends down a message that tells you exactly where you are. Look at it,' he said, pointing to the face of the GPS, where two illuminated rectangles provided ever-changing digital readings. 'On the side there,' the pilot said, turning his attention from the waters in front of them and pointing to the face of the instrument, 'that's the latitude reading. And that's the longitude. It'll keep changing as long as we keep moving.' As if to show just how this worked, Foa swung the boat hard to the right, and then just as quickly to the left. If the latitude and longitude readings changed, Brunetti took no notice, for he was busy grabbing the railing again to keep from toppling out of the launch.

Brunetti handed the object back to Foa and devoted his attention to Murano, which they were approaching at considerable speed. 'You want to go back to where we went the last time?' Foa asked.

'Yes. And I'd like you to come with me.'

Foa made no attempt to hide the pleasure this gave him. He slowed the engine and slipped the boat up to the dock, then shifted into reverse until they were motionless in the water. A side current brushed them against the embankment; Foa leaped out and made the boat fast to a ring in the paving, then secured it at the bow with another rope.

Brunetti slipped the GPS into the pocket of his jacket and climbed up beside Foa. Together they started back towards De Cal's factory. 'You want to talk to the old man again?' Foa asked.

'No,' Brunetti answered. 'I want to find where these points are.' He took out his wallet and extracted the piece of paper on which he had written the coordinates.

Foa took the paper and read the sets of numbers. 'The latitude and longitude are right for the *laguna*,' he said, then added, 'They've all got to be right around here.' Brunetti, who had a vague idea from having checked the nautical charts, nodded.

Together they skirted the factory building and went around

to the left, towards the barren field behind it. The side of the building that they walked along, Brunetti was glad to notice, had no windows.

They stopped just where the dry grass began, and Brunetti took out the GPS. He started to hand the piece of paper to Foa, but he realized that the pilot would be more familiar with the instrument so gave him that, instead. Foa took one final look at the paper and set off in the direction of the water.

He walked across the field, his eyes fixed to the instrument, moving at an angle that took him slightly to the left, towards the *laguna* to the north of the island. Halfway between De Cal's factory and the water, he stopped. When Brunetti joined him, Foa pulled the hand that held the paper towards him and checked the second number.

His attention on the GPS, Foa moved to the left, heading for the fence that had once stood between De Cal's property and the land next door. All that was left to indicate its previous existence or function was a line of bleached stakes and sticks, like the bones of some desiccated land animal long ago devoured by marauders. As if to provide a clearer demarcation between the two properties, nothing grew on the strip where once the fence had stood: the grass began only about a metre to either side of the tangled sticks.

After a time, Foa stopped and studied the instrument, then moved a few steps closer to the fence. 'What was the last digit, sir? Of the second number?'

Brunetti glanced at the paper. 'Point ninety.'

Foa took two small sideways steps until he was astride the rotting pieces of fence. He kicked them aside. He looked at the GPS and moved minimally to the right in response to whatever he read there, then called back to Brunetti, 'OK, this is it. Whatever this guy thought was important, this is the first place where he wanted you to look.' He took the paper from Brunetti, studied it for a moment, then turned and looked at De Cal's factory. 'The second lot of coordinates has got to be inside that building,' Foa said.

He checked the GPS, and looked around them again. 'The third place is probably inside that one,' he said, pointing to the factory that stood on the other side of the field, to the right of De Cal's.

Brunetti gazed around them. Could it be that something was visible from this point that might not be seen from another angle? They both turned in full circles and, without even discussing the possibility that they were meant to see something, dismissed it. Brunetti turned back towards De Cal's factory, and as he moved, both of them heard the squelching sound his foot made as he raised it. Neither had been aware of the dampness when they got there, but when they looked down and moved their feet, they saw the water quickly seep in to fill their footsteps.

The idea came to them simultaneously. 'I've got an empty bucket in the launch, Commissario. In case you'd like to take some of this stuff to Bocchese.'

'Yes,' Brunetti said, not at all sure what would be there but absolutely certain that something would be. He waited while the pilot headed for the factory and cut around it in the direction of the launch. Every so often Brunetti shifted his feet and heard and felt the sibilance of the mud.

Foa was quickly back with a pink plastic bucket and a small spade, the sort of thing a child would use for building castles on the beach. When Foa saw the attention Brunetti devoted to these objects, he pressed his lips together nervously and said, 'Well, I take the boat home with me on weekends sometimes, to work on the engine.'

'Does your daughter help you?' Brunetti asked.

'She's only three, sir,' Foa said with a smile. 'But she likes to come along when I go out in the *laguna* to dig for clams.'

'Better to go out there in a boat you know is safe, I suppose, especially if you have a child,' said Brunetti.

Foa answered with a smile. 'I buy my own gas,' he said,

and Brunetti believed him. He liked the fact that Foa felt it important to tell him.

Brunetti took the shovel and dug it into the mud at their feet. Foa held the bucket for him as he spilled in a few shovelfuls, then placed the blade of the shovel flat on the ground and allowed some water to seep in. He added this carefully to the mud.

A man's voice spoke from their left. 'What are you doing?'

Brunetti stopped and stood upright. A man was approaching them from the factory he had been told belonged to Gianluca Fasano. 'What are you doing here?' the man demanded, clearly not at all impressed by the sight of Foa's police uniform. He was tall, taller than Vianello, and thicker, as well. The thick ridge of bone above his eyes cast them into shadow, even in this morning light. His lips were thin and cracked, and the skin around them looked irritated.

'Good morning,' Brunetti said, walking towards the man and putting out his hand. His gesture surprised the man into taking it. 'I'm Commissario Guido Brunetti.'

'Palazzi,' he said as he shook Brunetti's hand. 'Raffaele.'

Foa approached, and Brunetti introduced the two men, who also shook hands.

'Could you tell me what you're doing?' Palazzi asked in a more moderate tone.

'I'm in charge of the investigation into the death of l'uomo di notte. He worked in your factory, too, didn't he?'

'Yes,' Palazzi said, then pointed down at the bucket. 'But what's that?'

'I'm taking a sample of the soil from Signor De Cal's property there,' Brunetti said, indicating with the spade the place where they had been when Palazzi first saw them.

'What for?' Palazzi asked with real curiosity.

'To examine,' Brunetti said.

'Because of Giorgio?' Palazzi asked.

'You knew him?' Brunetti asked.

'Oh, we all knew him,' Palazzi said with a bittersweet smile. 'Poor guy. I've known him for what, six years?' Palazzi shook his head, as if surprised to discover how long he had known the dead man.

'So you knew him before his daughter was born?' Brunetti asked.

'The poor devil,' Palazzi said. 'No one deserved that.'

'Deserved what, Signor Palazzi?' Brunetti asked and set the bucket on the ground, the better to convey the idea that he was there for a long conversation. Foa moved his feet apart and relaxed.

'The baby. That she should be born like that. I've got two kids, and thank God they're normal.'

'Did you ever see Signor Tassini's daughter?'

'No, but he told me about her. He told us all about her.'

'Did he tell you why he thought she was that way?' Brunetti asked.

'Oh, Lord, he told us all a hundred times, told us until none of us would listen to him any more.' Palazzi thought about this and then said, 'I'm sorry now we didn't listen to him, now that he's gone. It probably wouldn't have cost us that much.' But then he thought better of it and said, 'But it was awful. Really. He'd start and he'd go on for an hour, or at least until you had to tell him to stop or you just walked away. He'd come in early sometimes, I think, just to talk to us about it, or stay after his shift was over in the morning.' Palazzi weighed it all up and said, 'I guess we stopped listening to him, or he realized we wouldn't listen to him. Anyway, he didn't have so much to say lately.'

'Was he crazy?' Brunetti surprised himself by asking.

Palazzi's mouth fell open at this affront to the dead. 'No. He wasn't crazy. He was just . . . well . . . he was strange. I mean, he could talk about things, just like one of us, but as soon as some subjects came up, he was gone.'

'Did he ever threaten his employer, Signor De Cal? Or Signor Fasano?'

Palazzi laughed at the idea. 'Giorgio threaten somebody? You're the crazy one if you can ask that.'

'Did they ever threaten him?' Brunetti asked quickly.

This question really did astonish Palazzi. 'Why would they do that? They could have fired him. Just told him to leave. He was working *in nero*, so there was nothing he could have done. He'd have had to leave.'

'Are many of you working *in nero*?' Brunetti asked and regretted the words as soon as they were out of his mouth.

There was a long pause, and then Palazzi said, in a very formal, controlled voice, 'I wouldn't know about that, Commissario.' His tone told Brunetti how little Palazzi would know from now on. Rather than insist, Brunetti thanked him, shook his hand, waited for Foa to do the same, then bent and picked up the pink bucket. He abandoned the idea of going into the factory buildings to try to find the spots that would correspond to the other sets of coordinates.

Palazzi turned and started to walk across the field towards Fasano's factory, and it was then that Brunetti noticed the sun-faded letters painted above the back of the building. 'Vetreria Regini,' he made out.

'Signor Palazzi,' Brunetti called after the retreating man.

Palazzi stopped and turned around.

'What's that?' Brunetti asked, pointing at the letters.

Palazzi followed Brunetti's gesture. 'It's the name of the factory, Vetreria Regini,' Palazzi called back, saying it slowly, as though he doubted Brunetti would be able to read it without help.

He prepared to move off again, but Brunetti called after him, 'I thought it was Fasano's. In his family.'

'It is,' Palazzi said. 'His mother's family.' Palazzi turned and walked away.

198

22

Brunetti resisted the temptation to remain on Murano and return to Nanni's for fresh fish and polenta. Instead, he told Foa to take them back to the Questura, and when they got there, he asked the pilot to take the bucket to Bocchese and ask him to find out what was in the mud and water.

Because Paola and the kids were at lunch with her parents that day, Brunetti ate at a restaurant in Castello, a meal he paid no attention to and forgot as soon as he left. After he had eaten, he walked down to San Pietro in Castello and went inside the church to have a look at the funeral stele with its carved Qur'anic verses. Continuing debate as to whether he was looking at evidence of cultural theft or multiculturalism in no way diminished his appreciation of the carving's beauty.

Slowly he made his way back to the Questura. Vianello came up a little before six, noticed the volumes of the *Gazzetta* on Brunetti's desk and asked what they were for. Brunetti explained, then asked the Inspector what he thought had gone on before the laws were passed.

'They did whatever they pleased,' Vianello said with predictable indignation, then surprised Brunetti by adding, 'but I doubt they did much harm on Murano.'

Brunetti pointed to the chair in front of his desk and asked, 'Why?'

Vianello sat. 'Well, it's a relative term,' he said, "harm.' When you compare it to Marghera, that is. I know that doesn't change what happened on Murano. But Marghera's the real killer.'

'You really hate it, don't you?' Brunetti asked.

Vianello's face was deadly serious. 'Of course I do: any thinking person would. And Tassini said he hated Murano. But he never acted like he hated it.'

Brunetti failed to follow him. 'I don't understand.'

'If he had really believed it – that working for De Cal had caused what happened to his daughter – he would have done something to harm him. But all he did was talk to the men who worked with him at the *fornace*. And tell them that De Cal was to blame for everything.'

'Which means?' Brunetti asked.

'Which means it was just his guilt talking,' Vianello said.

This had always been Brunetti's opinion, so he let it pass unquestioned. 'But why do you hate Marghera so much?' he asked.

'Because I have children,' Vianello answered.

'So do I,' Brunetti countered.

'When you get home,' Vianello said, his voice suddenly moderate, 'ask your wife if she got the supplement to today's *Gazzettino*.'

'What supplement?'

Vianello got to his feet and moved over to the door. 'Just ask her,' he said. Standing at the door, he went on, 'I spoke to a few of De Cal's workers. They say business is bad, and everyone I spoke to heard he was selling, but everyone had heard he was asking a different price, though all of them were well above a million.'

200

'Anything else?' Brunetti asked.

'Tassini had been Fasano's *uomo di notte* only a month or two.'

'Before that?'

'He was already working as De Cal's *uomo di notte*; before that he worked in the *molatura*.'

'Is that a step up or a step down?' idle curiosity prompted Brunetti to ask. 'He had a wife and two kids to support.'

Vianello shrugged. 'I don't know. The guy who used to work for Fasano retired, and Tassini asked if he could have the job. At least that's what two of them told me. They said he liked working nights because it meant he could read, but they made it sound like he wanted to grow a second head.' Vianello laughed at this, and so did Brunetti, and the tension between them evaporated.

After the Inspector left, Brunetti used his curiosity about the *Gazzettino* supplement as an excuse to leave work early, which brought him home an hour before his usual time.

He went down to Paola's study and found her at her desk with what looked like a manuscript in front of her. He kissed her proffered cheek, then said, 'Vianello told me to ask if you read the supplement that came with the *Gazzettino* today.'

Her confusion was momentary, but then she set the manuscript to one side and bent to replace it with a disorganized pile of papers and magazines from the floor. 'He would ask about it, wouldn't he?' she asked with a smile, beginning to shuffle through the papers.

'What is it?'

She continued to hunt through the pile until she pulled something out and held it up in triumph. '*Porto Marghera*,' she read aloud, '*Situazione e Prospettive*.' She held it out so he could read the title on the cover. 'Do you think it's coincidental that this was given out with the newspaper at the same time as the trial is taking place?'

'But the trial has been going on for ever,' Brunetti objected. The trial against the petrochemical complex for its pollution of the land, the air, and the *laguna* had been dragging on for years: everyone in the Veneto knew that, just as they knew it would drag on for many more, or at least until the statute of limitations ran out and its spirit was subsumed into that heaven where expired cases went.

'Then let me read you one thing, and you tell me if you think it's coincidental,' she said, flipping the supplement over and running her eyes down the back cover. 'At the end, the writers express their thanks to those who have helped in the preparation of this supplement – a document that is meant to inform the people of the Veneto of any environmental danger resulting from the existence of the industrial plant in their back yard.' She glanced at Brunetti to see that she had his full attention and then continued. 'And just who is it that they thank for this cooperation?' she asked, running her finger, he assumed quite unnecessarily, down the last page. 'The authorities of the industrial zone.'

When Brunetti remained silent, she tossed the supplement on to her desk and said, 'Come on, Guido, you have to tell me that's wonderful. That's genius. They prepare a document about this percolating industrial complex that's three kilometres from us, probably filled with enough toxins and poisons to eliminate all of the north-east, and who do they ask for information about how dangerous those substances might be if not the very authorities who run the complex?' She laughed out loud, but Brunetti did not join her.

Like the presenter of a television quiz show, she paused and gave him a mock-serious look, as if hoping to provoke a response by a display of eager curiosity. When he remained silent, she said, 'Or think of it this way: the next time Patta wants some crime statistics, he should ask the boss of the local Mafia, or the Chinese Mafia, to prepare them for him.'

She raised the supplement above her head and said, 'We're all crazy, Guido.'

Brunetti sat on the sofa, silent but attentive. 'Let me read one more thing, just one,' she said, opening the booklet. She flipped forward a few pages, then back. 'Ah, here it is,' she said. 'Just listen to this: "How to behave in case of an emergency."' She pushed up her glasses, pulled the supplement a bit closer, and continued to read aloud. '"Shut yourself in your house, close the windows, turn off the gas, don't use the phone, listen to the radio, don't go outside for any reason."' She turned to him and added, 'The only thing they don't do is tell us not to breathe.' She let the supplement drop and said, 'We live less than three kilometres from that, Guido.'

'You've known about this for years,' Brunetti said, letting himself sink deeper into the sofa.

'Yes, I've known about it,' she agreed. 'But I didn't have this,' she said, picking up the booklet again and opening it to the last page. 'I didn't have the information that thirty-six million tons of "material" flow through there every year. I've no idea how much thirty-six million tons is, and God knows they don't tell us what it's thirty-six million tons *of*, but I suspect it would take considerably less than that, in the case of fire, to . . .' Her voice drifted off.

'What makes you think something like that will happen?' he asked.

'Because I spent an hour and a half today trying to give the new expiry date of my credit card to the phone company,' she shot back.

'The connection?' he inquired with Olympian calm.

'They sent me a letter, telling me the card had expired and asking me to dial their free number. When I did, I got the usual menu of cheerful suggestions: press one for this and two for that and three if you want to sign up for new services. And then the line died. Six times.'

'Why did you try six times?'

'What other choice is there? Even if I want to tell them to cancel the service, I still have to speak to them and tell them to do so and send the final bill to the bank.'

'And when is it that you are going to explain the connection with Marghera?' he asked, aware suddenly of how tired he was and how much he longed not to be involved in this conversation.

She removed her glasses, the better to see him or the better to fix him with her basilisk eye. 'Because the same people work in both places, Guido. The same people set up the programs and work on the safety systems. At the end of all of this, I was told, by the human being I finally managed to talk to, that I had to send the expiry date of the card to a fax number because their system did not allow her to take the information over the phone.'

Brunetti rested his head against the back of the sofa and closed his eyes. 'I still don't get the connection,' he said.

'Because the person who failed to put the fax number on the letter they sent me could just as easily be the man whose job it is to turn a handle or a knob at one of the factories in Marghera and who, instead of turning it like this,' she said and waited for him to open his eyes. When he did, he saw her grab a giant, invisible wheel and turn it to the right. 'Turns it like this,' she continued, turning her hands to the left. 'And there goes Marghera, and there goes Venice, and there go all of us.'

'Oh come on,' he said, tired and irritated by her histrionics, 'you're being a catastrophist.'

'Just like Vianello?' she asked.

Brunetti no longer remembered how he had been dragged into this, but he no longer cared what he said. 'In his wilder moments, yes. You are.'

A tense silence had replaced the eager humour of her first remarks. Brunetti leaned down and fished up that week's

Espresso. He flipped it open and found himself looking at the movie reviews. Doggedly he concentrated on reviews of films he would never, even in his wildest moments, think of seeing. Having finished reading these, he fanned through the pages and came to the lead story: the Marghera trial. He shut the magazine and let it drop to the floor.

'All right,' he said. 'All right.' He let some time pass and said, 'I've had a long day, Paola. And I don't want to spend what little is left of it arguing with you.'

His eyes closed, he heard her rather than saw her come close, and then he felt her weight on the sofa beside him. 'I'll go make dinner,' she said. Her weight shifted, and then he felt her lips on his forehead.

An hour later, as they sat down to dinner, Brunetti watched his children as the family ate and drank, and he listened to them complain about their teachers and the pressure of homework that seemed never to ease.

'If you want to go to the university,' he said, 'then homework's the price you have to pay.'

'And if I don't go,' Chiara asked, 'then what?' Brunetti failed to detect defiance in her words; he noticed that Paola had tuned into the question.

'Then I suppose you try to find a job,' Brunetti answered in a voice he attempted to make sound factual rather than critical. The choice seemed obvious enough to him.

'But everyone's always saying that there aren't any jobs,' Chiara complained.

'And that's what's always in the papers,' Raffi added, his fork poised over his swordfish steak. 'Look at Kati and Fulvio,' he said, naming the older brother and sister of his best friend. 'Both of them are *dottori*, and neither one of them has a job.'

'That's not true,' Chiara said. 'Kati's working in a museum.'

'Kati is selling catalogues at the Correr, you mean,' Raffi

said. 'That's not a job, not after six years at the university. She'd make more money if she sold shoes at Prada.' Brunetti wondered if Raffi considered that a better job.

'Prada's not the smartest place in the world to work if you want to get a job as an art historian,' Chiara said.

'Neither is the bargain basement at the Correr Museum,' her brother shot back.

Brunetti, who had seen the last exhibition there and paid more than forty Euros for the catalogue, hardly saw the museum shop as a bargain basement, but he kept this thought to himself and, instead, asked, 'What about Fulvio?'

Raffi looked down at his fish, and Chiara reached out to take some more spinach, though her knife and fork had been neatly lined up on her plate before. Neither answered, and the atmosphere filled with a palpable awkwardness. Brunetti pretended he had noticed nothing and said, 'Well, he's sure to find something. He's a bright boy.' Then, to Paola, he said, 'Would you pass me the spinach? If Chiara decides to leave any, that is.'

As she passed the dish to him, Paola gave every indication she had registered the response to Fulvio's name by ignoring it and saying, 'It's the same with my students. They write their theses, get their degrees, begin to call themselves *dottore*, and then think they're lucky if they can find a job as a substitute teacher in some place like Burano or Dolo.'

'Plumbing,' Brunetti interrupted, holding up a hand to gather their attention. 'That's what I tell my children to study: plumbing. There's always work to be had. Lots of interesting company and plenty of work. Nothing good can come of reading all those books, sitting in libraries, talking about ideas: it's bad for the brain. No, give me a real man's job: fresh air, good pay, honest hard work.'

'Oh, *Papà*,' Chiara said, as usual, the first to get it, 'you are so silly sometimes.' Brunetti feigned not to understand her and tried to convince her that she should stop studying mathematics and learn to weld. Dessert interrupted his performance, and by then the ghost of whatever Fulvio was up to had been driven from the feast.

It was not until they were in bed, Brunetti exhausted by his day, that he asked, 'What about Fulvio?'

The light was already out, so he felt rather than saw her shrug. 'My guess is drugs,' Paola said.

'Using them?'

'Could be,' she answered, not at all persuaded.

'Then selling them,' he said and turned on to his right side to face her dim outline.

'More likely.'

'Poor boy,' Brunetti said, adding, 'poor everyone.' He shifted on to his back and stared up at the ceiling. 'Do you have any idea if . . .' he began, wondering at the extent of the boy's sales and whether it was a matter he should interest himself in professionally. And who would Fulvio's customers be? The very question released the worm that was forever poised and ready to begin crawling towards every parent's heart.

'If what you want to know is whether Raffi is interested, I think we can be fairly sure he isn't. He doesn't use drugs.'

The policeman in Brunetti wanted to know why Paola could say this: what was her source, and how reliable? Had she questioned Raffi himself, or had he volunteered the information, or was her witness some other person with knowledge of the case or the suspects? He stared at the ceiling, and as he watched, one of the lights shining in from the other side of the *calle* was extinguished, leaving him in comforting darkness. How foolish, how rash to believe a mother's word as to the innocence of her only son.

He stared at the ceiling, afraid to question her. The window was ajar, and through it came the bells of San Marco, telling them that it was midnight, time to be asleep. Over it, he heard Paola say, 'It's all right, Guido. Don't worry about Raffi.' He closed his eyes in momentary relief, and when he opened them again, it was morning.

23

On his way to the Questura the following morning, Brunetti began to consider how best to raise the subject of Fasano with Signorina Elettra. He did not understand the reason for her apparent regard for the man: she usually had enough sense to hold politicians in utter contempt, so why had she chosen to stand up in defence of this one? Given the peculiarities of Signorina Elettra's prejudices, it might be nothing more than the fact that Fasano had not yet made an official declaration of his desire to enter into politics, and until such time she might be willing to continue to treat him as human.

Brunetti had been seeing Fasano's photo and reading his name in the *Gazzettino* for years. He was tall, athletic, photogenic, was said to be a good speaker and a well-regarded employer. Brunetti had met him and his wife at a dinner some years before and had a vague memory of him as being affable and of her as an attractive blonde, but he could summon up little more than that. He might have talked with her about a play they had both seen at the Goldoni, or perhaps it had been a film: he could not retrieve the memory.

He went into Ballarin and asked for a coffee and a brioche, still trying to recall anything else about the man that the waves of gossip had washed up into his memory over the years. Brunetti had the brioche halfway to his mouth when it occurred to him that the best way to gather information would be to go and talk to the man. He stood for a few seconds, brioche poised in the air, his head tilted to one side. A man eased by him to get to the bar and Brunetti caught a glimpse of himself in the mirror. Quickly he finished the brioche and the coffee, paid, and started back toward Fondamenta Nuove and the 42.

The route from the Sacca Serenella ACTV *embarcadero* was by now familiar to Brunetti. At the end of the cement walkway, instead of turning to the right and to De Cal's factory, he went to the left and approached the other building, which he had previously ignored. Built of brick, the factory had a high peaked roof with a double row of skylights. As with most of the *fornaci*, the entrance was through a set of sliding metal doors.

As he approached, he recognized Palazzi standing in front of the building, smoking. 'Good morning,' Brunetti said to the workman and raised a hand in greeting. 'Looks like it'll be a nice day.'

Palazzi returned an amiable enough smile, dropped his cigarette and stepped on it, grinding it into the earth with his toe. 'Habit,' he said when he saw Brunetti watching this. 'I used to work in a chemical plant, and we had to be careful with cigarettes.

'I'm surprised they let you smoke there at all,' Brunetti said.

'They didn't,' Palazzi said and smiled again. At the sign of Brunetti's answering grin, he asked, tilting his head backwards, towards the field that ran from the factories down to the water, 'You find anything out there?'

'No results yet,' Brunetti said.

'You expecting to find anything?'

Brunetti shrugged. 'The guy in the lab'll tell me.'

'What're you looking for?'

'No idea,' Brunetti admitted.

'Just curious?' Palazzi asked, taking out his cigarettes. He shook some forward in the packet and held them out towards Brunetti, who shook his head.

When Brunetti said nothing, Palazzi repeated, 'Just curious?'

'Always curious.'

'Because of Tassini?'

'Partly, yes.'

'What's the other part?'

'Because people don't like it that I come out here.'

'And ask questions?'

Brunetti nodded.

Palazzi lit his cigarette and pulled deeply on it, leaned his head back and let out a long series of perfect smoke rings that slowly expanded to the size of haloes before evaporating in the soft morning air. 'Tassini asked a lot of questions, too,' Palazzi said.

'About what?' The sun had grown warmer since Brunetti got off the boat. He unbuttoned his jacket.

'About everything,' Palazzi said.

'Such as?'

'Such as who kept the records of what sort of chemicals came in and went out and whether any of us knew anyone in the other factories who had kids with . . . kids with problems.'

'Like his daughter?' Brunetti asked.

'I suppose so.'

'And?'

Palazzi tossed his half-smoked cigarette beside the shreds of the other one and ground it out, too, then rubbed at the space with his toe until all sign of the cigarettes had been obliterated. 'Tassini didn't work with us until a couple of

211

months ago. He was over at De Cal's for years, so we all knew him. Then, when the night man here retired, well, I suppose the boss thought it made sense to get him to work here, too. Not all that much for *l'uomo di notte* to do, after all.' Palazzi's voice softened. 'We knew about his daughter by then. From the guys at De Cal's. But like I told you yesterday, no one much wanted to listen to him or talk to him or get involved in his ideas.' Brunetti nodded to make it clear that he understood their reluctance, hoping to make Palazzi feel less uncomfortable about speaking of Tassini like this so soon after his death.

After a reflective, or respectful, pause, Palazzi added, 'And we all sort of felt sorry for him.' In response to Brunetti's inquisitive glance, he added, 'Because he was so clumsy: he was pretty much useless around the *fornace*. But all *l'uomo di notte* has to do is toss things in and stir them around, then keep an eye on the *miscela* and stir it whenever it's necessary.'

'Did he ask questions about anything else?' Brunetti asked.

Palazzi thought about this. He stuffed his hands into his pockets and studied the toes of his shoes. Finally he looked at Brunetti and said, 'About a month ago, he asked me about the plumber.'

'What about him?'

'Who he was – the one for the factory – and when was the last time he did any work here.'

'Did you know?' When Palazzi nodded, Brunetti asked, 'What did you tell him?'

'I told him I thought it was Adil-San – they're over by the Misericordia. It's their boat that comes out for pick-ups or when anything goes wrong: that's what I told him.'

'And when were they last out here?' Brunetti asked, though he had no idea why he was pursuing this.

'About two months ago, I think, around the time he started working here. The grinding shop was closed for a day while they worked on one of the sedimentation tanks.'

212

'Did Tassini know about that?'

'No: he was working nights, and they were finished and gone by the middle of the afternoon.'

'I see,' Brunetti said, though he didn't.

Palazzi looked at his watch. Seeing him shift his weight prior to moving on, Brunetti asked, 'Your boss around?'

'I saw him come in a while ago. He's probably in his office. Would you like me to find out?'

'No, thanks,' Brunetti said easily. 'If you'll tell me where it is, I'll find him. It's nothing important, just some bureaucratic questions about Tassini and how long he worked here.'

Palazzi gave Brunetti a long look and said, 'Odd that the police should send a commissario all the way out here to ask bureaucratic questions, isn't it?' He smiled and Brunetti wondered which of them had been conducting the interrogation.

He thanked Palazzi again, and the man turned and went back inside the factory. Brunetti followed him through the sliding doors and into the now-familiar gloom of the work space. The open rectangles of the furnaces glared at him from the far end of the room, light-rimmed figures moving around in front of them. He stood and watched them for a few minutes, saw them bend carefully forward and slide the canes into the glaring light of the furnaces in the familiar rhythm. Something about the way they moved caught at his memory, but all he saw were men twirling the rods and inserting them into the fire, continuing to rotate them until they pulled them out, never pausing in the constant rotation: precisely what he had seen often over the last few days. He turned away.

Four doors stood along the right wall. Fasano's name was on the first. Just as he was about to knock, Brunetti realized what he had just seen in the glare of the furnaces. The *maestri* used their right hands to hold the end of the long rods, levering them from the position of greater strength. The glove and protective sleeves were worn on the left, the side closest

213

to the fire. But Tassini had held his glass, and the phone, with his left hand, so he should have been wearing the sleeve and glove on the right.

Brunetti knocked, then entered at a shout. Fasano stood by the single window, bent close to something he held towards the light. He was in shirtsleeves and waistcoat, his attention devoted entirely to the object in his hands.

'Signor Fasano?' Brunetti asked, though he recognized him from his photos and from their one meeting.

'Yes,' Fasano answered, glancing across. 'Ah,' he said when he saw Brunetti, 'you're the policeman who's been coming out here, aren't you?'

'Yes. Guido Brunetti,' he said, choosing to make no reference to the long-ago dinner party.

'I remember,' Fasano said. 'At the Guzzinis', about five years ago.'

'You have a good memory,' Brunetti said, which could mean either that he did or he did not recall the meeting.

Fasano smiled and walked over to his desk. He set the object on it – a tall filigree vase that tapered to a lily-like opening at the top – then came across and offered his hand to Brunetti.

'How may I help you?' Fasano asked.

'I'd like to ask you about Giorgio Tassini, if I might,' Brunetti said.

'That poor devil who died over there,' he said, part question, part statement, pointing with his chin in the direction of De Cal's factory. 'It's the first time anyone's been killed out here for as long as I can remember.'

'"Out here," meaning Murano, Signore?'

'Yes. De Cal's never even had a serious accident before this,' Fasano said. Then he added, with something between relief and pride, 'Nor have we.'

'Tassini hadn't been working for you very long, had he?' Brunetti asked, 'before this happened?'

Fasano gave him a nervous smile and then said, 'I don't mean to be offensive, Commissario, but I'm not sure I understand why you're asking me these questions.' He paused, then added, 'Instead of De Cal, that is.'

'I'm trying to get an idea of what Tassini did, Signore. Or, in fact, anything about him that might help me understand what might have happened. I've already spoken to Signor De Cal, and since Tassini also worked for you . . .' Brunetti let the sentence drift away.

Fasano looked away. Unconsciously mimicking Palazzi's uncertainty, he put his hands in his pockets and studied the floor for some time, then looked at Brunetti squarely and said, 'He was working *in nero*, Commissario.' He took his hands out of his pockets and raised them in a consciously theatrical gesture. 'You're going to find out sooner or later, so I might as well tell you.'

'It's nothing that concerns me, Signor Fasano,' Brunetti said with easy grace. 'I'm not interested in how he was paid, only in what may have caused his death; nothing else.'

Fasano studied Brunetti's face, obviously weighing how much he could trust this man. Finally he said, 'My guess is that he was making glass.' When Brunetti did not respond, he clarified this by adding, 'Objects, that is. Glasses, vases.'

'Did he know how to?' Brunetti asked.

'He'd been working next door for years, so I'm sure he'd have picked up the basic skills, yes.'

'Did you ever see him working the glass? There or here?'

Fasano shook his head. 'No, I saw almost nothing of him here, after I hired him,' he said, sounding nervous when he used the word 'hired'.

'He worked nights,' Fasano went on quickly, 'and I'm here only during the day. But it's what most of the men who work the night shift do. They make a piece or two during their shift, let it cool, then take it with them in the morning when they go home. It's pretty much accepted, at least here, by me.'

215

'Why?'

Fasano smiled and said, 'So long as they don't put the name of the *vetreria* on it or try to sell it as the work of one of the *maestri*, it's harmless enough. I suppose, over the years, we've all come to turn a blind eye to it, and it's now a sort of thirteenth pay packet for them, certainly for those working the way he was.' He thought about this for a while, then added, 'And from what the men have told me, it sounded like Tassini had a hard time of it, what with his daughter and all, so why not let him do it?' When Brunetti did not comment, Fasano said, 'Besides, without the help of a *servente*, there really wasn't much he could make except the most simple sort of plate or vase.'

'Did the other workers know what he was doing?'

Fasano considered the question, then said, 'My guess is that they would have known. The workers always know everything that's going on.'

'You sound very untroubled by it.'

'I told you,' Fasano said, 'he deserved a bit of charity.'

'I see,' Brunetti said, then asked, 'Did he ever talk to you about his theory that his daughter's problems were the result of the working conditions here?'

'I told you, Commissario: I spoke to him only when I hired him, and he was here just two months.'

With an easy smile, Brunetti said, 'I'm sorry; I didn't express myself clearly. I know he was here only a short time. I suppose what I should have asked was whether you ever heard talk from anyone that he was saying such things?' When Fasano did not respond, Brunetti gave a complicit smile and said, 'The workers always know what's going on.'

Fasano's hands went back into his pockets and he returned his attention to the tips of his shoes. His head still lowered, he finally said, 'I don't like to say these things about him.'

'There's nothing you can say that can do him any harm, Signore,' Brunetti said.

Fasano looked up at that. 'Well, then, yes, I did hear talk. That he believed he had breathed in chemicals and minerals while he was working for De Cal and that that was the cause of his daughter's . . . of her problems.'

'Do you think that's possible?'

'You ask me a difficult question, Commissario,' Fasano said, trying to smile. 'I've looked at the statistics for the workers out here, and I've never seen anything that would suggest . . . well, that would suggest that what Tassini believed is possible.' He saw Brunetti's reaction and added, 'I'm not a scientist and I'm not a doctor, I know, but this is something that concerns me.'

'The health of the workers?' Brunetti asked.

'Yes. Of course,' Fasano said with sudden heat, adding, 'and mine.' He smiled to suggest he was joking. 'But it's not working on Murano that puts them in danger, Commissario: it's working so near to Marghera. You read the papers; you know what's going on at the trial.' Then, with a rueful half-smile, he amended that to, 'Or not going on.' He took a step to his left and raised a hand in the direction of what Brunetti thought was north-west. 'The danger's over there,' he said; then, as if unwilling to leave Brunetti in any doubt, specified, 'Marghera.'

He saw that he had Brunetti's attention and went on, 'That's where the pollution comes from; that's what puts my workers at risk.' His voice had grown stronger. 'Those are the people who dump and pour and pollute, toss anything they want into the *laguna* or ship it south to be spread on fields. Not here, believe me.'

Fasano stopped, as if he had realized how heated his voice had become. He tried to laugh off his enthusiasm but failed. 'I'm sorry if I get excited about this,' he said. 'But I've got kids. And to know what they're pumping into the atmosphere and the water, every day, well, it makes me . . . I suppose it makes me a little crazy.'

'And there's nothing coming from here?' Brunetti asked.

Fasano answered with a shrug that dismissed the very possibility. 'There was never much of a problem with pollution here. But now they've got us so closely watched and measured and weighed, well, there's no chance we could get away with polluting anything.' After a moment, he added, 'For the sake of my children, I'd like to be able to say the same about Marghera, but I can't.'

Brunetti had built up, over the years, the habit of suspicion, especially when people spoke of their concern for the good of others, but he had to confess, if only to himself, that Fasano sounded very much like Vianello on the subject of pollution. And because of the trust Brunetti had come to invest in the Inspector, Fasano sounded sincere.

'Could pollution from Marghera have been the cause of Tassini's daughter's problems?' Brunetti asked.

Fasano shrugged again, then said, almost reluctantly, 'No, I don't think so. Much as I believe Marghera is slowly poisoning us all, I don't think it's responsible for what happened to the little girl.' Brunetti asked for no explanation, but Fasano went on to supply one. 'I've heard about what happened when she was born.'

When it was obvious that Fasano would not elaborate, Brunetti asked, 'Then why did he blame De Cal?'

Fasano started to answer, stopped himself and studied Brunetti's face for a moment, as if asking himself how far he could go with a person he did not know very well. Finally he asked, 'He had to blame someone, didn't he?'

Fasano turned aside and walked back to his desk, where he bent over the vase he had placed there. It stood about fifty centimetres tall, its lines perfectly simple and clean. 'It's beautiful,' Brunetti said spontaneously.

Fasano turned with a smile that softened his entire face. 'Thank you, Commissario. Every once in a while, I like to see if I can still make something that isn't all squashed to one side or that has one handle that's bigger than the other.'

'I didn't realize you actually worked the glass,' Brunetti said, making no attempt to disguise his admiration.

'I spent my childhood here,' Fasano said, not without pride. 'My father wanted me to go to university, the first person in our family, so I did, but I always spent my summers here, at the *fornace*.' He picked up the vase and turned it around twice, studying the surface. Brunetti noticed that it had the faintest cast of amethyst, so light as to be almost invisible in bright light.

Still turning the vase and keeping his eyes on it, Fasano said finally, as though he had been thinking about it since Brunetti had first posed the question, 'He had to believe himself. Everyone here knows what happened when the little girl was born. I think that's why everyone was usually so patient with him. He had to blame something, well, something other than himself, so he ended up blaming De Cal.' He set the vase down on his desk again. 'But he never did anyone any harm.'

Brunetti stopped himself from suggesting that Tassini had done his daughter more than enough harm and said only, 'Did Signor De Cal ever have any trouble with him?'

He watched Fasano consider how to answer this. Finally the man said, 'I've never heard that he did.'

'Do you know Signor De Cal?'

Fasano smiled and said, 'Our families have had factories side by side for more than a hundred years, Commissario.'

'Yes, of course,' answered a chastened Brunetti. 'Did he ever say anything about Tassini or about having trouble with him?'

'You've met Signor De Cal?' Fasano asked.

'Yes.'

'Then can you imagine the workman who would give him any real trouble?'

'No.'

'De Cal would probably have eaten him alive if Tassini had so much as suggested he was responsible for the little girl.' Fasano leaned back against his desk, bracing his hands on either side of him. 'That's another reason why Tassini had to keep telling other people, I think. He couldn't say anything to De Cal. He must have been afraid to.'

'It sounds as if you've given his accusations some thought, Signore,' Brunetti said.

Fasano shrugged. 'I suppose I have. After all, we work around these materials all the time, and the idea that they might be harmful to me, or to us, is one I don't like.'

'You don't sound like you believe they are, if I might say so,' Brunetti observed.

'No, I don't,' Fasano said. 'I've read the scientific papers and the reports, Commissario. The danger, I repeat, is over there.' Half turning, he pointed to the north-west.

'One of my inspectors believes it's killing us,' Brunetti said.

'He's right,' Fasano said forcefully. But he said no more, for which Brunetti was almost thankful.

Fasano pushed himself away from his desk, 'I'm afraid I have to go back to work,' he said.

Brunetti expected him to walk around and sit at the desk, but Fasano picked up the vase and went and stood by the door to his office. 'I want to grind off a few imperfections,' he said, making it clear that Brunetti was not invited to join him.

Brunetti thanked him for his time and left the factory, heading back towards the pier.

24

Brunetti took the 42 back to Fondamenta Nuove and then, because it was near, walked towards the Fondamenta della Misericordia. He stopped for a coffee and asked where Adil-San was, learning not only where to find them but that they were honest and busy and that the owner's son had recently married a girl from Denmark he had met at university, and it wasn't expected to last. No, not because of the girl, even if she was a foreigner, but because Roberto was a *donnaiolo*, and they never change, do they, they never stop chasing women? Nodding his head in acknowledgement or appreciation of this information, Brunetti left the bar and took the first right, following the canal until he saw the sign on the opposite side. Up and down a bridge and then back and into the plumbers' office, where he found a young woman sitting behind a computer.

She looked up and smiled when he came in, asking what she could do for him. Her mouth was perhaps too big, or her lipstick too dark, but she was lovely, and Brunetti found himself flattered by her attention. 'I'd like to speak to the manager, please,' he said.

'Is this about an estimate, sir?' she asked, her smile growing warmer and suggesting to Brunetti that perhaps her mouth was really just the right size.

'No. I'd like to ask him about a client,' he said taking his warrant card from his wallet.

She looked at it, at him, then back at the photo. 'I've never seen one of these before,' she said. 'It's just like on television, isn't it?'

'A bit, I suppose. But not as interesting,' Brunetti said.

She looked at the card again, then handed it back to him. 'I'll go and tell him, all right, Commissario?' she asked and got to her feet. Thicker in the waist than he had expected, she was still pleasant to watch as she crossed the room and pushed open a door without bothering to knock.

In a moment she was back at the door. 'Signor Repeta can see you now, Commissario,' she said.

When Brunetti entered, a man about his own age was just getting to his feet behind his desk. He came towards Brunetti. Like the girl in the outer office, he had a large mouth; her dark eyes, as well.

'Your daughter?' Brunetti asked, waving towards the door, which was now shut.

The man smiled. 'Is it that obvious?' he asked. Like her, his entire face softened when he smiled, and he had the same thickness of build.

'The mouth and eyes,' Brunetti said.

'"Signor Repeta," she always calls me when we're working,' the man said with a smile. He wore a pair of black woollen trousers and a pink shirt with sleeves rolled back to the elbows, exposing the thick forearms of a worker. He motioned Brunetti to a chair, retreated behind his desk and asked, 'What can I do for you, Commissario?'

'I'd like to know what sort of work you do for the Vetreria Regini,' Brunetti said.

It was obvious that the question puzzled Repeta. After a

222

moment, he answered, 'What I do for all of the *vetrerie* I have a contract with,' he said.

'Which is?'

'Oh, of course,' Repeta said. 'There's no way you'd know that, is there? Sorry.' He brushed his right hand through his greying hair, leaving part of it standing up in spikes. 'We service their water systems and dispose of the waste from the grinding room.'

Brunetti gave a layman's smile and held up his palms, then asked, 'What does that mean to someone like me, Signore?'

Like many men wrapped up in their work, Repeta struggled to find the words with which to make things clear. 'I suppose all the service part means is that we make sure they can turn the water in the factory on and off and adjust the rate of flow in the grinding shop.'

'Doesn't sound very complicated,' Brunetti said, but he said it gently, as though both of them took the same delight in its simplicity.

'No,' Repeta admitted with a smile, 'it's not complicated, not at all. But the tanks are.'

'Why?'

'We've got to see that the water flows from one to the next slowly enough to allow for sedimentation.' He saw the look on Brunetti's face and picked up a letter lying on his desk. He glanced at it, flipped it over, and picked up a pencil. 'Here, look,' he said, and Brunetti moved his chair over next to the desk.

Quickly, with the ease of familiarity, Repeta drew a row of four equally sized rectangles. A line, presumably meant to indicate a pipe, led from a point near the top of one to the next, and then another led to the third; after the last one, it slanted down and disappeared off the bottom of the drawing.

Pointing to the first rectangle, Repeta said, 'Look, the water from the *molatura* flows out of the grinding shop and into the first tank, carrying away everything that's been ground off.

223

The heavy particles begin to sink to the bottom, while the water flows to the next one, where more of it drops down and is deposited. And so on and so on,' he said, tapping the point of the pencil against the third and fourth rectangles.

'At the end of it, all of the particles have settled to the bottom of the tanks, and the water that flows out of the last one,' he said, trailing the pencil along the diagonal line that flowed off the page, 'goes into the drain.'

'Clean water?' Brunetti asked.

'Clean enough.'

Brunetti studied the drawing for a moment and then asked, 'What happens to the sediment in the tanks?'

'That's the second part of what we do,' Repeta said, pushing the paper away from him and returning his attention to Brunetti. 'They call us when they've drained the tanks and we go out and take the sediment away.'

'And?'

'And deliver it – well, it's really a kind of heavy sludge – we deliver it to the company that disposes of it.'

'How?'

'They fuse it, melt the glass particles and the minerals get fused into the glass.'

'What minerals are there?' Brunetti asked, interested now.

'As many as are used in making glass,' answered Repeta. 'Cadmium, cobalt, manganese, arsenic, potassium.'

'How do they get into the water?'

'Because they're in the glass. When it's ground, the particles are carried away by the water and out into the tanks.' He put the paper back in front of him and pointed with the pencil to the first rectangle, then tapped it all along the row. 'The water also keeps the powder from getting into the lungs of the men doing the grinding.'

'How many *vetrerie* do you do this for?'

'More than thirty, I'd say, but I'd have to look at my client list.'

'And how often do you make pick-ups?'

'That depends on how much work they have. Maybe every three months, maybe six. We go out whenever they call us. It depends.'

'Does that mean the same day?' Brunetti asked, thinking of a plugged sink in the kitchen, running over.

'No,' Repeta said and laughed. 'They usually call us and make an appointment a week before they need us. That also gives us the chance to schedule five or six pick-ups in one day.' Repeta glanced across to see that Brunetti was following and added, 'Saves us money, doing it that way. The charge for the trip is standard, no matter how much we pick up. I mean, we charge according to the weight of what we take away, but the charge for the pick-up is always the same, so it's best for them to have us come only when their tanks are full.'

'One of the men I spoke to said he saw one of your boats out at the Vetreria Regini two months ago,' Brunetti said. 'Was it a pick-up?'

Repeta shook his head at that. 'I don't know,' he said, shoving his chair back and moving around the desk. 'Let me ask Floridana.' He was gone before Brunetti could say anything.

While he waited for Repeta, Brunetti looked around the office: travel posters, no doubt from an agency; a window so dusty it allowed only minimal light and sound to filter in; and three metal filing cabinets. No computer and no phone, which surprised Brunetti.

Repeta came in, a sheet of paper in his hand. 'No,' he said as he approached Brunetti. 'It seems they needed someone to fix a leak.'

'What sort of leak?'

He passed the paper to Brunetti. 'One of the tanks. That's why they called us.' The words on the paper meant little to Brunetti, and he handed it back.

225

Repeta went back behind his desk. He closed his eyes, saying, 'Let me think about the way their tanks are.' His face became completely expressionless and remained that way for some time, and then he opened his eyes. 'Yes, I remember. The tanks are raised up on metal feet, about five centimetres from the ground, but they're flush against the wall at the back.' He looked at the receipt again. 'From this, I'd guess that a seam, probably at one of the angles, came loose or corroded.' He showed Brunetti the paper again, saying, 'See? It says they had to solder a leak in the back of the third tank. That's probably what it was.'

'Does your invoice say who did the work?' Brunetti asked.

'Yes. Biaggi. He's one of our best.' Brunetti, who had once paid a plumber one hundred and sixty Euros to replace a faucet, was unsure what that might mean.

'Would it be possible for you to ask him exactly what he did?' Brunetti asked, remembering Tassini's coordinates.

Repeta gave him a strange look but got to his feet again and went to the outer office. Brunetti returned to the study of the travel posters, aware of how little desire he had to spend time on a tropical beach.

After a few minutes, Repeta was back, saying, 'He's out in the shop. Be here in a minute.'

While they waited, Brunetti asked about the disposal of other substances from the *vetrerie*, asking if Repeta also disposed of the acids. Those, he learned, were handled by an even more specialized firm, one that transferred the liquid to tanker trucks for delivery to facilities in Marghera that saw to the disposal of toxic substances.

Before Brunetti could learn any more, he heard a voice from behind him.

'You wanted me, Luca?'

Say 'plumber', and this was the man who would appear on the inner eye. Not particularly tall, but thick from shoulder to hip – thick of nose as well; slightly balding, rough skinned,

226

with enormous hands and forearms, Biaggi stood at the door. He smiled at Repeta, as though amiability were his usual condition.

'Come in, Pietro,' Repeta said. 'This man wants to know what you did out at Fasano's place last time you went.'

Biaggi took a few steps into the room and nodded to Brunetti. He tilted his chin and studied the ceiling, as if searching there for a copy of the invoice. He pursed his lips in a surprisingly feminine gesture, brought his chin back down and said, 'The third tank had a leak, and his manager needed us to solder it. His boss was on vacation or something. Anyway, he couldn't be reached, so the manager called us. Good thing he did, too, because they could have had a real problem if they'd waited a couple more days.'

'Why is that?' Brunetti inquired.

'Water was already leaking all over the floor: grey stuff, so it was coming from the sediment, or at least from the new water coming into the tank that still had sediment in it.'

'What did you do?' Repeta asked.

'Usual stuff: turn off the water of the *molatura*. We sent the guys out for a coffee and told them to come back in an hour. No use having them standing around doing nothing or trying to help.'

'Who was with you?' Repeta asked.

'Dondini.'

'What did you have to do?' Brunetti interrupted to ask. Before Biaggi could begin to explain, Repeta told him to come and sit down, which he did, spreading himself into a chair and seeming even larger once he was seated.

'First thing I saw was that it was going to take a long time, more than an hour.' He looked at Brunetti, smiled, and said, 'Before you start thinking this is the way plumbers think, Signore, let me tell you it was true. Those tanks are too close to the ground, so you can't get under them, and they're fixed to the walls, so you can't get behind them to

227

have a look. Only way to work on them is to drain them and see what's going on.'

'Even with all the sludge in them?' Brunetti asked, pleased with himself for sounding in command of the subject.

Biaggi smiled. 'We had to drain it first. Luckily, it had only been a month or so since we were out there, so the sediment wasn't very high. Most of what was in it was water, so we turned it off in the grinding shop; then we bailed it into the next tank until we got down about forty centimetres. That's where the leak was.'

'In the soldering on the angles?' Repeta asked.

'No,' Biaggi answered. 'It looks like they used to drain the tank out of the back, straight through the wall. Or else it was used for something else before they put it there to filter the water from the *molatura*. I figure that's why they had to change the position of the pipes.' Biaggi dismissed the subject. 'None of my business, is it?' he asked Brunetti, who shook his head in agreement.

'I don't know who did the job, but it was a mess,' Biaggi continued. 'Someone had cut a round plate out of tin or something, then they soldered a kind of flange thing on to the back, so the circle could be swung back and forth over the opening of the pipe to open and close it. But they didn't know what they were doing when they put the pipe in: they didn't use enough solder, and so it had started to leak.'

'And what did you do?' Brunetti asked.

'I closed it off.'

'How?' Brunetti asked.

'I pried off the circle thing and covered over the hole in the pipe. I used plastic and a good adhesive, so it'll last as long as that tank will,' Biaggi said proudly.

'And the other tanks? Did they have the same problem?'

Biaggi shrugged. 'I got called to fix a leak, not to check their whole system.'

'Just where was this hole?' Brunetti asked.

228

Biaggi repeated his gesture in attempting to recall the tanks, then said, 'About forty centimetres down, maybe a little less.'

'What sort of liquid would there be at that depth, Signor Biaggi?' Brunetti asked.

'Well, if they're at full production, and a lot of water is coming in,' he began, then added for clarification, 'that would be if the water was running for three or more people in the *molatura* – in that case, with full flow, it would be water with a lot of sediment in it.'

'And if there were less work going on?' Brunetti asked.

Again, Biaggi made that very feminine pursing of his lips. 'There'd still be a fair amount of sediment in it.'

'Where did the old pipe go?' Brunetti asked.

Again, Biaggi played the scene back, then said, 'The angle was bad from where I had to stand, so I couldn't see into it, how far it went or where it went. Into the back wall. That's all I'm sure of. But it's sealed now. There's no chance it will leak again.'

'Could you say how long ago the original work was done?' Brunetti asked.

'You mean the soldering?'

'Yes.'

'No, not exactly. Ten years ago. Maybe more, but that's just a guess. No way to tell, really.'

Biaggi glanced at his wristwatch, leading Brunetti to say. 'Just one more question, Signore. Would it be possible for someone to find that pipe?'

The question confused the man and he asked, 'You mean the opening in the tank?'

'Yes.'

'But why would anyone want to do that?'

'Oh, I don't know,' Brunetti answered easily. 'But if they wanted to, could they find it there in the tank?'

Biaggi looked at his employer, who nodded. He looked at his watch again, rubbed his hands together, making a dry,

229

sandpapery noise, and finally said, 'If he knew it was there, I suppose he could find it with his hand, by hunting around. The water's off at both ends at night, so I guess if he opened the drain at the end and let the water run out, he could have a look, at least down to the level of the sediment. Then, when he wanted to fill it up again, all he'd have to do is close the drain again and go into the other room and turn the water on and wait until the tanks were full again. Easy.'

With a smile he attempted to make reassuring, Brunetti said, 'I'm sorry, but I've just thought of another last question, but I promise it really will be the last.'

Biaggi nodded, and Brunetti said, 'Did they give you any idea of how long the tank had been leaking?'

'A month or so, I'd say,' came Biaggi's quick response.

'You seem very sure of that,' Brunetti observed.

'I am. It looked like someone tried to fix it. That is, it looks like someone tried to solder the disc into place over the hole in the pipe, but there was no way that was going to work. When I asked about it, the manager said the guys had been complaining about the wet floor for a couple of weeks.' He gave Brunetti an interrogative smile, as if to ask if he'd answered enough questions, and Brunetti smiled in return, got to his feet, and held out his hand.

'You've been very helpful, Signor Biaggi. It's always nice to talk to a man who knows his job.'

When Biaggi, made faintly uncomfortable by praise, had left, Repeta asked, making no attempt to disguise the curiosity Brunetti's questions had provoked in him, 'Are you a man who knows your job, Commissario?'

'I'm beginning to think so,' Brunetti said, thanked him, and went back to the Questura.

25

Brunetti's mind turned to tactics. Patta was sure to reject the idea that a man like Fasano – already possessed of some political clout and on his way to acquiring more – could be involved in crime. Nor was he likely to authorize Brunetti to conduct a full investigation based on nothing more than bits and pieces of information and the patterns into which they might be made to fit. Evidence? Brunetti sniffed at the very word. He had nothing more than suspicions and events that could be interpreted in a particular way.

He dialled Bocchese's internal number. The technician answered with his name.

'You have time to look at that sample yet?' Brunetti asked.

'Sample?'

'That Foa brought you.'

'No. I forgot. Tomorrow?'

'Yes.'

Brunetti knew he should stop thinking about this until he had the results of Bocchese's analyses: before that, he could have no certain idea of what had gone on or what had gone

into the field behind the two factories. De Cal grew wild at
the thought that his son-in-law, the environmentalist, would
some day be involved with his factory and would sooner sell
it than let it pass to his daughter and thus to her husband.
Sell it instead to Gianluca Fasano, rising star in the polluted
firmament of local politics, his advance heralded by his deep
concern for the environmental degradation of his native city.
Some environmentalists were apparently more equal than
others to De Cal.

None of this would have merited a second glance, were it
not for Giorgio Tassini, a man whom the random forces of
life had driven into an erratic orbit. Searching for proof that
would free him of the guilt of having destroyed his daughter's
life, what had he stumbled upon?

Brunetti tried to recall his conversation with Tassini, unsettled by the realization that it had taken place only a few days
before. When Brunetti had asked him if De Cal knew about
the pollution, Tassini had replied that *both* of them knew what
was going on, leaving Brunetti to draw the obvious conclusion that he meant De Cal's daughter. But that was before
Foa had given Brunetti a detailed map of Murano, one that
provided latitude and longitude readings as well as the location of all buildings, and confirmed that the last coordinates
on Tassini's paper indicated a point within Fasano's factory.

His phone rang as he sat at his desk, staring at the map
and shifting and reshifting the pieces of information in his
mind. Distracted, he answered with his name.

'Guido?' asked a voice he recognized.

'Yes.'

Something in his tone provoked a long pause. 'It's me,
Guido. Paola. Your wife. Remember me?'

Brunetti grunted.

'Then food? You remember food, Guido, don't you?
Something called lunch?'

He looked at his watch, amazed to see that it was after

two. 'Oh, my God,' he said. 'I'm sorry. I forgot.'

'To come home or to eat?' she asked.

'Both.'

'Are you all right?' she asked with real concern.

'It's this thing with Tassini,' he said. 'I can't figure it out, or I can't find any proof of what I think is true.'

'You will,' she said, and then added, 'or else you won't. In either case, you will always remain the bright star of my life.'

He took this as it was meant. 'Thank you, my dear. I need to be told that once in a while.'

'Good.' There followed a long pause. 'Will . . .' she started to say.

Brunetti spoke at the same moment. 'I'll be home early.'

'Good,' she said and hung up.

Brunetti looked at the map again. Nothing had changed, but it all suddenly seemed less terrible, though he knew this should not be so.

When in doubt, provoke. It was a principle he had learned, over the years, from Paola. He checked Pelusso's office number in his address book.

'Pelusso,' the journalist answered on the third ring.

'It's me, Guido,' Brunetti said. 'I need you to place something.'

Perhaps responding to Brunetti's tone, Pelusso did not ask the sort of ironic question an opening like this would usually provoke him to. 'Where?' was all he asked.

'Preferably on the front page of the second section.'

'Local news, huh? What sort of thing?'

'That the authorities – I don't think you have to name them, but it would be nice if the article could suggest it's the Magistrato alle Acque – have learned of the presence of dangerous substances in a field in Murano and are about to begin an investigation of their source.'

Pelusso made a humming noise, as if to convey that he was writing this down, then asked, 'What else?'

'That the investigation is related to another one currently under way.'

'Tassini?' Pelusso asked.

After only minimal hesitation, Brunetti said, 'Yes.'

'You want to tell me what this is about?'

'Only if it doesn't appear in the article,' Brunetti said.

It took Pelusso some time to answer, but he finally said, 'All right.'

'It looks like Tassini's employers were using some sort of illegal system to get rid of dangerous waste.'

'What were they doing?'

'Same thing they did until 1973: just dumping it all into the *laguna*.'

'What sort of waste?'

'From the *molatura*. Ground particles of glass and minerals,' Brunetti answered.

'Doesn't sound very toxic to me.'

'I'm not sure that it is,' Brunetti agreed. 'But it's illegal.'

'And *che brutta figura* if one of those employers is the same man whose name is now beginning to be linked to the environmental cause,' Pelusso observed.

'Yes,' Brunetti said, realizing as he said it that he was saying far too much, and to a journalist. 'This can't appear,' he added. 'What we're saying now.'

'Why do you want it printed, then?' Pelluso asked, voice stern with unexpressed displeasure.

Brunetti chose to answer the question and ignore the way in which it had been asked. 'It's like opening an ant hill. You do it, and then you wait to see what happens.'

'And who comes out,' Pelusso added.

'Exactly.'

Pelusso laughed, his irritation forgotten, then said, 'It's not even three. I'll have it in tomorrow morning. Nothing easier; don't worry.'

It was only then that Brunetti thought to ask, 'Will there

be any trouble if the whole thing's false and there's no sign of pollution?'

Pelusso laughed again, harder this time. 'How long have you been reading the *Gazzettino*, Guido?'

'Of course,' came Brunetti's chastened response. 'How silly of me.'

'No need to worry, really,' Pelusso said.

'But you might be questioned about your source,' Brunetti said, in what he tried to make a joking tone. 'And then I'd be looking for a job.'

'Since the information came to me from a source inside the mayor's office,' Pelusso said indignantly, no doubt in the voice he would use were he to be questioned by his employers, 'I can hardly be expected to reveal it.' After a moment, Pelusso continued, 'It'll run right next to the story about the Questura.'

'What story?' Brunetti asked, knowing this was what his friend wanted him to say.

'About the women at the Ufficio Stranieri. You've heard about what's going on, haven't you?'

Relieved at his own ignorance, Brunetti could say, honestly, 'No. Nothing.' When Pelusso remained silent, Brunetti asked, 'What is it?'

'I've got a friend who's familiar with the office,' Pelusso said, leaving it to Brunetti to translate what 'friend' might mean to an investigative journalist.

'And?'

'And he told me that two women who have been there for decades asked for, and were given, early retirement this week.'

'I'm sorry, Elio,' said an impatient Brunetti, 'but I don't know what you're talking about.'

Not at all unsettled by Brunetti's tone, Pelusso continued. 'My friend said they'd been accepting payments from people for years for filing their applications for residence and work permits, and keeping the money.'

'That's impossible,' Brunetti protested. 'Don't they have to give them receipts?'

'The story I was told,' Pelusso went on with sweet patience, 'was that they were the only ones working in the office, and they'd ask for cash from the people who came in alone or without an Italian agent. The story I heard said that one of them would ask for the payment, and then send the applicant to the other woman, who had a register, and signing this register was supposed to be their receipt. Seems they'd been doing it for years.'

'But who'd believe that? Signing a register?' demanded Brunetti.

'People in a strange country, they don't speak much Italian, and it's a city office, and there's two women saying the same thing. Seems to me lots of people would sign it. And it seems they did.'

Brunetti asked, 'So what happened?'

'Someone complained to the Questore about it, and he had them in his office the same day. With the register. They're both on administrative leave now, but they retire at the end of the month.'

'And the people who signed the register? What happens to them? Did they get their permits?'

'I don't know,' Pelusso said. 'You want me to find out?'

For a moment, Brunetti was tempted, but good sense intervened and he answered, 'No. Thanks. It's enough to know it happened.'

'The dawn of justice in our fair city,' Pelusso said in a portentous voice.

Brunetti made a rude noise and replaced the phone. He dialled Signorina Elettra's number and, when she answered, asked, 'Your friend Giorgio still work at Telecom?'

'Yes, he does,' she said but then added, 'Of course, it's no longer necessary for me to consult him.'

'Don't tease me today, please, Signorina,' Brunetti said,

heard how that sounded, and quickly added, 'by suggesting that you've suddenly taken to using the official channels to obtain information.'

If she heard the gear shift in his voice, she chose to ignore it and said, 'No, Commissario. It's that I've found a more direct way to access their information.'

So much for using official channels, Brunetti thought. The gypsy children were not the only recidivists in the city. 'You've got Tassini's home number. I'd like you to get numbers for Fasano and De Cal: home, office, *telefonini*. And I'd like you to check for calls between any two of them,' he said, wondering why he had not thought to do this before. Though never saying so directly, Fasano had certainly made it sound as if he knew little more about Tassini than that he was working off the books and had a handicapped daughter, nothing more than what everyone at the factory would know.

'Of course,' she said.

'How long will it take?' he asked, hoping he might have the information the following morning.

'Oh, I'll bring it up in fifteen minutes or so, Commissario,' she answered.

'Much faster than Giorgio,' Brunetti said in open admiration.

'Yes, that's true. I'm afraid his heart wasn't in it,' she said and was gone.

It took closer to twenty minutes, but when she came in she was smiling. 'De Cal and Fasano seem to be quite good friends,' she began, putting some papers on his desk. 'But I won't spoil it for you, Commissario. I'll leave you to read through the lists,' she said, adding more paper. He looked at the numbers and times on the first sheet, and when he glanced up, she had gone.

Indeed, De Cal and Fasano had spoken to one another with some frequency during the last three months: there were at

237

least twelve calls, most of them made by Fasano. He looked at Tassini's number: during the years of his employment by De Cal, he had called the factory seven times. No call had been made to him either from De Cal's office or from his home.

With Fasano, however, the case was rather different. Tassini had been working there only two months when he died, yet the records from his home phone showed that he had called Fasano's *telefonino* six times, and the factory twice. Fasano, for his part, had called Tassini at home once ten days before he died and once on the day before. In addition, at 11.34 of the night Tassini died, Fasano's *telefonino* showed a call to the De Cal factory.

Brunetti pulled out the Yellow Pages and looked under *Idraulici* then dialled the number for Adil-San. When the young woman with the pleasant smile answered, Brunetti give his name and asked if he could speak to her father.

After a bit of music and a few clicks, Brunetti heard Repeta say, 'Good afternoon, Commissario. How can I help you now?'

'One quick question, Signor Repeta,' Brunetti said, seeing no reason to waste time in a formal exchange of pleasantries. 'When I was over at your office, I didn't ask enough about the procedure when you empty the tanks.'

'What is it you'd like to know, Commissario?'

'When you do it, how do you empty the tanks?'

'I'm not sure I understand your question,' Repeta said.

'Do you empty them completely?' Brunetti explained: 'So that you can see inside them, that is.'

'I'd have to look at their bill,' Repeta said, then quickly explained: 'I don't know what system we use with each of the clients, but if I look at the bill, the costs are detailed, so I'll know exactly what we did.' He paused a moment and then asked, 'Would you like me to call you back?'

'No, that's all right,' Brunetti said. 'Now that I've got you on the line, I'd rather wait.'

'All right. It should take only a few minutes.'

238

Brunetti heard a clack as Repeta set the receiver down, then footsteps, then a rough noise that could have been a door or drawer opening. And then silence. Brunetti gazed out of his window at the sky, studying the clouds and thinking about the weather. He tried to force his mind into a straight line, thinking of nothing but the clear sky and the coming and going of clouds.

The footsteps returned, and then Repeta said, 'From what I see on the invoice, all we do is pick up the barrels of sludge. That means they clean out the tanks themselves.'

'Is this normal?' Brunetti asked.

'Do you mean do the other *vetrerie* do it this way?'

'Yes.'

'Some do. Some don't. I'd guess about two-thirds of them opt to have us clean out the tanks.'

'Another last question,' Brunetti said, and before Repeta could agree to answer it, he asked, 'Do you service De Cal's factory?'

'That old bastard?' Repeta asked without humour.

'Yes.'

'We did until about three years ago.'

'What happened?'

'He didn't pay for two pick-ups, and then when I called him, he said I'd have to wait to be paid.'

'And so?'

'And so we stopped going there.'

'Did you try to get your money?' Brunetti asked.

'And do what, bring charges against him and spend ten years in the courts?' Repeta asked, still without any sign of humour.

'Do you know who makes the pick-ups now?' Brunetti asked.

Repeta hesitated, but then said 'No', and hung up.

26

The expected summons came at eleven the next morning, by which time Brunetti had read the article – which did not carry Pelusso's byline – three times. An organization in the city administration, it stated, alerted to a case of illegal dumping at a glass factory on Murano, was about to open an investigation. There followed a catalogue of the various inquiries already being conducted by the Magistrato alle Acque, thus leaving no doubt in any reader's mind – though without saying so – that this was the office involved. Because the cases cited all involved the dumping of toxic materials, the reader again was led to believe that the same was true this time. The final paragraph stated that the police, already conducting an investigation into a suspicious death, were also involved.

'The Vice-Questore would like to see you,' Signorina Elettra said when she called his office. Nothing more, a sure sign of trouble at hand.

'I'll be right down,' he said, deciding to take with him the folder into which he had put all of the information he had accumulated since first being sucked into the wake of Giorgio Tassini.

Patta's door was open when he got there, so Brunetti could do no more than smile at Signorina Elettra, who surprised him by holding up her right hand, fingers lifted in a wide V. *Vittoria?* Brunetti wondered. More likely *vittima.* Equally possible, *vendetta.*

'Shut the door, Brunetti,' Patta said in greeting.

He did as he was told and went and sat, unasked, in the chair in front of Patta's desk. How like being back at school this always was, Brunetti reflected.

'This article,' Patta said, tapping a well-manicured forefinger on the first page of the second section of the *Gazzettino.* 'Is it yours?'

What could Patta do to him? Expel him? Send him home to get a note from his parents? His father was dead, and his mother was an empty shell, her mind filled with the tiny filaments of Alzheimer's. No one to write a note for Guido.

'If you mean in the sense that I'm responsible for it,' Brunetti said, suddenly tired, 'yes.'

Patta was obviously taken aback by Brunetti's response. He drew the newspaper towards him and, forgetting to put on the reading glasses he kept on his desk for effect, read through it again. 'Fasano, I assume?' he asked.

'He seems to be involved,' Brunetti said.

'In what?' Patta asked with real curiosity.

It took Brunetti almost half an hour to explain, starting with his trip to Mestre to speak on Marco Ribetti's behalf – he left Patta to conclude that they were old friends – and finishing with the phone records and a drawing of the sedimentation tanks in Fasano's factory.

'You think Fasano killed him?' Patta asked when Brunetti finished.

Becoming evasive, Brunetti answered, 'I think a case could be made from what I've just told you that he did.'

Patta sighed. 'That's not what I asked you, Brunetti: do you think he killed him?'

'Yes.'

'Why not the other one, what's his name?' he asked, looking down at the papers and shifting them around until he found it. 'De Cal?'

'He had no contact with Tassini,' Brunetti said, 'other than as his employer, and he barely knew who he was.'

'What else?' Patta asked.

'What would it cost him to be convicted of environmental pollution? A fine? A few thousand Euros? Besides, he's a sick man; no judge is going to send him to jail. He has nothing to lose.'

'Not like Fasano, eh?' Patta asked with what sounded to Brunetti like satisfaction.

Brunetti was uncertain whether Patta referred to the fact that Fasano had a lot to lose or that he was a healthy man. 'He does have everything to lose. He's President of the glass-makers on Murano, but I've been told that's just a stepping-stone,' Brunetti said.

Patta nodded. 'And where do you think he intends to go?'

'Who knows? First higher in the city, as mayor, and then Europe, as a deputy. It's the path they usually take. Or perhaps he'll do both, and continue to run the factory, as well.' Brunetti turned his thoughts away from the shoals of politicians who managed to hold two, three, even four full-time jobs. 'He's hitched himself to the environmental move-ment, but he's still a businessman interested in making a profit. What better combination for our times?' Brunetti asked, thinking it was unusual for him to speak so openly to Patta, of all people.

Patta looked at the papers again. 'You mentioned samples. Sent to Bocchese. Have you got his results yet?'

'I called when I got in, but the tests weren't finished,' Brunetti said.

Patta took his phone and asked Signorina Elettra to connect him with the laboratory. Almost at once Patta said, 'Good morning, Bocchese. Yes, it's me. I'm calling for Commissario Brunetti, about those samples he sent you.'

Patta looked over at Brunetti, his face as smooth as he tried to make his voice. After a moment, he said, 'Excuse me? Yes, he is.' Patta's eyes took on a stunned look, as though perhaps Bocchese had told him the samples contained plague or botulism. 'Yes,' he repeated, 'he is. One moment.' He held the phone across his desk, saying, 'He wants to talk to you.'

'Good morning, Bocchese,' Brunetti said.

'Is it all right if I tell him?'

'Yes.'

'Pass me back, then,' Bocchese said.

Expressionless, Brunetti handed the phone back to Patta.

Patta put it to his ear again, and said, 'Well?' making his voice brusque and authoritative. Brunetti could hear Bocchese's voice, but he couldn't make out what he was saying. Patta pulled a sheet of paper towards him and started to write. 'Say that again, please,' he said.

As Brunetti watched, the letters started to appear upside down: 'Manganese, arsenic, cadmium, potassium, lead.' More followed below, all sounding harmful, if not lethal.

Patta set the pen down and listened for some time. 'Above the limits?' Bocchese answered this at some length, and then Patta said, 'Thank you, Bocchese,' and hung up. He turned the paper so that Brunetti could more easily read it. 'Quite a cocktail,' he said.

'What was Bocchese's answer when you asked if they were above the limits?' Brunetti asked.

'He said he'd have to go out there to take a larger sample, but that, if this is an indication, then the place is dangerous.'

Brunetti knew that was a relative term. Dangerous to whom, to what sort of creature, and after how long an exposure? But he had no desire to jeopardize his truce with Patta, so he said only, 'He'll need a judge to authorize him to go out and take samples.'

'I know that,' Patta snapped.

Brunetti said nothing.

Patta reached over and tapped the newspaper again. 'Then this is all lies? There's no investigation?'

'No.'

He watched Patta weigh this information. Brunetti's answer had destroyed Patta's hopes of following in the wake of some other investigation, leaving the Vice-Questore no choice but to be a shark and not a scavenger. He looked at Brunetti, placed his open palm on the papers Brunetti had shown him, and asked, 'You think you've got enough to link him to this dumping?'

The dumping, Brunetti knew, could have served as a motive for Fasano to eliminate Tassini. Prove that it had been going on and that Tassini knew about it, and there was a chance that they would find some other link between Fasano and Tassini, perhaps some physical evidence – perhaps someone who remembered seeing Fasano near the factory on the night Tassini died? Brunetti no sooner considered this possibility than he asked himself what could be considered strange about an owner's presence near his own factory? He decided to answer the question as asked. 'Yes. If he's not personally responsible, his factory is. Someone used that pipe, and perhaps three other pipes, to get rid of the sediment from the *molatura*.'

'Just like in the good old days,' Patta said with no indication that he spoke ironically, then asked, 'How much would this save him?'

'I don't know.'

'Find out. Find out how much it costs for each pick-up.' Patta paused, gave Brunetti a long, evaluating look, then said, 'I know him from the Lions Club, and he's never been seen to pick up a bill. I wouldn't be surprised if the cheap bastard did it to save a couple of hundred Euros. Maybe less.'

Brunetti could have been no more startled had he heard an English lady-in-waiting call the Queen a slut. Fasano was both wealthy and powerful, and had he just heard Patta refer to him as a 'cheap bastard'?

'What else, sir?' Brunetti asked, stunned to monosyllables.

'Nothing for the moment. I'll take care of getting a judge to sign the order to send Bocchese out there to take more samples. In fact, you'd better tell him to get rid of the samples he has. This is a new investigation, and I don't want there to be any evidence that we looked into this before.'

'Yes, sir,' Brunetti said, getting to his feet.

'And I want you to talk to those plumbers again, but I want you to do it here, with a video camera running.' Brunetti nodded, and Patta said, 'Make sure he describes that pipe in the back, and if he knows, ask him what minerals are in the stuff he hauls away and how dangerous they are. And ask him again when he thinks that cover was put on the pipe.'

'Yes, sir,' Brunetti said.

'I'll have the order for you after lunch, and as soon as you have it, I want Bocchese out there,' said Patta with increasing urgency. Then he added, 'And I want him to take people from the Environmental Agency with him. I don't want there to be any question about those samples, that they've been contaminated in any way. In fact, maybe the environmental people can take their own samples and do their own tests, along with Bocchese.'

'All right,' Brunetti said.

'Good.' Patta gave a particularly eager smile. 'That should be enough.'

'To do what, sir? Show there was a reason why he murdered Tassini?'

Patta could not have been more astonished had Brunetti's hair suddenly burst into flames. 'Who said anything about murder, Brunetti?' He tilted his head and looked at Brunetti as though he had doubts as to whether they had been in the same room together all this time, talking about the same thing. 'I want him stopped. If he gets into office and brings a new junta into power with him, then what happens to the connections I've spent ten years building up?' Patta demanded aggressively. 'Have you thought about that?'

He saw Brunetti's expression and went on, 'And don't you for an instant believe he's using this environmental nonsense for political ends, Brunetti. He really believes it.' Patta threw up his hands at the very thought. 'I've listened to him talk: he's like all converts, all fanatics. It's all he cares about, so if he's elected mayor, you can say goodbye to the idea of the subway in from the airport or the dikes in the *laguna* or licences for more hotels. He'll turn this city back fifty years. And then where will we all be?'

Stunned beyond speech, Brunetti could do nothing more than say, 'I don't know, sir.'

Patta's phone rang, and he answered it. When he heard the voice on the other end, he waved a hand at Brunetti, as if to flick him out of the room. Brunetti left.

27

Brunetti was a wide reader and so was familiar with the Juggernaut, the idol of Krishna carried on a monstrous carriage in a Hindu procession, under the wheels of whose passage the overly pious would hurl themselves and the careless often be crushed. This image came to Brunetti as he observed Patta's investigation of Fasano's environmental crimes, watching as all questions that might lead to an investigation of Tassini's death, one by one, fell or were tossed under the wheels.

From the moment that Bocchese, accompanied by chemsuited inspectors from the Environmental Agency, arrived at Fasano's factory, armed with a warrant signed by the most fiercely environmental of the local judges, Fasano fought a rearguard action. Accompanied by his lawyer and no doubt alerted by the article in the *Gazzettino*, he met Bocchese in the field behind his factory. At first he attempted to prevent the Inspectors from setting foot on his land, but when Bocchese showed his lawyer the judge's order, Fasano had no option but to relent.

As the technicians began to dig and collect, label and store, Fasano pointed out that they were working along the line that divided his property from De Cal's, and so whatever they were looking for – he made a great display of confusion and astonishment here – must have been put there by his neighbour. The technicians ignored him and left his questions unanswered until he and his lawyer went back inside his factory, leaving them to their task.

Brunetti thought of Juggernaut again two days later, when the *Gazzettino* published a photo of the giant digger that was systematically following the line of pipe that led from the abandoned field, discovered to be highly contaminated, back towards the *vetrerie*. As it drew closer to the factories, the accompanying article revealed, it had uncovered a joint where two smaller pipes met, one running from De Cal's factory and one from Fasano's.

Brunetti studied the photo, aware that those thick Caterpillar treads, so hot in their pursuit of Fasano's political destruction, buried all hope that Patta would take an interest in Tassini's death. Always one to seize the main chance, Patta gave himself up to his desire to prove Fasano's involvement in the very crime he had based his political career on condemning: the environmental degradation of the *laguna*. A conviction for an environmental crime would put paid to Fasano's political aspirations, and that was enough to satisfy Patta as well as whatever powerful interests he hoped to please with Fasano's destruction. In contrast to that certain goal, a solution to the mystery of Tassini's death was no sure thing, only a long and complicated investigation that was not certain to lead to a conviction. So let it go, forget it, call it accidental death and file the papers away.

Brunetti followed the case from a distance, and was able – with the help of Signorina Elettra – to read the transcripts of the videotaped sessions during which Fasano, and then

De Cal, were questioned by a magistrate and Lieutenant Scarpa.

De Cal admitted everything from the beginning, said he had been doing what any sensible businessman would do: using the cheapest means to solve a production problem. The pipes had been there in his father's time, and he had continued to use them. When the judge ordered that his sediment tanks be drained, they were all shown to have a second set of very narrow drainpipes leading into the wall, each about forty centimetres down. Each pipe had a simple disc soldered into place beside it, just as had the pipes in Fasano's factory: rotating the disc back and forth over the end of the pipe would open or close it, thus regulating the flow of water that carried the residue under the field and out to the *laguna*. The swampy area in the field had been caused by a leak in the century-old pipe: the digger followed it all the way down to the water's edge, where the water trickled into the *laguna* from beneath an abandoned dock.

When told that he would be fined, De Cal remained entirely untroubled, no doubt aware of how derisory such a fine would be. When asked by the magistrate if he knew whether Signor Fasano had been using the same system, De Cal laughed out loud and said that he would have to put that question to Signor Fasano.

Fasano's response to the magistrate's questions was entirely different. He explained that he had taken over the running of his factory only six years before and that he knew nothing about the pipes. They must have been put there by his father, a man who – though Fasano revered his memory – was a man of his time and thus not concerned with the ecological problems of Venice. Of course Fasano had been told about the leak in the sedimentation tank and about the plumber's visit. His manager had dealt with the problem while Fasano was on a business trip to Prague and had told him about it when he returned. It was his manager's job,

Fasano said, to deal with all of the minor details of running the *vetreria*. That was why he employed him.

Scarpa, no doubt resentful of Fasano's high-handed attitude, interrupted to ask – Brunetti, reading the report, could hear the sarcasm in the lieutenant's voice – if it was his manager who had dealt with the death of one of his employees.

'Poor devil,' ran the transcript. 'I came back from my place in the country that morning and learned about it when I got to the factory. But, no, Lieutenant, I did not leave it to my manager to deal with. Even though I barely knew the man, I went over to see what I could do, but his body had already been taken away.'

Apparently stung by Fasano's tone, Scarpa asked no further questions and the magistrate returned to the sedimentation tanks and the set of swinging discs over the openings to the pipes. All of them had been shut when Bocchese's men discovered them, and Fasano continued to maintain that he knew nothing about them. It was as Brunetti read this interchange that he first began to suspect that Fasano might get away with it. His revered father, or perhaps his no doubt equally revered grandfather, would have been responsible for those pipes, and they would have been used when it was still legal to empty into the *laguna*. There was no clear evidence that they had been in use recently, and so Fasano's ecological commitment was in no way compromised.

The magistrate asked nothing about Fasano's connection with Tassini and presented no evidence that he and Tassini knew one another as anything other than employer and employee. The magistrate made no mention of the phone calls between Tassini and Fasano: had he done so, Brunetti could easily imagine Fasano protesting that he could not be asked to recall every conversation he had with his employees. Neither Patta nor any judge in the city would authorize an investigation based on such an absence of evidence.

250

To what extent the investigation of the contamination of the *laguna* would affect Fasano's political ambitions, Brunetti had no idea. It had been some time since criminal association or the evidence of criminal behaviour had served as an impediment to political office, and so it was entirely possible that enough of the voting public would be prepared to elect Fasano mayor. Should this happen, then Brunetti would be best advised to take what small comfort he could from Patta's discomfiture and, for the rest, follow the advice Paola had passed on from her recent rereading of one of Jane Austen's novels: to save his breath to cool his tea. Besides, Patta would far rather see Fasano elected mayor than have to deal with the scandal and clamour of a murder investigation involving a rich and powerful man who was connected to men of far greater wealth and power.

His mind filled with these prospects, Brunetti felt a desire to leave the Questura, an urge so strong that it propelled him to his feet and down the stairs. Even if he did nothing more than go down to the corner to get a coffee, at least he would feel the sun on his face and perhaps catch a whiff of the lilacs from across the canal. So much seemed to have happened, and yet it was still springtime.

Indeed it was lilac he encountered, though he did so while still inside the Questura. Signorina Elettra met him on the steps, wearing a blouse he did not remember seeing before: on a field of crème silk, pink and magenta panicles vied with one another, though the victory was won by her taste.

'Ah, Commissario,' she said, as he held the door open for her, 'I'm afraid I've got bad news for you.'

Her smile denied that, and so Brunetti asked, 'Which is?'

'I'm afraid you didn't win the lottery.'

'Lottery?' Brunetti asked, distracted by the lilacs and by the sudden warmth in the air as they stepped outside.

'The Vice-Questore's received his letter from Interpol.' She wiped away her smile and said, 'I'm afraid he was not selected for the job in England.'

They were standing still, the light reflecting on to their faces from the canal. 'That news is that nation's loss, I fear,' Brunetti said in a suitably serious voice.

She smiled and said that she was sure the Vice-Questore would be strong, then turned in the opposite direction and walked away.

Brunetti noticed Foa standing on the deck of his boat, following Signorina Elettra with his eyes. When she turned the corner, the pilot returned his attention to Brunetti. 'Give you a ride somewhere, sir?' he asked.

'Not on duty?' Brunetti asked.

'Not until two, when I have to pick up the Vice-Questore at Harry's Bar.'

'Ah,' muttered Brunetti in acknowledgement of the appropriateness of his taste. 'Until then?'

'I suppose I should stay here and wait to see if there are any calls,' the pilot said, his heart not in it, 'but I'd rather you asked me to take you somewhere. It's such a beautiful day.'

Brunetti raised a hand to shield his eyes from the young sun. 'Yes, it is,' he agreed, succumbing to the contagion of Foa's restlessness. 'How about up the Grand Canal?' he asked for no real reason.

As they passed Harry's Bar, where Patta sat with some presumably powerful personage, Brunetti began to notice the return to life taking place in the gardens on either side of the canal. Crocuses tried to hide themselves under evergreens; daffodils didn't even bother. The magnolia would be out in a week, he noticed; sooner if it would only rain.

He saw the plaque marking the home of Lord Byron, a man who, like the young Brunetti, had once swum in these waters. No more.

'You want to go out to Sacca Serenella?' Foa asked with a

252

glance at his watch. 'Lunch there and back on time?'

'Thanks, Foa, but I don't think I'll be going out there again. At least not for work.'

'Yeah, I read about it, and Vianello told me a bit,' Foa said, waving at a *gondoliere* who passed at some distance in front of them. 'So they get to pollute all they want and get away with it?'

'The pipes in Fasano's factory were shut off, no one knows when. Could have been years ago,' Brunetti explained. 'And there's no evidence that he knew anything about it. Might have been his father; might even have been his grandfather.'

'Cheap bastards, each and every one of them,' Foa said.

'Says who?'

Foa took one hand from the wheel, unbuttoned his jacket and loosened his tie in homage to the sun. 'The father of a friend of mine who lives out there: he knew them both, the father and grandfather. And an uncle of mine who worked for the father. Said they'd do anything to save fifty lire.' As an afterthought and with the beginning of a laugh, he added, 'And a friend of mine I was at school with.'

'What's so funny?' Brunetti asked, attention on the trees in a garden to his left.

'He's a captain with ACTV now,' Foa said with a residual chuckle. 'Lives on Murano, so he knows Fasano, and his father knew the father, and so on.' This sort of familiarity was common enough, and Brunetti acknowledged it with a nod.

'He told me a couple of days ago that he had Fasano on his boat about a week ago, trying to dodge the fare. Got on without a ticket, then tried to say he forgot to stamp it. But he didn't have a ticket to stamp in the first place.'

'The captain checks them?' Brunetti asked, wondering who, if this were the case, had been left to drive the boat.

'No, no, the guys who check the tickets. Usually they only work during the day, but the last month or so they've been checking tickets at night because that's when people don't

253

expect to be checked.' Foa broke off to shout a greeting to a man passing in a transport boat riding low in the water, and Brunetti thought the topic was over.

But Fao continued. 'Anyway, he recognized Fasano, who was standing on deck when it happened, and after the route was finished – because he knew who he was – he asked the ticket checkers what he'd said. Usual stuff: I forgot to stamp my ticket, forgot to ask to buy one when I got on board. But they've heard it all,' Foa said with another laugh. 'One of them once had a woman say she was on the way to the hospital to have a baby.'

'What happened?'

'He made her open her coat, and she was as thin as . . .' Foa began, glancing at Brunetti. 'As thin as I am,' he finished.

Perhaps to cover the awkward pause, Foa went back to his original story. 'So they asked to see his identity card, but he said he didn't have it with him. Left his wallet at home. But then he found some money and paid the fine right then. Nando said Fasano was so cheap he thought he'd give his name and then try to get some friend of his to fix it for him, but he paid right then before they could take his name and send him a notice and the fine.'

Brunetti turned his head from the contemplation of the progress of spring and asked, 'What boat?'

'The 42,' Foa said, 'going out to his factory.'

'At night?'

'Yes. That's what Nando said.'

'Did he say what time it was?' Brunetti asked.

'Huh?' Foa asked, coming up behind a transport boat and slipping past it.

'Did he say what time it happened?'

'Not that I remember. But they usually knock off at midnight, guys on that shift,' Foa said, with a long toot on his horn at the boat they were passing.

'Exactly when was this?' Brunetti asked.

254

'Last week some time, I'd say,' Foa answered. 'At least that's what Nando said. Why?'

'Could you check?'

'I suppose so. If he'd remember,' Foa said, puzzled by his superior's sudden curiosity.

'Could you call him?'

'When?'

'Now.'

If he found this request strange, Foa gave no sign of it. He pulled out his *telefonino* and punched some numbers, studied the screen, then punched in some more.

'*Ciao*, Nando,' he said. 'Yeah, it's me, Paolo.' There was a long pause, after which Foa continued, 'I'm at work, but I've got to ask you something. Remember you said you had Fasano on a boat last week, when he got a fine for not having a ticket? Yes. Do you remember what night it was?' There followed a silence, after which Foa pressed the receiver to his chest and said, 'He's checking his schedule.'

'When he comes back, ask him what time it was, please,' Brunetti said.

The pilot nodded and wedged the phone between his shoulder and his ear, and Brunetti looked at the façade of Ca' Farsetti, the city hall. How lovely it was, white and permanent, with flags snapping in the wind in front of it. To govern Venice was no longer to govern the Adriatic and the East, but it was still something.

'Yes, I'm still here,' Foa said into the phone. 'Tuesday? You sure?' he asked. 'And what time? You remember that?' There was a short pause and then Foa said, 'No, that's all. Thanks, Nando. Give me a call, all right?' There were a few more words of affectionate friendship, and then Foa slipped the phone back into his pocket.

'You hear that, sir? Tuesday.'

'Yes, I heard, Foa.' The night Tassini died, the night Fasano, during his interrogation – videotaped and the transcript

255

signed by Fasano – said he had been away from the city. 'And what time?'

'He says it was some time close to midnight, but the exact time would be on the receipt for the fine he paid.'

'His receipt?' Brunetti asked, breathing a silent prayer that this would not be the only copy.

'Sure, on his. Cheap bastard will probably try to take it off his taxes somehow – say it was a business trip or something. But the time'll be on the copy in the ACTV office, too.'

'With his name on it?'

'No, Nando said he didn't give his name: just paid the fine. But one of the ticket collectors recognized him, too. He and Nando laughed about it after he got off.'

Their boat passed under the Rialto Bridge, entered the sweep that would take them past the market and then up to the third bridge. After a few moments, Brunetti looked at his watch and saw that it was a little after one.

'If you don't mind turning around, Foa, I'd like you to take me to Harry's Bar.'

'You going to join the Vice-Questore for lunch?' Foa asked, slowing the motor and looking behind him to see when he could make the turn.

Brunetti waited, unwilling to distract the pilot during this manoeuvre. Finally the turn was made and Brunetti was going in the right direction. 'No, as a matter of fact,' Brunetti said with the beginnings of a smile, 'I think I'm going to ruin the Vice-Questore's lunch.'